CEREMONY OF INNOCENCE

CEREMONY OF INNOCENCE

GLADYS SWAN

SERVING HOUSE BOOKS

Ceremony of Innocence

Copyright © 2021 by Gladys Swan

All Rights Reserved

Published by Serving House Books

Copenhagen, Denmark and South Orange, NJ

www.servinghousebooks.com

ISBN: 978-1-947175-52-5

Library of Congress Control Number: 2021934015

Member of The Independent Book Publishers Association

First Serving House Books Edition 2021

Cover Painting by Gladys Swan

Serving House Books Logo: Barry Lereng Wilmont

What business has innocence here? What relation to the
innumerable spirits of darkness?

—Samuel Beckett

A. A violent order is a great disorder.
B. A great disorder is an order. These
Two things are one. (Pages of illustrations.)

—Wallace Stevens

I have given you as a covenant to the people,
a light to the nations,
to open the eyes that are blind,
to bring out the prisoners from the dungeon,
from the prison those who sit in darkness.

—Isaiah. ch. 42 v. 6 & 7

I.

The Center

No doubt it was inevitable that a woman of her particular innocence should stumble across the prisoner: ponder the elements of his story, encounter an ideology that violated the rights of certain segments of humanity. Their fate in the hands of bureaucrats shuffling papers, wielding pens and stamps and official seals, men working busily, working mightily for those standing above them, who could lift off the tops of their skulls and watch the machinery, shift the gears, interchange parts, seal them up again. All prisoners, it seemed, locked away by politics and protocol. (Except for one, there was always one who managed to escape.) And the rest—complicitors, there to deny and deny.

And this prisoner, one denied again and again. At a further remove, behind bars, his identity reduced to the size of a cell, to the dimensions of his body. Who had paled to oblivion behind the walls. And who, even more if he were set free, would be in danger of being forgotten altogether.

Meanwhile there was the struggle to hang onto something, in the midst of all that was falling apart, coming down: the Berlin Wall, the Europe of the past fifty years. A time of exhilarating chaos: barbed wire being torn out, borders opening, people flooding across, streaming in the direction of new hope, in this century of the refugee. New bids for power, one Germany instead of two. Old enemies released from old constraints to torment one another once again. The great seethe and heave of it all, possibility and menace in the same twist. The seemingly impregnable structures having the ground ripped out from under them and those released from their bonds being able to stand naked, with all new emotions. And in the midst of it still the little life to be lived. After all, you had to do that.

In the beginning you were always lost. She knew that. As soon as you cut the leading strings and allowed between your past and your future the great stretch of the Atlantic, you knew that. As soon as you crossed a border, decided not to go back, but stood on a distant shore in a moment of vertigo and panic, you knew in your deepest bones. And were in danger of floating away, your bones had grown so light, as hollow as birds'. What was to hold you after all? Love, she said vehemently. Love. When you love a man, you are held down in this street by your own boots, walking in a known direction. You carry a talisman through the indifference of strangers: a light that breaks beyond the swirl of faces appearing only to disappear and brings into the world a shining difference. Florrie had some of these beliefs.

For this was not her city, not the sound of her own speech in her ears. Even after six months, she could look up into the faces glowing with the cold and see no one familiar to her. She could say, I am in a strange country. And if the Queen walks these streets, familiarly as a citizen, if in some odd moment you pass by royalty and are assured the country is in the hands of a good queen, you are still a stranger. But love, oh, love, could create a place for this madwoman.

Love had transformed her into a stranger to herself. She was a tall woman with a lean body, energetic in movement, but not wholly assured, as though she were still trying to learn to get it right, whatever it was. Love had given a light to her expression. She had a good face: sympathetic and open, that in a past on the other side of the Atlantic had encouraged her clients to tell her their stories. But for the past few months she smiled or laughed for no reason at all, or from thinking about how it had happened, how she had come to Copenhagen for a conference for therapists, the beginning of a month's leave for her to recover from the burnout she was experiencing from her work; how she had met Eric at the Embassy party, and how, toward the end of the month, she had resigned from the clinic. It was the most impulsive thing she had ever done. Taking her life and wrenching it from its moorings. She'd never done anything that wasn't guarded and sensible, against being asked to pay for the consequences of a bad mistake. She had tried to cushion against that by talking to her colleagues who had taken over her clients during her absence, asking about their progress, offering her suggestions. It wasn't as though they were being abandoned, she told herself, but just moving their troubles to another ear. Even so . . . Love made you selfish, she'd have to grant that.

But in her defense, it seemed to her she'd missed youth, its chances for discovery, its pleasurable innocence.

And what better way to recapture it than through love? But the treasure itself—Once you had it as your very own, suddenly threats appeared where none existed before. Was she unduly fearful? But ever since the letter had come, an anonymous letter, she had been unsettled—even though the accusations were patently absurd. It had left her vulnerable, her uncertainty deepened by longing, for Eric had been away when she received it. And just when she was on the verge of seeing him, giving a rest to her confusion, his plane was delayed by bad weather. She'd waited for him for hours at the airport and gone home almost in tears. He'd called her sometime after 2:00 a.m. and wakened her out of a fitful sleep. Her relief made her tremble—things could right themselves again. He'd catch a few hours' sleep in the back of the shop and then be there for her.

And the letter, in the light of day, in the light of his return and recovered rationality, was insignificant. Probably he'd just laugh at it, tell her to laugh and forget it. But who could have written it, and why would anyone want to? The question nagged at her. Someone who had a grudge against her, against Eric? Someone jealous of their love? She began to scold herself. She should not let anything darken her thought. Eric would be there for her, the two of them joined together once more.

It was a Monday morning early in January, suddenly cold after a mild year's end, and during the night snow had finally come. She was hurrying down Komagdesgade toward the bookshop where she would find Eric, no doubt still asleep. She would prepare to open the shop.

It was uncanny, she couldn't help thinking. Whoever had written the letter knew her with a certain intimacy, but had accused her of things that had no basis in fact.

Could anyone have been into her desk, her journal? Someone who'd been in her apartment during the past weeks? Beryl? Surely not Beryl. She had told Beryl about people she corresponded with, mentioned names of men, various friends. But Beryl wouldn't spy on her . Or Helga—unthinkable. Both were close friends, established in their own lives and loves—Beryl at the Embassy library; Helga, an independent journalist. They were her close friends.

The only snag belonged to the night of the party—and that was too ridiculous an incident that she'd tried to put out of her mind as quickly as possible—Jimmy and the rest. One after another she called up the images of her friends, theirs: hers and Eric's. Trying to press for the rotten spot beneath the surface. What would give rise to this little piece of malice? Who was capable of it? Against Eric too—who beamed his generosity in every direction. And while he was away. His first trip back to the States since he'd come to Denmark.

She tried to take hold of herself. She wouldn't give whoever it was the power to spoil their reunion. When he'd called her the night before, he said he'd brought back something for her. She gave herself to anticipation to hold her against the cold, against the dark morning, against lies.

Jimmy? She wondered, sinking back into her predicament. Would it be worth his while to send such a letter? A nasty joke? A sop to his narcissism? She didn't think he'd go to that kind of trouble, though his wandering, casual glance had lighted on her, and he'd put himself forward to make time with her in the kitchen. The presumption! Quite as boundless as his ego.

It was quite ridiculous, that New Year's party: something to amuse her in Eric's absence. With his friends, now hers, handed on as a common possession: a small group of Americans on the edge of things. She was not certain what they meant to her, people thrown together by their common origins, perhaps not those you'd single out at home. Not even Beryl, perhaps, though she admired her level of culture and her frankness. Helga was a different matter. She'd been born in Europe of American parents, but educated in the States. She seemed at home anywhere, and had a kind of courage and passion for truth that set her apart. Florrie admired her. She was glad to have them for friends, and they had interesting things to say to one another. So the party was a mixed bag.

She put Jimmy aside, involved as he was with his current flame, a college girl, who had camped that night on pillows and blankets on her living room floor.

"You don't mind, do you?—putting us up tonight. It's a long way to go on such a cold night."

She had minded, oddly enough, though it was late, and she should have been glad to accommodate them. Even before he'd made any advances, she felt encroached upon. She had no real excuse.

To her surprise, he had rousted himself out later that morning to help her push aside enough dishes and wine bottles to make coffee. As she stood at the sink, he'd come up behind her, parted the hair at the back of her neck, and started kissing her neck. Startled, put off balance, she turned and found herself surrounded, pressed into a kiss that nearly suffocated her. Aroused, breathless, she pushed him away.

"Are you crazy? What do you think you're doing?" She was furious.

"I knew it," he said, "All that passion just going to waste. It's not a shame—it's a damned crime."

He was so obvious, she was caught between laughter and contempt. "Come on, don't give me that crap."

"Listen, Christ-a-mighty, don't get sore. I'm all on your side. You're giving out the fire. I'm just giving you the news."

She looked at him. His eye wanted to take her in, into some fascination. She pulled away. "On a morning after a New Year's party? You must still be drunk."

"Maybe that's when you know things best," he countered, undaunted. "Eric's a chump. He doesn't know a damned thing. Doesn't have the foggiest idea what he's got. Doesn't know what to do with it. If he hadn't got there first . . ."

"Get out of here will you?" She turned back to the dishes. "What nonsense."

Apparently it didn't matter what she said. Bolder than an oncoming train. Nothing mattered beyond the demands of his inner life in any given moment. She wanted some way to get round him and avoid flattering him by some means short of physical violence "You think you can get on with me by dumping on Eric? Now how about getting Carla up and taking yourselves out of here. The party's over, and I've got things to do."

Following her from stove to sink, putting his hands on her shoulders, Jimmy was ecstatic. "I adore it. I really do. Loyalty— that's the bedrock. It's the lever you grab hold of to move the world."

She wriggled out from under his hands, and he let his arms flop to his sides. Maybe she should have kicked him one. "Does Carla admire it also?"

"Trying to prick the balloon, huh? Throw a little acid in the face? Catch me in a piece of hypocrisy? I'm ahead of you, kid. And it ain't what you think. Carla and I have our arrangements. She knows exactly what to expect from me. And she's happy as a clam, you bet."

He didn't owe her any explanations, she assured him.

"Look, Florrie, don't be a fool just because Eric is. It don't fit no requirements."

Slang to undercut her. To amuse, woo her towards intimacy?

"Eric couldn't appreciate the Venus de Milo if she grabbed him by the balls and said, 'Com'ere, baby.'"

"Wouldn't that be a little difficult for her?"

"And that Beryl bitch . . . "

"Jimmy, do shut up." She didn't want to yell at him, give him that power over her. She stood looking into his handsome, meaty face. No wonder the women were magnetized by him. The cleft chin did it every time. Just let a woman turn in his direction. And then he would seize her up greedily, hold her in his gaze, make her feel her seductiveness. It was all her doing, her fault for enticing him.

"Women love me," he said, as though he'd read her mind, "because I love them. I know them—what they really want, what they need. More than they know themselves." He looked at her narrowly, then took a lighter tone, "What's in them? Dynamite." He acted out an explosion for her.

At that moment Carla came straggling in. "Hi," she said weakly. "I have got the prize headache."

"Poor baby," Jimmy said, going to her, massaging her temples.

Then Florrie threw them both out, looked around at what was left to do, figured it could wait and went back to bed. But she lay awake in spite of her efforts to relax.

Ridiculous, the whole thing. But had it prompted the letter: Your affairs are too well-known. The men who have come under your spell. Your willingness to take what belongs to others. The emotional corruption of your victims. Those whose loyalty you've betrayed will know soon enough.

And names were named. Altogether bizarre. When she'd first read all this, she let out a hoot, it had to be some sort of joke. But she'd seen enough craziness to know better. And if this meant she now had to train a suspicious eye on everyone she knew, here, as she was trying to gain a foothold on a new life, well, it was a low blow— that's what it was.

Her immigrant and vulnerable state registered every shock and tremor. She needed Eric to dismiss the Jimmy business with a wave of the hand, tell her it was the sort of thing that could happen in the aftermath of any boozy party, in the lingering drunken haze. Jimmy never hid his predilection for women. A man on the prowl. Some innate sense of superiority gave him a tougher hide than most. Nothing fazed him, according to Eric, and resistance apparently whetted his appetite for the chase. Or else he simply moved on to the next: there would always be women.

Eric had his number. The two of them had their understanding; Eric found Jimmy useful. Sometimes he gave Jimmy money if he was short, and in return Jimmy would keep the shop open on an occasional afternoon when Eric had to be away. From Jimmy you didn't ask for loyalty, the notion didn't apply. He wandered outside all categories, no doubt making up the rules as he went along. Even so, for him to turn in her direction. But then the letter—perhaps Eric was in a better position to know what she, what they, had to look out for. A raptor.

At least her eye had grown sharper now. What she wanted had come into clearer focus. And she was going to muster her forces. Even against the voices of reason and caution? Florrie, Florrie, what do you want? Her father's voice, hovering just above her, rousing her up from the dream she had drifted into. Her father, but petulant and irritated. Why don't you come home where you belong? In her dream she sat awake in her childhood room, only now, as she looked upward from her bed, its ceiling was a vault of sky with a few cold stars. And the walls were gray and indistinct. She could tell it was winter, and she lay shivering in her bed. What is it you want?

Oh, don't ask, she cried, looking around wildly in all directions, as though she'd lost something of great value. Where's the moon, oh where is it? she demanded. I can't see it. Even as she cried out, the sky whitened and turned menacing. For a moment as she looked around, she didn't know where she was.

"Florrie, hello. Are you off to the shop?"

She stopped short as her name broke in upon her. This voice was mild, if a bit eager. Only Koenig. She was used to him, he came in so often to stand near the coffee pot at the back of the shop and talk to Eric, now to her. He was almost a fixture. For some reason, she was always glad to see him, though she could never think of anything of interest to say to him. He would come in from the street, perhaps to escape something other than the cold, though he was always dressed as if for an important occasion. He would take off his coat and gloves and hold his hands above the heater. Then she or Eric would offer him a cup of coffee. Did he have a home, she sometimes wondered, where he was not welcome? Actually, she imagined him alone in a room piled with books overflowing the shelves and piled in stacks on the floor, and Koenig seated in a worn and solitary chair, stuffing himself with ideas, until either the books ran out or his intellectual loneliness ran him out. He was always ordering books and then looking for some excuse to stand around talking to Eric and her, or even to the occasional acquaintance who wandered in.

"Oh, hello," she said. She didn't want to pause, she had too much on her mind. Invariably there was a conversation, always rather hesitantly begun, as though some great obstacle had first to be lifted out of the way. If she tried to look encouraging, he would nod, as though weighing the consideration that she meant well by him never, it seemed, quite coming to a final conclusion. It had to be done over again each time. It made him a bit ponderous. Or else he met what she said with immediate agreement, followed by a pause, perhaps to give him time to find the words for the exact contradiction or some irony or bit of subtlety. She was used to the American gregariousness; hers was a nation of extroverts.

"Your book came in," she told him.

"Yes, thank you." He looked at her expectantly as if she might say something more personal. Finally he said, "I'll be coming by to pick it up later."

"I don't think the shop will be open today."

He didn't contradict her. "Eric phoned."

"Oh," she said, disappointed in spite of herself, certain they'd have the day together without interruption. Very likely he'd called everybody in a great gesture of goodwill and delight in being back, all eager to talk about the trip, forgetting fatigue, even forgetting her. She couldn't really begrudge him that. Not entirely. They'd come trooping by, all his friends, ready to talk and drink schnapps and beer or the bottle of Jack Daniels he promised to bring back. Henry and Yvonne, Jimmy, Koenig and the rest. She could picture them there in the shop, bibulous and full of welcome, wanting all the news of home, what he'd seen and done.

For he was back now, the keeper of the lighthouse, as she saw him, where the beacon shone for a little colony of foreigners, expatriates. Back with a gesture of largesse and camaraderie. And she was happy. It was wrong to be proprietary about him, possessive of this space as if she'd created it. She'd been invited into it, after all. She strived only to let it be, this vessel that contained the future. She wanted only that: a future that kept on giving her Eric and the bookstore. Her old life lay shriveled in a corner, like an outworn skin she no longer claimed.

It was curious—No matter where you were, you began gathering things, at first only a couple of plates and cups, some utensils, a coffee pot. A chair. A comforter for the bed. Towels. You started with a room nearly empty and then suddenly yearned in the direction of things that didn't yet exist but were there in potentia. Gleams of possibility; brilliant sparks. You stood waiting for them to break open, expand, become the future. Now they'd get an apartment together. Surely it was time: they'd talked about it often enough. And the sheer inconvenience they'd borne while they looked into this and that, she having to travel back to her place, Eric camping in the back of the bookstore—all the awkward separations. The times she stayed there with him, the two of them sharing a mattress designed for one, arms and legs entwined, neither of them getting any sleep. For a time you could do that in the name of love. You could laugh when you tumbled out of bed. Gypsies, both of them, having landed here to make a life.

She entered the shop and paused a moment. There: the familiar shape of his head, the line of his arm. She caught him in his being there, caught him with the simple awe of having absence filled, the great hole of it. And she realized that his time away from her, much as she had filled it with reading and dreaming and putting herself in the way of her friends, was an anguish. They looked at one another, and his face came back in its familiarity as she adjusted to her present sense of it. He got up from behind his desk before she was fairly in the door, and then, with her arms around him, came the feel of him actually there, the familiar smell of him, reminding her where to put herself in relation to him. "I'm so glad you're back," was all she would allow herself to say.

He kissed her. "Your face is all cold," he said, bending his fingers against her cheek.

She nuzzled against his fingers, held onto him and then let go. "I've missed you so much." She'd have liked to take his face into her hands, stare into it, take from it greedily whatever he'd brought back to her. But somehow she didn't dare ask for more just then. Her heart quickened with her impatience. "How was the trip?" she said, standing back to take off her coat and boots. "Tell me everything."

"It was a good trip," he said, as though that was all he could say about it. "Wait," he said, coming out of the pause almost as if he'd been rescued from it, "I've got something for you."

He went into the back and returned with a round object wrapped in layers of tissue paper. "I thought you'd like this to look at."

It was hard in her hand as she undid the paper, and then the divided halves of a geode fell open in her hands like an egg. "Oh, how lovely," she said surprised by his choice, but ready to be appeased by the crystals lining the center. "I'm always amazed at these things," she said. "Hiding all this at the core till you break it open. Imagine, everything built up around the hollow." She turned one of the halves, trying to catch the light in the crystals.

"You said your dad had a whole shelf of them."

Yes, she'd told him that. "Probably where I got my love of rocks. I left my collection with my friend Emily."

She smiled up at him. "I kept talking to you while you were gone. Long conversations—enough to burn your ears across the Atlantic. All about what we'd do when you got back."

"And I missed you," he said measuredly.

"I'm so glad," she said. Of course he had to miss her, even with all the excitement of the trip. She looked at him hungry for that quality in his face, in his eyes that had specifically to do with her. Looked for it behind their separation, his fatigue.

"You must be worn out," she granted him. "I can take over everything today. You're mad, you know, opening the shop today. Have you made coffee?"

"I completely forgot. God knows I could use some. How could I forget coffee?"

The prospect of it clearly excited him. "I got all involved with opening the mail, sorting through book orders." He laughed. "I'm crazy with exhaustion."

"You're a monster to yourself," she chided him and hurried off to make coffee. "Tell me about—," home, she started to say, "—everything."

"I caught a couple of book fairs," he said vaguely, searching for something in a stack of papers. He started to sit down, but instead leaned against the side of the desk. "You can't believe the stuff. So much of it. Incredible. You can't even begin to keep track. I've been away too long," he said, almost to himself. "So much always coming out. Good stuff too, in out-of-the-way places. I looked over some of the small presses. Really first-rate. Got together with Jack—You remember, I told you about that crazy guy I used to hang out with. He's quit writing poetry."

"The one who fled to Canada."

"Yeah, well, he's back in Syracuse now. Says literature is a luxury for the effete these days. The only thing real is politics . . ."

"I hope you drove some sense into his head."

He shrugged. "He's passionate about it. Committed. Got a lot invested in trying to change things. After all, the stagnation—"

He seemed to be getting off on a single track. She wanted to argue. "But aren't there some reasons to try to influence the culture? Art has always done that."

"He got some people together—I told you about that group of activists that used to meet. I hadn't been in touch with some of them for God-knows-how-long. And my closest friend in college—he came down from Boston."

He stood as if he were still in their midst, listening to their voices. She could sense certain invisible filaments connecting him.

She had to break in. "How did it feel, seeing them? Going back? Did it feel strange?"

She herself was light years away from home. If she went back now, even with so short a space, she'd be a stranger. Too much had happened.

He was moving restlessly back and forth while she ground the coffee beans and measured out the coffee.

"At first," he said, pausing to consider. "I felt I'd been gone a century. Painful, like standing in a glare, being asked embarrassing questions. I felt as though I'd lost touch. So many things left behind, broken off . . ."

He seemed to be falling into regret. Then his expression changed, moving toward enthusiasm. "Only after a week or so, I felt like I'd never been anywhere else. Strange, isn't it?"

They broke off while she helped a customer, then other people came into the shop. There was a little hubbub of noise, people greeting him, asking about the trip and the holidays before. He talked and joked as usual, and sometimes when she looked in his direction he smiled at her. But at odd moments when she caught his expression, it was clear that some part of him hadn't made the journey back across the Atlantic. It fed into a remoteness she recognized. From time to time, she'd had the fleeting impression he kept some part of himself from her. Now something hung in the air unspoken. His eyes didn't follow his smile; she couldn't catch the drift of his mood. Nervous, unsettled—caffeine hitting his fatigue. When the shop was quiet again, she said, "Why don't you go catch a nap. You look ravaged."

"I haven't slept much," he admitted. "After I got back here, I just stared at the ceiling. Things kept grinding away in my head. I couldn't get rid of them."

"Awful when that happens." She recognized the state he was in and how it mated something of her own.

"Florrie," he said, coming over and putting his hands on her shoulders, "I hate coming back this way—it's got me all torn up."

Indeed his misery rose up to meet her, a tumbling sorry mess.

She was in the dark. "Eric, darling, what's the matter? I hate to see you this way."

"I know this is an awful shock, but I'm thinking of selling the shop."

"What! But why?" A chill went through her—she felt the blood leave her face. "Surely—"

"I know," he said. "I feel awful. I can't even tell you. It's just so . . . overwhelming."

The misery? Where had it come from, or, worse yet, had it been there all along, hidden from her, a secret thing? "But why? You've got such a good thing here. And you know I'm behind you all the way."

He shook his head as if to shake off a bad dream. "I kept thinking while I was there: this store, this life—it isn't real. I know what it means to you. . . . I can't explain. I know I'm a monster. But I'm thinking of going back to the States."

Considering the state of her inner life, it was the worst possible moment for Koenig to make his appearance. And the unease she felt in his presence overlaid by her current distress was like a raw spot. His eyes were beacons searching the premises, boring right through her, as if she were merely an obstacle to a view of what he sought but couldn't find. Perhaps he found fault with her clothes, her earrings. Or her mental capacities, which by now he must have assessed and found wanting. He had read more of American literature than she had, and was always trotting out some recent interest, in that hesitant manner of his. Herzog was surely Bellow's masterpiece. He wanted to reread Faulkner. Did she appreciate Henry Adams? Would there ever again be an image as powerful as the Virgin?— he was weary of the Dynamo. Industrial complexes rather than cathedrals. A world of computers and mechanized armies. Would there ever be anything to get one past the ruins? He had held out his arms as though ruins lay in all directions. He seemed to look to her as an American for some kind of inspiration, as to a source of enlightenment, an oracle perhaps ready to yield something more than a riddle. He spoke of ruins as if whole cities hadn't risen up after the war. As if the tumbling down of old walls hadn't left place for the new—even in Albania. He troubled her. He made her want to hold out her hands, palms up, and disclaim all responsibility. And then run for refuge. Only now she was stopped in front of the large hole only she appeared to be staring into. Ruins.

Bombs go off this way, the sudden act of terrorists. And cars and buildings and bodies are ripped apart. Like a war with the present—not to allow it to go on and become the future.

But there he was, Koenig as he'd promised, stepping down into the basement shop in a thick coat that made him resemble a large bear. He stood for a moment dusting the snow from the sleeves, a powdering on the fur collar, taking off his astrakhan and looking around with a face made ruddy by the cold. He seemed to brighten when he saw her—he always looked a little pale, a little frayed, as from the vestiges of an old illness. She looked over at Eric, who seemed greatly relieved to have the outside interruption.

"How are you, old man. Good to see you," he said.

Koenig removed his gloves, then took out a handkerchief and blew his nose. Discreetly, she thought, the way he did everything. She couldn't help staring at him, she was too miserable to think straight. Master of the social graces. Discretion molded into a reserve that looked to her like a highly polished piece of silver. Except when he talked about books or the latest article he was writing on the environment. Perhaps then a certain purity of enthusiasm acquitted him of the need for safety. Or perhaps he was merely trying to save the globe singlehandedly.

"Happy New Year, Eric." They shook hands as Eric rose from behind his desk.

"And my dear Florrie," he said. "You are as beautiful as your name, and how dull-witted of me not to have brought you a rose." Coming over, he kissed her hand. "For the New Year," he said.

His greeting surprised her. Perhaps he thought better of her than she did herself. He dismayed her because, for reasons she couldn't fathom, he made her feel guilty, as if in some obscure way she were failing him, even betraying him. And since, at that moment, everything had failed her, she couldn't bear it.

"Thanks," she said, holding up her hand. "I'll use it to light my path in days to come." Why had he taken the trouble to make the moment into an occasion, given it a touch of elegance even. As though you could snatch up any little particle from the surface of things and turn it into art or perhaps artifice. To flatter her? After all, he'd just seen her in the street."

'Well, it's the New Year," she said. "If anything's rotten in Denmark, we can bury it under the snow." This time she didn't blink from his gaze. Let him enter from any moment of the twenty hours of darkness. Let him quote all the wisdom in his head, backed by any book of manners on the shelf. The phony. She was being unjust, she knew. But she'd have been glad to lash out at anyone unlucky enough to cross her path just then, with an insult so withering the American image in the country would require several years of diplomacy to repair the damage. The phone rang, and Eric went to his desk to answer it, leaving her and Koenig to make the next advance.

"You're looking a little pale," Koenig said, his smile qualified by an expression of concern. "I hope the weather hasn't been too hard on you."

He'd taken the weapon from her hand. It was all she could do to keep from burying her face in the vest he was wearing and letting go.

"I always look bleached out in the winter." It was a lie. Lies for her, manners for him. "Oh, dear," he said. "Now I must find something to complain about."

"Eric, are you working her too hard?" Koenig said, glancing over at Eric, who was now opening a package. The effort at humor could only irritate her, the more for being made in a British accent that had somehow won past his Czech and German origins.

"Every chance I get— You see how she resists me though. Spends all her time chatting with the customers. Here's your book, Anton," he said, coming forward.

24

Their banter was a conspiracy against her. She hated them both.

"Good. Very good of you to order it."

Eric held up the volume. "Terror and Resistance: A Study of Political Violence." Timely, all right."

"Yes," Koenig agreed, taking it from him, looking at the cover. "Yes, I thank you for taking the trouble—"

It could have been any morning of the past six months: passersby in the street outside, things coming and going. Inside, a little pool of quiet surrounded by books. Classics of fiction and poetry, philosophy and history, all in English, along with the latest books by American and British authors—books that had created the order around her. All the knowledge that had been brought between covers, emotion as well as thought: the best that had been thought and said. All beside the point. Gone aground on the moment. Tomorrow, maybe a month or six months from now, it could all disappear.

"I read the notice on the window," Koenig said, "about the Czech poet who is going to read. What do you know about him?"

"Only a little. A refugee—for some years now. I think he was in Yugoslavia for a time," Eric told him, "then managed to get to West Berlin. He's kept very quiet. Family back there, I think. Other connections."

"Interesting. Yes, I will come. I've never heard of him," Koenig said, as though he should have.

"His work is just now being translated into English. It's very political, as you might guess."

And all that created such a moment could disappear, she was thinking. Could disappear because things broke in—in the middle of a pleasant hour, in the middle of a sentence, things broke in, and suddenly chaos was come again. I hate to tell you this, but I'm thinking of selling . . .

Of course, anything was possible. Stamp out one set of possibilities and there was another rising up: forget the books. A month from now it could be a sausage shop or the home of herring and eels. Nothing was impossible on the side of things breaking up, falling apart, disappearing. Nothing was ever impossible—was that what the shop signified? She still couldn't believe it: that he'd throw it all away, that part of his life, his work. Cast it aside like a handful of pebbles. Did he value it so little, and himself? To throw it all away, and for what? To sink back into the past? Impossible. But then came the shrug that said it all: why should it be impossible to make an end, break things up? She was being naive.

"Your family's from there, isn't it?" Eric said.

"My mother's. She left some years ago. Luckily."

Czech on one side and what on the other?

"My father was German. He came as a boy with my grandparents."

There was nothing you could define, nothing you could count on. Everybody was leaving for somewhere else, and pretty soon no nationality would ever be the same. All the races would be warring in the blood. And what bookstore then? She bent to unpack the rest of a carton of books and mark off the titles on the invoice blurring before her eyes. She resisted such knowledge, resisted to the core.

She'd protested. "But you've done so beautifully. You've built up a wonderful clientele—it's a real center of culture here. All your friends, think of them."

Politics. He wanted to fight for some higher good, join the fray. But wasn't there an equal benefit in expanding the imagination, enriching the culture, raising questions? Sometimes people who came into the shop spoke to her with such warmth and gratitude about its existence she felt a personal responsibility for it. For its being there. For her being there, one more among the expatriates or visitors passing through, or foreigners who had lived in England or America or who'd learned English well enough to want to be put in touch with the latest works of authors they admired or reclaim writers from the past they wanted to read now. Familiar ground.

It wasn't only a question of the bookstore, her job, her future in Copenhagen. Minor considerations. They'd had love—what about that? Seize the day. No more waiting for life to begin. These past six months—we were happy together.

He went to the back room to get another carton, a piece of that familiar ground. They were restocking the shelves now that she had finished taking inventory while he was away. Yes, only now he'd met her with that misery that had risen up between them. Now he was ready to tell her he was sick of the whole business.

The growing weariness—she tried to take it in. There was no question of responsibility, what something might mean to them, to her, to a community. That's what he seemed to be saying. There was only sickness. Why hadn't she noticed the symptoms? A lessening of light on the forehead, a slackness. A fainting of vitality. She had missed all the clues. When had they last made love? True, they had been busy. When had their love leaked away? Even now as he talked to Koenig, she could not take her eyes from him as she tried to locate a telltale sign of his malaise.

A wave of fear rose in her chest. She was looking into a breach, into a space where she'd be quite alone. She must hold onto some kind of hope, some sense of possibility. So she had once counseled others.

"Have you ever been back?" Eric was asking Koenig.

"Oh no, too dangerous entirely. My mother left everything behind. I barely escaped a few months later. Only now, who knows? I might go back, at least for a look at my old life, see if I can connect with some of my old friends. I'd like to talk to Havel."

"A hero," Eric said. "A true leader of his people. And a writer, think of that."

"Yes, think of it. They had his plays."

Koenig excused himself to go off to the toilet, and Eric came over to her. "Nothing's written in stone, you know" Again the shrug. "And I'm not going to rush out in the next five minutes and throw all the books into the street. But I've started thinking and making some inquiries."

And what was she supposed to make of that? He was thinking and she was thinking, as though their thoughts were grinding together like stones. I'm thinking of going back to the States. Thinking.

He'd been here how long now—five years, seven years? Had put his losses behind him, vehemently in fact. He was never going back. The country was falling apart, what with drugs and decaying cities and violence in the streets and a president who was wrecking the economy, selling the country down the river: Vietnam and Watergate had shown us our moral bankruptcy. Poor old America. No, he'd never go back.

"I thought you came here to escape the evils of a corrupt society." His phrase.

So he had. But now, he confessed, he felt cut off. There was a kind of life in the culture after all, maybe something more than the glow of rotting wood, and maybe you had to be part of it. " I don't know, I'm confused." He came over then and put his hands on her shoulders and gave her the second kiss of the morning, this time less eager, a sop to her feelings. The first kiss had belonged to another dimension, or so it seemed. She'd run the gamut now what with his and Koenig's. And neither could be trusted.

Koenig was now browsing among the books while Eric worked through his orders. Where indeed had he come from and what had he left behind? What ruins, what trail of wreckage?

Around them all was calm, the morning moving towards its haphazard close. What would she do now?

"Funny, my grandparents came from here, yet this doesn't seem like home. Almost six years here and I still butcher the language. And there's Lily—I'll miss her childhood if I stay away any longer. I feel restless, like I'm living in a little stagnant pool I've created around me."

And there it was. Whatever they'd had, she and Eric—love (could you call it that?)—he'd leave that behind too, just as he'd left a divorced wife and a child on the other side of the Atlantic. She couldn't expect—what? Permanence. Perhaps he'd loved her, maybe even did still, but if it had been a mighty wave at the beginning, it had flopped on the beach, and she was looking at the receding water sucking sand, and the last little fringe of foam.

"And if you go?"

"You're free to do as you like."

Free? She wanted to yell at him. A whole mouthful of accusations. "But not free to go with you?"

He didn't answer. He was a tall, solid-looking man with clear eyes of palest blue that held no malice, even as they held nothing you could pin down, everything they took in just floating under the surface. He was thirty-eight, a year older than she, but he looked younger in a lackluster way, as though he were moving back toward his boyhood from a certain failure of nerve. It was clear now that he lived on the verge of things, met the passing moment with a sense of the temporary, even though the temporary was now six years old. The temporary was a child too, a foster child that could be sent packing. In a single moment, the world had shifted its furniture. Now she saw—had he so seen from the beginning?—that everything between them was simply an affair that could end at any moment. Was that his passion? Perhaps such a perspective gave the only intensity or finally simply allowed it to flow into indifference. And yet love, had it been love, was like a deep sea under you; that was how she saw it or wanted to see it. If it were that deep sea, they could have gone anywhere together, sustained, buoyed up by the depths of their emotional life.

"I thought we understood each other. No promises, nothing binding."

No, nothing binding. She had thought love was enough—the cement and the mortar, the wave and the deep sea. Now she was looking at it all as though she and Eric and the shop itself were already a memory. It gave everything a strange spectral quality, as of time floating with no happening, no ground under her feet.

"And even if I stayed, I figured the time would come when you'd go back."

"Do you think I live what you're living?" she said sharply. "It's because of all this that I stay." She had indicated the store, with its shelves of books and the whole climate around them—where love had been. The books had formed a world. Everything could exist between their pages, even horrors, but at least, enormities though they might be, something contained them: they'd become

29

knowledge. This, too, she tried to hold onto, this flimsy belief that it made a difference.

She looked out. Now Koenig was browsing among the recent arrivals, while Eric sat deep in concentration. He paused to remove his glasses and polished them with a handkerchief. Is that all I mean to you? But she would never ask such a question. It was abject to have to inquire from anyone how do I rate in your scale of existential values? Go look in a mirror, Bright Eyes—check out your narcissism. She was a psychologist, that is, had been one. Now she had a problem, a question of soul. Was the word archaic?

"Indeed, you are pale," Koenig said when he came up to her again. He'd crept up on her blind side and startled her.

She resisted concern or sympathy, for fear it would open upon what had best be concealed. She didn't know him, this stranger with his reserve. Perhaps he struggled to keep up the same kind of reserve. Just now he was holding a book on American foreign policy he was ready to buy.

He claimed once to have spent time in America. But it was Europe that had bred him. He'd alluded to being in Germany at some point after the war. Mentioned relatives here and there. Various travels: Vienna, Rome, Barcelona. In these pieces of disconnected narrative, she could pin nothing down, find no pattern. None of it touched her: she acknowledged no claims. The rest lay unspoken, belonging to the polished vessel of his reserve. She couldn't tell his age—late forties perhaps, but he looked older. What was he but one more person on the move? Like herself in that. What was he looking for? she wondered.

"I imagine you're glad Eric's back and that things have slowed down a bit."

More chitchat. "Yes, things kept us pretty busy."

No wonder she looked a little peaked. Even so, she had the impression she was confronting superior knowledge that shaded off into irony. Her inner life seemed open to view, like one of those stomachs with a window in it. But Koenig couldn't possibly know. He and Eric had been friends for some time: Eric had said as much. Though for the past six months Eric's time had been pretty well devoted to her. She remembered that Eric had been particularly charming just before he left for the States. Had he made up his mind even before he left?

"But actually," she said. "I know how to take care of myself. Indeed I'm very good to myself."

"May I offer you a further opportunity for self-indulgence? A coffee and perhaps something tasty to go with it? I suspect, you see, that you are undernourished. That you need my tender care." He used the lightest touch, how much of it dissembling? Still the words were a lash against her hide. "But really I would enjoy your lovely company." He stood smiling down at her.

The invitation was so unexpected she hardly knew what to say. He'd never done that before, though he'd been in the shop often enough. She drew a deep breath. "Yes," she said, suddenly taking him up on it. "I'd be delighted."

"I'm stealing the work force," Koenig said to Eric as she slipped on her boots and coat, hat and gloves. Koenig opened the door for her. "Be back soon," she said.

❖

"Where would you like to go?" Koenig asked her.

She was grateful for the question "Oh, I know just the place." Now she had purpose and could lead him to one of her discoveries. She tried to relax and allow herself pleasure in being with this man, let go of preconceived ideas. He offered her his arm, and she let him guide her through the crowded street. She got into the measure of his stride.

She put aside all expectation. It was a relief to be in a neutral space, to remove herself, as well as she could, from the heavy weather of the bookshop, to have Koenig as a distraction.

She was glad to be out in the sunlight after the clouds that had bound the city for the past few days. The streets had been cleared, so walking was easy, and the stores were filled with people. Perhaps the sun had brought them out, to make the most of light before the darkness dropped like a curtain in the middle of the afternoon. She was still not used to that.

She tried to account for things, to give them to the light of reason. Eric had always had his moods—he said it was because he was a Gemini—and some part of him, she knew, had never been available to her, even though he talked about Margaret and the divorce, the chaos of their married life, fractured by nagging and blame and manipulation His irritability she'd put onto the pressure of the holidays.

Christmas in a foreign country, even if both Santa Claus and God had dropped away, reminded you of things. You remembered then that you were a stranger. Christmas had been rather hard for both of them. Then he was off across the Atlantic.

"Look," Koenig said. In the window was an elaborate castle of gingerbread, a street of gingerbread houses all decorated with icing and candies. He turned to her as though he were offering her a gift.

"Lovely," she said. She had seen it before, this piece of delight for children. For this was the city of Hans Christian Anderson, and she had been trying, was perhaps trying still, to create her own fairy tale.

At first you plunge into the world. And you must see it, experience the wonder of it. If ogres and witches darken your path, rise up, rise up and defeat them. Help people cure their sickness: she had started out thinking she could do that. As a psychologist, she had seen all kinds, the breakdowns that broke people down: couples running from one another towards divorce, children menaced, abused, violated, and all the rest, young and old, married and single, those caught in the meshes of betrayal and abandonment. They'd handed her their stories, somehow to be revised, given happy endings. All their stories piling up till she was totally empty, till she had none of her own. Till all the stories coalesced in the same disembodied voice that spoke in her head, sought her out before sleep to continue the litany of grief and longing. Then she'd come to Denmark, no doubt hoping to leave all the stories behind and open a new chapter of her own. If at first you want to see the world, embark on discovery. Then what do you do to escape it? You find a pastry shop with a gingerbread house. She had found the best.

"I found the pastry shop where we're headed not long after I got here. Right after I met Eric and started wandering around his neighborhood. One of my most important discoveries "

"It reveals your character," Koenig teased her. "You want all the sweets." He had the manner of a man trying to be lighthearted without quite knowing how.

"Absolutely. I have a sweet tooth you wouldn't believe. I am like a child in this city."

"How long have you been here now? Not quite a year?"

"A year in April. But I may go—somewhere else." She hadn't meant to say it.

"Oh, I hope not," he said, turning to her. "I have grown accustomed to your presence. I do not like changes." There was a hint of dismay. "Where will you go?"

The walking street was thronged with people—a busy time of morning. The old buildings displayed their modern items, clothes, furnishings, elaborate displays of food. The two of them moved into the street, which, though crowded, allowed for easier walking than the sidewalks.

"I don't know. Right now I'm not sure of anything."

"Sometimes I think I should go myself," Koenig said. "I think my eye has grown dull from seeing the same things over and over. It takes a kind of openness, perhaps even childlike, to see the world with fresh eyes."

"I don't think I have that anymore."

"Nor do I."

"Oh, I think you do. It's in your eyes."

Did he really believe that? "What nonsense. I'm approaching forty, and I read the newspapers."

He gave a little ironic laugh. "Ah, the newspapers . . . The breakdown. Things falling apart. Not just the family and the village, all blown to smithereens. Pick your part of the globe, indulge your preferences. Ashes, ashes, all fall down. But the self, the essential being—that, too, exists," he said, summing up.

"And who would put it together again all those fragments?" she questioned him.

We try, she thought—with a sense of irony and with passion. Now Eric wanted to be among the world-savers, forgetting what might be sacrificed in the process.

"Forgive me," Koenig said. "I think I read too many newspapers." Indeed one was rolled up, sticking out of his pocket. In what language? she wondered.

"Actually, I still believe the child always exists as part of the soul. That is, if it is allowed to be," he said. "Le genie est le retour a l'enfance a la volonte. Genius is the ability to return to childhood at will. The Americans—"

"—are still children," she offered.

Again he gave a little laugh. "I think you are twisting my words. Oh, you have the infantile sorts—they are everywhere creating their tyrannies. No, I think you, and others of your nation, in your enthusiasm, your openness, still look for the good in people, for something to be done or salvaged. And for possibility."

He was looking to her for that? To warm his hands at her fire? Well, he was too late. Maybe they'd changed places. "And people here?"

"Maybe down deep—here, other places. But there is a reserve, a suspicion. Too many people have had experiences . . . In the end perhaps all of us will have our taste of them—the war, " he said grimly, but left it at that.

"You're a cynic then?"

"Of course not," he said. "Cynics don't take beautiful young women for pastries."

She laughed. "Maybe only to tease them, take their revenge." And Eric, Eric, what are you? More cynical than the rest? A jack-in-the-box springing out, now here, now there. A man without a country. One of the homeless of the world? No, she wanted the benefit of the fairy tale ending. Could it be that two days from now the mood would pass? I don't know what got into me. Then. I love you.

A window full of pastries announced the bakery. They paused in front of the window, where, for a moment, both of them stood mesmerized. The window was filled with pastries enough to tease anyone's palate or imagination. And suppose now she hadn't a penny, but only a terrible hunger, and was standing there in the cold—the little match girl. Koenig would rescue her: Ah, my beauty.

"I don't think I have ever been here," he acknowledged. "All my years in this city."

They stamped the snow off their boots and went inside, into a narrow little shop with a bakery in front crowded with customers, as it usually was. Loaves of bread dark and light, seeded or filled with raisins, nuts, and other ingredients were stacked in the shelves behind the class-topped case in which the cakes and pastries were arranged. Pastries with centers like jewels. She couldn't help feeling a rush of pleasure. Women behind the counter rushed back and forth taking, orders, serving their waiting customers. She and Koenig stood in line waiting behind those choosing their daily bread or pausing for the indulgence of a pastry with raspberries or apricots or almonds inside.

The warm air surrounded and entered her, and she gave herself to it gratefully. She was chilled inside her coat, and her fingers tingled from their contact with warmth.

"It smells so lovely," she said. "If I close my eyes, it reminds me of my grandmother's kitchen." Air rich with yeast and cinnamon, with suggestions of nuts and honey, apples and chocolate. "I love to come here and sit and watch people. You match their characters with the pastries they choose."

"And what have you learned?" He was smiling down at her almost expectantly, as though he was discovering her power to amuse him.

"I won't know till I've tasted all of them. What will you have?"

"A chocolate eclair. I have a taste for chocolate," he said.

Sometimes when she and Eric had come in, they had changed halves of the pastries they had, so that each could have a taste of the other's. And she had been so happy she almost forgot what she was eating. Anguish went through her.

"And what will you have?"

Her eyes moved over the trays, over puffs of whipped cream and planes of chocolate icing, over glazes with nuts and cherries, over rich little pockets of apricot and raspberry jam. I'm thinking of going back to the States. Suddenly a bitterness rose in her throat, and everything melted together before her eyes: He will sell the shop, he will go away, and I'll be all alone. Not simply alone. He'd put Koenig up to this: to smooth over the breach, to cosset her.

"Sometimes I used to have the fantasy of being in a bakery at five in the morning when all the cakes and rolls come out of the oven, and choosing one of everything."

"All the sweets. And what would it prove of your theory?"

He was smiling at her, challenging her. What was he asking of her? What could she reveal that would answer? She turned to the woman about to take her order. "I'll have one of each."

"Do you wish to take them with you?"

"No," she said, "I'll have them here."

She didn't look to see what was in Koenig's face as he took out his wallet and paid for them. With deliberate casualness she walked back to a table, took off her things and sat down. Perhaps it would take the waitress two or three trips to bring all her pastries. And everyone in the shop would stare at her appalled, while she sat there quietly, as though about to participate in a ritual, some vital ceremony of innocence. She would spread them all out in front like jewels and sit and gloat over them for a time, then carefully take a bite of each, just to see, and eat them slowly one after the other, until, as she glutted herself, the world felt solid beneath her feet—until she was no longer hungry.

❖

She had to talk to someone. Helga had dropped by the bookshop while Florrie was out and left a message saying that she would call and they would get together after things had settled down a bit. Helga had been off in Eastern Europe for several weeks. Florrie was glad for a little space. She hoped to be in a better frame of mind when she saw Helga again, for Helga was savvy about matters Florrie was just learning to be interested in. Most Americans, Helga felt, had very little sense of what Europeans experienced during the past century—what it was like to have a modern war fought on your territory. The bombings and invasions, the slaughter of whole populations, the leveling of cities, and torments of the prisons and death camps, Nor did they understand what tyranny was like—censorship, imprisonment, torture, murder—the way it warped and broke people's lives and divided families. The lies, the fear, the betrayals. "There was a taste of it during The McCarthy Era—people's careers and lives ruined—some sent to prison. But it's an episode mostly buried—a danger not kept in mind."

Whenever Helga returned from her travels, she had she had stories to tell that made Florrie see things differently.

But Beryl was available and told her to come for a cup of tea. With her, Florrie shared things on a more personal and intimate level, glad for her opinions and advice—someone to confide in. But she was careful to distinguish between the need for some people to cling to one another and real friendship.

Beryl Sommerville offered something more, even as she might prove capable of something less. She was not a clinging sort, and though she was still quite young—in her early thirties—she was one of those who appear somehow invulnerable to circumstance, who have found their way to where they are by some natural bent and have maintained a certain singleness of purpose that gave the impression of sincerity.

She was welcome in the homes of a number of well-placed Danes, otherwise not noted for an eagerness to admit outsiders: professional people mostly, who liked the American because she had a respect for tradition and showed such a genuine instinct for social convention she was never guilty of the faux pas the inept fall into unaware. Perhaps it was owing to her Southern upbringing, though after she graduated from Agnes Scott College, where her mother had gone, as well, she'd abandoned the family domain and struck out for Washington, D.C., where her uncle had connections. Then she strayed off to Denmark. "But I always was something of a maverick," she liked to say, and gave one of her lovely, rippling laughs. Since then she'd been in charge of the library at the American Center.

Her manner was gracious without being effusive, and men, in particular, were charmed by her. She had lustrous blonde hair that shone with a reddish glow in certain lights and one of those satiny complexions that made Eric tease her that she'd come to Denmark just to get out of the sun. Fortunately for her own predilections, someone was generally on hand to admire that beautiful hair and skin and to squire her around. She reveled in the company of men, particularly those who took her to dinner at restaurants like Kohl's for their sole cooked in lobster sauce and a bottle of Pouilly Fuisse, or else to the theater. She was a passionate theater-goer.

Florrie saw her as a woman who had a sure eye for where lay the vein of ore, and once having staked her claim, the benefits came like quicksilver. Living right, she concluded, was an art, and dubbed herself an amateur. Only Beryl's voice somewhat put her off: breathy and sweet, almost childlike, as though it were formed by some notion of how a well-behaved little girl ought to speak.

And when that voice said, "Why you poor thing, to have come so far for so little," as though everything Florrie had tried for wasn't worth the candle to begin with, she couldn't accuse Beryl of any studied cruelty. She kept a plain tongue and spoke her mind.

Florrie shifted uneasily on the antique brocaded sofa and took up her cup of tea from the marble-topped table at her side. She saw herself like someone who'd blundered into a social gathering with her dress inside out and only half buttoned: to have spoken of love, of all that Eric meant to her, must have made her ridiculous indeed. In spite of everything there is always something comic in the spurned lover mourning over lost love.

Beryl did a sigh that gave out a certain tiredness. "Yes, I know Eric. He's always expecting some female to come along and save him."

"Save him?"

"Yes, from himself. Some people absolutely require it, you know. They turn everything into a mess, only they can't keep it to themselves. The mess just becomes their lives, and they simply can't wait for the lucky person to share it with, invite into it."

Florrie stood up and walked past the baby grand to the window. Outside, it had stopped snowing, but a layer of gray cloud hung over an already darkening city. Even now she couldn't take on Beryl's turn of mind. If men and women were always looking to one another for new beginnings in the fond hope of canceling out what went awry in the past, she wasn't prepared to fault them. Didn't love have the power to create something new—if it was love?

"I see you can't help moping around about it," Beryl said, "but believe me there's not a man alive that's worth it."

Extraordinary, the vehemence that came through the voice men found so enchanting. From a woman perfectly adored by them.

"You mean that?" Florrie said, intrigued.

"Right to the core," came her response. "If we were made out of Adam's rib, why that's probably the best part of their anatomy. At least, I can think of some others I'd call defective—their brains, for instance," she said, "and their hearts, for another."

Florrie refrained from requesting any further examples. she was surprised

"I kicked out two men who treated me like that rug over there—" She pointed towards an oriental rug patterned in rich blues and wheat, pale orange and gold, "—something to cross on the way to whatever was uppermost in their minds. And since then, I figured I'll do my part, but when it's over . . . " She snapped her fingers, "then that's it, honey—lots of good fish in the sea. Or no worse anyway."

When Florrie didn't respond, she said, "It's simple. You just make up your mind to it. After my marriage broke up, I didn't date anybody for a whole year. I needed the discipline. I figured when I could do it without desperation, then I'd go out. And when I was ready, I had a new man in a week."

Florrie had a sudden fantasy of turning her life over to Beryl to make a clean sweep of things, empty it out like a closet. She could picture an arc of departing contents—old guilt and regrets, bits of longing, outworn notions and keepsakes, obvious failures—all bound for the trash. "You're amazing," she said. "You should put out your shingle, you'd make a fortune."

"No," she said, waving a hand with long, impeccable fingernails, "I'm too busy trying to keep my place on the top of the ant hill. For the rest, I'm content to be a spectator."

Her expression took on a certain grimness Florrie hadn't been aware of before. "Eric is a desperate man," Beryl said. "I'm just surprised he's stuck it out this long. I think anything calling for the long term makes him antsy."

She should leave, Florrie thought, before she had to sweep up pieces of herself. Why wasn't it she hadn't heard any of this before?

"For a time it was a divorced woman," Beryl said, warming to the subject. "Anna—I quite liked her. She wrote poetry and Eric was translating some of her work."

"He never told me about her," Florrie said.

"Why should he, why should anybody watching the spectacle? It might just be taken as nobody's business, an interference."

She should go, she knew she should. "And so he just abandoned her?"

"Not so simple. She was seeing another man, and Eric found out."

Florrie gave a splutter of laughter. "I can't believe it."

"Well, he's one of your idealistic types—you ought to know. He believes in the purity of the image."

"I can't believe this," Florrie said. "It's all so— It's not what he let me see. I wonder if he suspects me. I wonder if the air has been poisoned. Whoever wrote the letter threatened to tell Eric my supposed affairs."

"What letter is that?"

"Why it's a real piece of blackmail," Florrie said, giving her the details. "And I can't imagine who wrote it. Somebody who wanted to break us up, obviously. But who would that be? The letter came addressed to Eric, but he told me to open the mail in case there were orders. But the person who wrote it knew enough to turn certain details of my daily life into lies."

"That is outrageous—really," Beryl agreed. Her tone changed entirely. "When did it come?"

"Just after Eric left. I've tried to think who's been in the apartment, when they'd have had a chance to rifle my desk. I keep a journal, put down things I've done, people I've met and been with. When I think about it, I get chills all down my spine. It's somebody's sickness, I realize. But still you feel—violated." She stood up to take her tea cup into the kitchen and compose herself.

"Good heavens, you've gone white as a sheet. Come sit down. No wonder you're in such a state. What you need is a drink. It's the cocktail hour anyway—in fact, it generally is. What can I fix for you?"

"I'd love a glass of wine," Florrie said, letting herself down into the sofa, sinking back as Beryl went to open a bottle and return with a tray with cheeses and thin slices of bread as well.

Red wine, rich and fruity, and she concentrated on the taste, held the glass to the light for the ruby glow. This apartment, a little island of peace, with its plants and paintings and antique furniture spoke of Beryl's exquisite taste . Beryl liked the finer things. One should not, it occurred to Florrie, disdain the value of objects. They might fade and break, but they didn't seize on destroying themselves or their surroundings as a matter of will. "It's just . . ." she went on, "who'd want to do such a thing? I'll grant it's a sickness—I know about such things. But who? Who'd want to break us up like that?"

"I might have a guess," Beryl said.

"Tell me."

"It's just a suspicion and I wouldn't want to point a finger."

"Jimmy," she said. "Do you think it's Jimmy?"

"Well, he's certainly capable of it," Beryl allowed. "Any man is." And she wouldn't be pressed any further.

When Florrie left, descending the stairs from the second floor of the fine, old, eighteenth-century house where Beryl had her flat, she'd been somewhat lulled by the wine. But when she stepped outside and was assailed by the cold, she entered a moment utterly blank. She tried to call to mind some image of warmth and light, but the dark space took her in, closed her off. She had to think where she was, ask herself where she was going, which way to turn, where the bus stop was. When she left the bus, she felt a sudden panic that she wouldn't remember her street and would be stranded outside unable to find her way. She was ready to weep tears of relief when she arrived at her apartment. She went to bed immediately but just before she sank into sleep like a stone, she thought, "I was a psychologist. How could I be so self-deceived?"

PEELING AWAY THE LAYERS

Build up the walls with silence, close the curtains. Mild for so long, it's cold outside now. I'm ill-equipped for winter here. I wasn't expecting to stay when I came in April and brought only a jacket and a heavy sweater. I've been wearing a winter coat I found in Eric's closet. Eric didn't know whose it was, but said I might as well use it. I'd been planning to buy one, but we were so busy during the holidays I didn't have time. I must do it now. The winter things I left back in Indianapolis are all stored now in Sarah's place, and it would be too expensive to have them sent now. I want a coat with a kapok lining and a warm hood for this region of snows and any other I happen to land in. Fortunately, I did buy a good pair of boots on sale. All my instincts are turning toward survival. I've got to start thinking about money and getting a job whether I stay here or not.

Today I stayed home from the shop and sipped tea and nursed the cold I've been catching. I called Eric and told him I wasn't coming in. He said he'd come by. Do I want to see him? Unfortunately, I do. I put on some Mozart to help me with waiting for him to come.

If I went to the window I could watch the snow and think about the uniqueness of each snow flake: the naked beauty of infinity. Till the darkness of winter distracted me. How long it must go on here, and I am a lover of light. Like some gay creature reveling in a long Indian summer, squandering my stock of warmth and light. Now I've been zapped by the cold. For six months I lived and played, how heedlessly, and now I retreat from the snow and write as though to draw back that perfect season.

You don't look for the end in the beginning. It was chance, a finger marking an oh-so-casual streak of circumstance. Some slight movement of the will and your life is changed forever. Who'd have thought? A gathering at the Embassy to launch the Danish issue of some literary magazine that the Embassy and the bookstore were sponsoring together. Why not go? After the rounds of psychological jargon, it seemed a lovely escape. I needed a new idiom. I've always leaned in the direction of literary expeditions. And then the chance to walk new streets, make a few discoveries.

I was standing next to a group of people as I drank my glass of wine, listening to one of the men telling a joke. It was funny, and when I laughed, I was invited to join the circle: a group of Americans, mostly my age, a couple of them younger, one husband and wife who'd been in Denmark for many years. I've come to know them now, though I've not seen Susan for weeks; Henry and Yvonne, the gypsy translators, rather sad people, Beryl, Jimmy . . . And one or two I'll never see again.

After they all went their way, Eric asked me to have dinner with him. He'd been standing next to me, a restless current, and I caught his interested glance in my direction a time or two. He took me to a small restaurant not far from the park, where we sat long at table over a very good ratatouille, accompanied by a light and fragrant white wine, then coffee and cake and brandy. His face seemed flushed—it could have been the wine—and he kept leaning forward as though not to lose a word I spoke. We kept looking at one another, trying to figure out, I think, what questions to ask, how to move ahead with a certain finesse when you really don't want to ask questions, but long to move to where nothing has to be said. A glow surrounded his face. I wanted to touch him, trail the tips of my fingers across his eyebrows and lips, then close my eyes and linger over the contours of his face. I wanted to touch my tongue to the rim of his ear, feel my fingers in his hair, so invitingly thick and curly. My face—I don't know what was in it, my blood tingling as it was, racing through my arms and fingers. Oh, desire, how long since I'd felt it! And as he walked me back to the hotel, the houses, each person who came towards me on the street, the slice of moon on the edge of the evening, the brace of poodles straining on the leash, the scent of spring unfolding itself all hurt me with an exquisite pleasure. More real than real. Oh, I was peeled raw, and the touch of those presences was unbearable. Inside and outside met, dissolving that thin separating membrane. Excruciating happiness.

The next day I cut the meetings right at noon and hurried off to meet him. I stood outside in the sun as he closed up the shop for the lunch hour, and we went for herring and beer at a tavern and ate it with thin slices of brown bread. He wanted me to come back at the end of the day, and for a space of hours I sat in the sun in a park, watching the ducks on the pond.

I have barely any memory of the conference dinner and the speaker I forced myself to listen to. Afterwards I hurried off to the bookstore. Eric had some schnapps a friend of his had brought him from Austria. "It's what you drink only with a very special person," he told me. "I must drink it with you." I watched him pour the pale, almost colorless liquid into the two small glasses, as though I was being offered some powerful potion. Was I ready? I was approaching a place from which, perhaps, I couldn't draw back. If I drank, could I go on living the life I led? The question seemed absurd—we'd known each other three days.

"Now," he directed me, "when you drink with someone here in Denmark, you must first look into their eyes, tip the glass, and then say Skoll.

"Then you drink."

We held out our glasses and drank, the liquor burning a track all down my throat. But then a kind of release.

Another layer was being peeled away; first one, now another. I had to marvel. They'd been there—they'd been part of me, like old scar tissue, protective but limiting. Now it struck me that if I let go and gave myself the freedom, I'd be open to discovery and, perhaps in time, find myself down to an unknown core. An experience beyond anything I knew. Both exciting and scary

In my work I'd always had faith in such a capacity, but for myself? How you could undo these entrenched ways of being . . . you couldn't be sure. One brief, disastrous excursion into marriage at twenty, and then the affairs that live off the tension of whether and when to go to bed with this one or that one, and what it will mean five minutes or five days or five months later. For somehow the disillusionment you thought to have left behind creeps up on you. I suppose that's what you call experience. Maybe I've kept looking at men for some sort of salvation, as though they could rescue me from being what I was, smooth my path, lift me up to where I could catch a glimpse of a higher reality. The quality product, you see, your best, most-heavenly-feathered love—from Eros' right wing. To save me from myself. Save me from being the good witch trying to patch up marriages; telling parents how to rescue their kids from dealing drugs and racing their wheels round in a drunken spree, cutting the narrowest margin against death for the sake of feeling alive. Save me from trying to set the world straight for all the homeless and abused children of whatever age.

Let us be, the two of us alone on the planet, having sloughed off the modern world. Let me be merely a woman loving loved by a man.

I was afraid too. Even if I found the man, would we just stare at one another like imbeciles, then finally throw off our clothes because we'd reached a conversational impasse?

Eric was different. "Believe me," he said, "we're here to make a difference to one another. When you're near, there's a powerful presence in the room. That's the power of Eros." And we did it justice.

It made her impatient, the sickness that filled her chest and sent her into painful coughing with phlegm, sickness whose taste almost suffocated her. Three days later Florrie was still in bed, her cold having become bronchitis. The third day Eric said he would come by to take her to the doctor. "Jimmy's back. He's going to take over the store while I'm gone," Eric told her over the phone. To take care of her, he wanted to do that. She yearned in the direction of hope. "Here, Jimmy wants to talk to you."

She didn't want him to. "Look—" But she was interrupted.

"Hello, sweetheart. You get well in a hurry, hear. Or I'll be around there to do something about it. Love you, my dove."

She hung up, seized by a fit of coughing. He aggravated her. What did he mean? His every exchange came as a push for further intimacy. Yet Eric had been standing there. Listening or not bothering to listen? Or maybe she was giving Jimmy more than his due. The truth was likely to be that she meant little to either of them.

After she took some cough syrup, she lay down again, to rid herself of the insinuating buzz of Jimmy's voice. The man who liked to boast that he'd been around the world and slept with a thousand women. Yes, he was exaggerating, but truly he'd lost count. They fell for him, they couldn't help themselves. But in turn, he loved them all—old and young, fat or thin, plain or knock-out. He was honored to have offered himself for their pleasure. As though he gave out some special scent, or some kind of magnetism that made him irresistible. He bestowed himself so generously, moving into their rooms or flats, and allowed them to take care of him so that he could dedicate himself to important work.

He'd left the States right after college, living all over Europe, at home anywhere—never in need, wanting nothing. And he would never go back. All the while, he'd been writing what was to be the erotic novel of the century. "Everybody thinks the barriers are down," he said. "Just because they've read D.H. Lawrence or Henry Miller or a few sex books. Or smirked over some porn and got turned on. Think they're sexual athletes. What do they know? Not a goddam thing—on the playing field or the battlefield."

The book had consumed him for over fifteen years. But now he was in the final stretch, he kept telling them all—on the verge of a major breakthrough.

"Most so-called civilized people get their kicks from money or blood. The feel of the green. Sex-y! Or from a bunch of hunks mauling each other on the football field . Or from patriotic war shit. Shooting the hell out of helpless populations. But the real thing—

You had to go to the depths for that." Of which he was qualified to speak. At least by his own boast. Perhaps, she acknowledged, you could borrow a certain warmth from all that heat, an indulgence she would gladly pass up. The feel of his hand on her shoulder made her shudder. Or his effort to kiss her—the way he leaned over and breathed on her neck. Something invasive about it. Like free samples of a drug too dangerous to use. She just wanted to push him away. And she resisted any suggestion of fascination, as though it might bind her like a spider's web.

Fortunately, there was no shortage of women. At the moment, Carla was the one held in thrall. She was young and sleek and knowing, a student at the University, an American. At parties she hung around while he talked offhandedly and took in whatever happened around her as if it confirmed what she suspected but offered nothing new. She bought Jimmy expensive presents she liked to have him show off: a hand-knit sweater, a suede jacket, a watch in a gold setting. "Look, see what Carla gave me," Jimmy would say, amused, as though she'd somehow missed the point. "Sweet kid, isn't she?"—giving her a look that fell just short of condescension. "Looks great on him, doesn't it?"

If Carla's tone suggested pride or pleasure, it was of a superior kind that had to do with the deeper motives of their relationship.

Carla was such a glorious creature Florrie wondered why some man wasn't smothering her in presents. A puzzle. She almost envied her, because she was convinced that, however superficial the attraction between them, for whatever gratifications, and even granting that moment in her kitchen, Jimmy wouldn't summarily abandon Carla for someone else

When Eric came, he put aside everything that had occurred between them and treated her as tenderly as a breakable object. After examining her and listened to her chest and her cough , the doctor recommended the medicine for "a rattling cough," Eric went to buy it

at the pharmacy next door, together with a syrup that would ease her throat. He then brought her back to the apartment and helped her out of coat and clothes and into bed. He filled a pitcher of water and set it with a glass on her night stand—she should drink plenty of that—and then gave her the phial of little round pills to dissolve under her tongue.

"I hope that'll begin to make you feel better," he said and asked her if she wanted something to eat. He'd brought her some bread and salmon, as well as apples and oranges. She appreciated what he had brought to her, but she wasn't hungry. He put the food in the refrigerator.

"Okay for the medical side," he said. "Now for the real cure—" and began taking out the rest of the things he'd brought. "I've got whiskey, I've got honey, and I've got a lemon. And I'm going to make you the best hot toddy you've ever swallowed."

"How lovely," she said. "I can't remember the last time I had one."

"It'll put you to sleep, and when you wake, you'll be a new person."

"I hope so. All I've done is sleep, and I long to be awake."

When he'd fixed the drink, he brought her a mug with a dish towel wrapped around it. "Careful now, it's very hot."

His tenderness, his seeming pleasure in taking care of her seemed better than any medicine. He knelt and kissed her on the cheek. "I do love you," she said, gratefully. "And I love you," he said.

"I hope so. Oh, it smells good," she said, taking it from him, breathing in the steam. A healing potion brought because she was sick. She wanted to sit there holding it, anchor the moment with him in it. But he wasn't leaving. He brought in the rocker from the living room that also served as her study and sat down.

In her weakness, she felt a whelming of gratitude that he had come like this, taken her to the doctor, made her this special drink. It was what she'd have been glad to do for him, what any two lovers might do for one another.

"You okay?" he said, when he noticed her wiping her eyes. "It's not too strong, is it?"

"No," she said. "It's wonderful, it really is."

"I used to take care of Margaret like this," he said, in one of his infrequent bursts of confidentiality. "She was sick a lot."

In her present state she had put him in mind of his ex-wife, as if such a state brought out the best in him. Or perhaps he'd merely been thinking about her, and it was to her Florrie owed his attention. She could not, though, in her present condition afford to throw Margaret in his face.

"Sometimes for days on end," he said. "She'd get those nervous attacks. A real frenzy. She couldn't breathe, and she'd be in a sweat, like something terrible was happening right before her eyes. I've actually seen her hair stand on end."

It was almost too much to take in, this unknown woman paralyzed by panic, or so it sounded, Eric hovering over her. She must have had a powerful hold on him—even now she could reach across the Atlantic and snatch him. "How awful," she managed.

"It was, it really was."

He rocked slowly back and forth, and she fell out of his attention. He was back there with those attacks. If he was making a bid for her sympathy, asking for some sort of acquittal, he'd certainly hit her at her weakest moment. Look, she wanted to say, do we have to talk about that? I'm the one lying here in this moment. But she let him go on: at least she'd know what she was up against.

"I'd get her to bed in a dark room and put cold compresses on her forehead and hold her hand. For hours like that."

"And how long did you go on doing that?" she asked hoarsely.

"Four or five years—I've lost track," he said, looking off into space. "She tried everything. Tranquilizers—they helped some, till she got immune. Various doctors. They couldn't find anything physically wrong. Stress possibly."

"That must've been hard on you," she said. The drink was making her drowsy, and now she wanted him to go. She wanted never to have met him. "I think I'll just . . ."

"No, actually," he said. "I felt very close to her then, just holding her hand. I liked taking care of her. She was so helpless."

"And you like taking care of me?" Her voice was a croak.

"Yes," he said, looking at her sympathetically. "Yes, I like that."

He would love her then, if she were sick all the time? If that's what he wanted, if that was her clue to binding him to her, it was too horrible to contemplate.

"Eric," she said suddenly, "is that what you want to go back to?"

She'd startled him. And he sat there resisting an answer. He'd let himself be sucked in. With so much sickness all around, it was such a struggle not to succumb to it. Was there anyone left whose sensibility hadn't been twisted out of shape? Except for the Danish king? And was it too much, too exclusive and selfish to try to isolate some small space, to create something green and growing?

"That's a question," he said, leaving her no wiser. "Feeling better?" he wanted to know.

"Sleepy anyway . . ."

"We've missed you. Everybody's asked about you. Henry and Yvonne—they're going to Italy for a couple of weeks. I can never figure out how they manage it with what they live on. Koenig was by. He asked me how you were. Helga's back—I know she wants to see you when you feel better.

He was trying to slip away from her. "Is it, Eric?" she insisted. "Is that what you want—more of that?"

A dark spot came to his cheek, as though it were being sucked into a hollow; he looked haggard.

She had to push in another direction, even if it took all her strength. "Eric, think what you're doing." It was hard for her to breathe. "You know the shop is really a center here. I've said it before. What it gives to people, how it brings them together, offers a connection. Books. Culture. Other ways of thinking. And the reading series—people coming from all over the city to hear. Do you remember the discussion of Mandelstam's poetry—how exciting it was?" She was left breathless.

He took her hand. "If I didn't need the money, I'd let you take over the shop."

"That's not what I mean." She put her hands to her temples. "Oh, my head is like cotton-wool and it's throbbing like crazy." She tried to say something about creating a life in a place, following its possibilities, but the words were lost in the throbbing. "I can't think straight." She closed her eyes.

"Florrie, you're sick and this isn't the time for heavy discussions. I'll say only that I've tried. I really have. But this isn't home for me. I don't know where home is, but it's not here."

"Nor with me," she said quietly.

"You're looking at failure," he said. After a pause, he said, "I know it doesn't look that way. The shop is doing well and—"

"We were happy," she reminded him. She had to remind herself as well.

"Yes," he acknowledged.

"Then why?" She wanted just to let him go, but she made herself sit up and kept drinking the warm liquid, to draw strength from it. She needed strength. She'd staked so much on living in the direction that had opened to her, on her ability to make a difference. Now it had become such a struggle.

"I can't answer. It just hit me when I was there."

"But it was your first trip in five years," she said with some force. "And it was bound to have an impact, to set you back on your heels even. It's like culture shock in reverse."

"I suppose so," he granted her.

"And you haven't allowed yourself any perspective. You came back and—wham." The irrationality of what had happened stunned her. "Think of that."

He shifted uncomfortably.

"We were just beginning to make plans. Think how it was with us. I stayed because of that."

"You make me feel like a worm, Florrie. Don't you know I can't stand it, this guilt I meet everywhere I turn. Always the mess that lies behind you. Guilt and more guilt." He'd stood up and walked away from her. She couldn't see his face.

"Maybe that's half the trouble, thinking you can leave it and just move on."

"Only that's what I've done, don't you see?"

"And you think you can go back now, that it's just been sitting there in a little pile waiting for you to come and clean it up?" she said, struggling to get the words out. "You know better. That's the past now. Maybe if we had an apartment together, our own place . . . where you'd sink your teeth into this life, here with me . . . "

The whole idea had him spooked, she could see that now—why they hadn't moved in together before this. He was trying to keep a slippery footing on both sides of the Atlantic.

"I'm confused, Florrie. I honestly am."

"I know," she said. "I understand that you're going through hell. But I do love you. I don't want to give you up."

"I love you too," he said, moving toward her, taking the empty cup from her hand. He leaned down and kissed her on the forehead.

"Don't throw it away," she said, "—what we've had. Give yourself some time—a few months. Give yourself that, give me that much. Promise."

"All right," he agreed. "You deserve it." He took her hand. "You deserve better than me. Don't think I don't know it. You sure you don't want something to eat?" he said gently.

"No," she said, giving him a smile. She'd gained an important concession, she was convinced of it. "I think I'll sleep now." And she lay back exhausted.

When she tried to look out the window, she saw that the snow had filled the bottom half and reduced the world to her one little room. She took up her notebook and tried to get something down:

I'm down in my cave and can't see out. I keep dreaming. Every time I sleep, I dream. I know that I want to come up for air, but I'm compelled. I can't write; my head aches so to drift downward.

A stone lay on her chest, and her efforts to heave it off sent her into violent fits of coughing, only for her to fall back again. When she attempted to look out, the furniture stood in the way, impeding her vision; beyond that, the walls. As she dozed and woke and dozed again, each spell of sleep pushed her deeper. A tunnel opened down into the dark, where things carried on a life of their own in their hiddenness. Now they glowed with a dark, spectral light.

She was looking for something her father had given her, an egg that was not just the New World, but something more—she had forgotten what. He was nowhere in the garden, and there were holes in the ground where the rosebushes had been. Her eye hurt: a sliver of glass was lodged there. She was momentarily blinded and couldn't see the new model he had made of the human embryo. Then she felt in her hand the egg, but it was made of stone, and she turned to see the grinning face of Jimmy Caledonia. "How do you like it, Sweetheart? I promised it to you all along."

She woke in a sweat and tried to calm herself with a glass of orange juice. When she slept again, her father was standing in front of her, much as she remembered him, railing against the world: they'd stolen everything from him, and she, too, had been carried off by aliens to another planet. He shook his fist at the sky.

She tried to stay awake, reminding herself that her father had been granted some recognition finally—given a room in the museum dedicated to his inventiveness. Just before he died, it was true. She thought of him with great tenderness, the boy who had found his way out of poverty to offer something unique to the world: a whole new way of looking at the development of the human fetus. She tried to remember his face and to recall her childhood self as she sat on his lap listening while he read to her, and later when he took her on rock hunting expeditions, or described the constellations for her as she looked through the telescope.

She fell asleep again trying to call to mind the names of the constellations she knew and match them with their particular configurations.

When she woke, it was to the sound of the buzzer announcing someone at her door. She shook off sleep, hastily slipped into her robe and went to press the button.

"Koenig," she heard from the other end and opened the door. Indeed there he stood in the doorway moments later, a bit of snow still on his boots. She roused herself, shook back her disheveled hair, felt the raw edge of the cold that clung to him and drew back to let him enter. "Come in, you must be cold. "

There was a moment's stupefaction while he took in her appearance, and she felt once again caught out, exposed. Then to cover her confusion, she said, "The last time I saw you, you were foolish enough to offer me a pastry."

Now he was offering her something further, for he was carrying a basket. "Not more pastries," she said, closing the door behind him.

He laughed, almost light-heartedly. "No," he assured her. "Now I know better."

She had to make an effort. "And you've come round again after you've been forewarned. Can't you recognize folly?" she said. "Whoever touches me touches folly." She wondered that he came, though she was grateful for a distraction. Her voice was growing rusty with disuse. "Do take off your things."

He set down the basket, removed his coat and hat and hung them on the coat tree.

"We're friends, are we not?" he said, as though it had not been established conclusively. "When Eric said you were sick, really sick, I thought about what it's like to be ill in a strange city."

He was rather an ugly man—something of the bulldog about his features—but when expression animated them, got past his reserve or his distance, he was, not handsome, but appealing. She could recognize a humanity in him. And she realized she was glad to see him. She hadn't really been abandoned. Her landlady had looked in. Beryl, who'd had to go to some embassy thing she couldn't get out of, still called her when she had a free moment.

Eric had promised to come by, but instead sent Jimmy around with some eggs and other provisions. He wanted to come inside, but she insisted all she wanted to do was sleep and for him to please go away. He was finally persuaded to leave. Eric did call to ask her how she was doing and apologized for not coming. He hadn't been able to get away, what with folks coming in for their orders and he being very much behind with the bills and correspondence . . . Mainly she wished Eric had come so that they might build on the good feeling that had been generated between them. She hoped there would soon be other opportunities.

She was relieved that Jimmy had been persuaded to leave. He would have cooked something for her. He wanted to talk: he always wanted to talk. With his special combination of gall and confidentiality, he gave the impression it was to you, sweetheart, only you, that he had to speak.

Once she was fully awake, she knew she was feeling a great deal better. But what she would talk to Koenig about she had no idea. He stood there in gray sweater, dark slacks and boots, more casual than usual, looking around her apartment on the first floor of the building.

One entered a vestibule that led into a narrow kitchen with a counter and stools where she generally ate her meals unless she wanted to watch something on the television in the living room. A doorway just before off the vestibule led into a living room made attractive with a comfortable sofa and chairs. Bookcases stood along the walls, and a folding table next to the window that could be opened when she had company for dinner. A narrow hall led to her bedroom, with a bathroom and a small room with a rocker and a desk she used for a study.

Mrs. Erland, her landlady, whose husband was a purser on a freighter, and her three children, who regularly tromped over her head and sometimes, when she met them, tried out their English on her, gave her privacy enough. She was comfortable in her space.

"What have you brought?" she asked Koenig as he headed for her kitchen counter.

"Something for you to eat. Soup and some bread—that's all."

"Do you always think it necessary to feed me?"

"Perhaps," he said, looking into her face as though to determine her case. She gave a little laugh, though she was grateful that he'd taken the trouble.

Illness made you vulnerable. I am a child in this city. At the moment, she admitted to feeling rather shaky. "I haven't felt much like eating. I couldn't taste anything. Mrs. Erland brought me some broth—she lives upstairs, but I slept past breakfast and lunch. I haven't eaten anything today."

"Then it's a good time to eat something. To give you strength," he said. "Shall I leave this and go?"

"No," she said. "I'd be happy for your company. You can make yourself a cup of tea. There are tea bags in the cupboard over the counter. Just put the kettle on."

She couldn't bear to have him just sitting there watching her eat.

"Very good—I will."

He put on the kettle, found the tea and drew a loaf of bread from the basket, found the cutting board and sliced two thick pieces. He'd brought butter and jam. He set the soup and bread in front of her on the small folding table Mrs. Erland had brought for her. She began to eat slowly, as though to savor every bite "It's so good," she said. He nodded. "I'm glad.

He was sitting in the chair that had been drawn up next to her bed, waiting for his tea to cool. She urged him to have a slice of bred and jam as well.

"Eric told me yesterday you hadn't recovered," he said, "and were alone. It is hard to be ill in a city where you are a stranger, especially in the winter."

Her situation had obviously made a strong impression on him. "People have been looking in," she told him. "All very kind." She'd tried not to weaken herself with fretting. A matter of survival. Either the body took on that task for you or turned against you, sometimes carrying on its battles in spite of you. She tried to stay content with that, allowing herself to drift between waking and sleeping. It took energy for anything more demanding, such as wrestling with troublesome questions.

He offered her more soup. She took a bit. "Do you like to cook?"

"In a way, yes—eating is such a privilege. But it is very boring to cook for oneself."

"Your family?"

He shrugged. "There is no one anymore."

Across from her, Koenig seemed too large for her room. Less a question of size, but by virtue of some moral or psychological dimension, or possible force of experience she had no way of gauging. Very likely he had earned his way to irony. He knew about winters, about being sick; perhaps he knew about hunger or persecution as well. He was seeing her at her worst, her most vulnerable, this American from whom he expected who-knows-what.

"Your father, what was he?"

"A very remarkable person in many ways." No, more than that. A model of the American genius, surely no less. It occurred to her that she would offer Koenig her father. In her own sorry condition she had nothing of her own; but her father, if nothing else, would give him a return for the soup. Maybe even what he was after.

"Wait," he said suddenly. "I almost forgot. I brought some fruit too. Would you like an apple or an orange?"

He'd thought of everything. "Oh, thank you, but I'm really satisfied. Fruit will be nice for breakfast. All of you are taking such good care of me."

"You must be careful in winter"—it was certainly on his mind—"not to get seriously ill, really run down. It takes strength to get through a winter." He seemed to allude to more than the realities of cold and ill health.

"Yes, it's hard," she said. "You're really closed in, and everything shrinks to how bad you're feeling." She stopped herself. Her worst days reduced her to dark imaginings. What if she got pneumonia, landed in a hospital, everything out of her control. Here in a foreign country facing an uncertain future. Then if Eric went back to the States. Would he do that? "It's good of you to remind me." To warn her, in fact. Not let her fall—she wasn't falling, was she? Was that why he'd come?

"I think you'd have liked my father," she said, picking up the thread of her thought "He was," she was inspired to say, "a true innocent. A rare adventurer. There was always a new world for him to discover. He gave me my name."

"Florence?"

She laughed. "You'll have to be more imaginative than that. To give you an idea of what he was like. He wanted to name me Florida. Florrie is a compromise he made with my mother."

"He came from there?"

She let out a peal of laughter. "Sorry, logic won't do the trick. Actually, he came from Louisiana. No, it was the idea of the place, the beginning of the New World—that's where the Spaniards first came ashore on the mainland, you know. To that tropical paradise full of birds and flowers. He wanted to celebrate that with me."

"A real contribution. Yes," Koenig reflected. "He was indeed a lucky man to be so inspired."

"That was his work." She looked at him expecting more, but he said nothing further. She felt he was holding something back.

"He could make a kind of leap," she insisted. "You told him what you needed, and he could see immediately what had to be done. This back in the thirties." It was what she'd so admired in him—an imagination, not only for what he could make and do, but what he could conceive about being human. A man self-created by genius and struggle. And the sort of childhood he'd given her as a result: full of books and games to challenge the mind and the curiosity to know. And he'd wanted to know everything. He was an omnivorous reader. There wasn't a meal that wasn't interrupted by a trip to the encyclopedia for something he had to know right then. He drove her mother nuts. And every night she went to sleep with the sound of his voice in her ear. One night she might be weeping over the fate of Ophelia or wondering at the devils planning the battle to regain heaven. Another, she might be escaping into sleep from Kropotkin's social theories.

Koenig gave a little laugh. "A bit overwhelming."

"Oh, it was," she said. "But he had such a hunger. And you see, he never forgot where he came from. He was sure that the great hope was other people just like himself. People who just needed an opportunity. They might be people who just did their ordinary

59

work, but he would say, 'Think what this does for our lives, what comforts we enjoy because of them—the way we can flip a switch and fill a room with light and turn it off again.'"

She particularly remembered the time they visited the Hoover Dam, how he insisted on meeting personally the man who threw the switch. "That's the fellow who gives us the light in our living rooms.' he said. She took that was the basis of his feeling for social justice, his great belief in the working class.

"Ah, yes." Koenig said. "I know something about that—the triumph of the proletariat. The brotherhood of the worker."

"Oh, but he was never taken in by ideology," she hastened to add, as though he'd missed the point. "He hated any sort of dogmatism. He held onto an idea so long as it worked, but when it didn't—poof, he let it go."

"That is pretty extraordinary," Koenig acknowledged, "like abandoning a beautiful woman." He smiled.

"One you allowed to seduce you?"

"I'm afraid so."

She did not ask him to elaborate. "There are personalities that can make a difference. Do you believe that? They can pick things up, turn them in the light, and something happens."

"Yes," he said, "only it's very rare. Some people manage to escape from the chains of the mind, while the rest of us chase a will o-the-wisp."

She didn't want to think that way. If you got to the end and there was nothing after all, what then? Time was growing short, and all the promise . . . "My father could move in all directions, you see. There was a whole world out there, and he wanted all of it." In addition to everything else, he was a passionate mountain-climber. He made himself a naturalist and could identify herbs and their medicinal use. Toward the end of his life he studied geology. He was especially fascinated with crystals. He kept bees, installed his own telephone company for the community where we lived then, in Idaho—they didn't have one, and he rigged one up. And kept a record of the star showers every August.

"My God!" Koenig said. "He was a phenomenon. You see them—

you never know where. Only in my part of the world, so much waste of talent . . . Suppressed, hidden. Except for those who fled. When the mind is imprisoned—and all of us make the prison . . ." He let the rest of it go. "And you are his daughter! That must be a bit daunting."

"He was so entirely convinced I'd go on, create beyond him. And he led me into everything he undertook." Now she wasn't certain it had been a blessing. "'You have all my science,' he said to me, 'and it's only the first movement for your mind. You'll leap beyond that, take the stars and juggle them like puff balls. You have another kind of mind. You'll dream beyond me.' That was him all over."

She had two older brothers, she told Koenig, who were too intimidated by him, with all his energy and enthusiasm, to follow in his footsteps. "And they resented him heartily. Resented me, too, for being the one he chose to take up where he left off." She was beginning to feel fatigued. "And sometimes I wonder about that myself ."

They'd gotten off easily, it seemed, dropped into an old pattern and gone on to lead their unpretentious lives with jobs and family. And her mother, who was the backdrop for all that labor and activity, had only to keep the family together and put food on the table. She had her clubs and diversions.

"I wanted to help people," she said, "help them improve their lives. But I had no great ideas. He was like a beacon. I can't do any of it. It would take, I don't know, a magician's gift. And something else, I wanted quite selfishly . . . " She broke off.

"It's hard to resist the lure. Yes," Koenig said, as though agreeing with himself. "But don't give up too soon. You're not at your best just now. It's hard to improve anything when you're suffering."

"It's not just that—" she said. The idea of her suffering surprised her. She had intended to give her father to Koenig as a kind of gift. But the way she had revealed herself was distressing.

"You see, he was able to bring a design out of the flux, to use his mind that way. I can't. There are too many things that don't fit."

"I know that too. And something of science. How hard it tries to reach for the underlying order. In spite of the irregularities that fall across the path. The order is God— And the will to impose it is human. And something else . . . The higher order goes quite beyond us."

He was, it seemed, making little circles all around her that she couldn't penetrate. She hadn't told him anything he didn't know, it occurred to her. On the contrary . . .

"My little life," she said miserably. "I didn't go the normal route— beyond one brief excursion into marriage." She hadn't meant to refer to it. "Family, children—I left those aside, for whatever I was chosen to do. Only what is it?"

What had been eluding her came together in a vivid set of images that lived beyond her childhood, from those days her father took her to the lab. It was an old building with wooden cabinets and metal casement windows, pull-down blinds and fluorescent lights. As soon as she entered, she somehow wanted to flee. It was the primate research center, where the fetuses necessary for research were bred and aborted, and it was filled with angry caged animals. Sometimes the monkeys bit whatever hand fed them or extended in their direction, and occasionally escaped. Then they had to be trapped, recaptured.

She'd been there once when one got loose, and she'd drawn back against the wall in terror, while the monkey leapt and swung around the cages and over the tables, screeching at the top of its lungs. The researcher and his assistant kept trying to corner it before it did any real damage, but her heart was with the monkey, wanting it only to get away.

And now she was forced to remember what a bitter, disappointed man her father had been in his later years, never really recognized for what he'd done. He'd just been a hired hand, not a proper scientist— Still pursuing his enthusiasms, he'd died virtually unknown. And now here she was.

"There is always so much death to carry," Koenig said gently. "Today I am not so dressed up. But I have watched you as you have noticed every detail of my attire. My silk tie. My cuff links. The color of my shirt—lavender, blue. I like those colors. My gray silk vest with its darker pattern. The texture of my jacket—cashmere. My penchant for ornament. Something very fussy, you must think. Or vain, the way I seem to revel in the rich stuffs of the world." He looked at her. "With them, I conceal the death that lives in me."

She was deeply shocked—she didn't know him at all.

CAMOUFLAGE
January 11th

And what is Koenig hiding behind his clothes? Some crime, some hidden guilt? Each time I've seen him he was wearing something that caught my attention, like a bird with a brilliant crest. I remember him from the first, a stocky man in a light summer suit and straw hat, very well dressed. He carried a pocket watch with a gold chain that caught my eye immediately. My father had one, and I felt an irresistible urge to ask him if I could look at his. I went up to see if I could help him. He was looking for an English translation of some stories by Danilo Kis, but we had nothing of his. I hadn't heard of him. When I asked to see his watch, Koenig drew it out and opened the case. It was an ornate watch of white gold with a design of peacocks engraved on the back. It had a set of chimes that might have graced a little music box.

One day I noticed he wore a set of cuff links with gold lions' heads, and a matching tie clasp. He wears rings: a yellow diamond, jade, various stones. I wonder where his money comes from.

If love is a peeling away, a descent to that bare and vulnerable core, it is a dangerous business.

Perhaps I'd do better to consider outer layers of disguise and what they conceal—and which may best be left alone. Forget the pastries and the subtleties of flavor that await the palate, but rather consider the implications of clothing, the nuances thereof.

Shall I school myself from the elegant matrons in their woolen suits, in well-fitted skirts, and silk blouses and sweaters like abstract paintings, with their gold chains and rings, some sparkling with diamonds. Women who have spent their lives handling good linens and silverware and dressed themselves and their children smartly and decorated their homes with the best of Danish modern. (The Danes are especially good at such things.) Women furnish their homes with the simple elegance that draws your admiration. And they pause in their shopping to treat themselves to a pastry, sit chatting pleasantly over their tea, cutting delicate bites with their knives and forks. They would know which pastry to choose, which gloves to wear, which sweater to select.

And if I choose yours, madam, would I come to feel at home here, discover a life of such intrinsic worth, I could cultivate a bearing, a mien that would allow me to travel through all adversities? Koenig has already done it.

At home it didn't work. There were riches all around—in the store windows, in the magazine ads, on television. I, too, loved to browse in shops. I love bright colors and beautiful clothes, the sort Koenig sees right through. I indulged myself. When a certain mood comes upon me, I go shopping for, say, a new sweater, a new pair of shoes. Yet it got harder. Whenever I reached for a hanger to bring out my beautiful purchase, the man who accosted me the day before was there before my eyes. In the tatters he was wearing in the street, asking me for money for something to eat. Breathing his foul breath, his speech slurred—so that I couldn't tell if he was only drunk or one of the schizophrenics lately turned loose into the streets. I wanted to get away from him, escape from his smell, that seemed to come from the rotting of his spirit. "Here," I said, handing him some change." "What am I supposed to do with that?" he demanded, flinging it back at me.

I saw my cowardice as I turned tail from all that misery. Only to be haunted by everything else: the child caught by a stray bullet. In her grief the mother pulled at her hair as though she'd pull it out by the roots. I sat for a long time looking at her picture. "What will I do without her," the mother wept. I thought of the child playing outside with the other kids, running, being chased, laughing then suddenly dropping to the ground and out of the world: the stroke that sends the future reeling into the tomb. The woman had come to me, but what could I offer her?

But finally it was my patient, the Cambodian woman, whom I sat and stared at. I could stare at her as long as I liked, because she had no defense against me. I could devour her and she couldn't see me. Sometimes I touched her hand or her arm, to give her a sense of my presence. At first it made her jump.

"Stress—you're under too much of a strain," my doctor said. He was an old man near retirement, an amiable man who spoke gently. I had come to be cured of headaches. I had imagined a brain tumor, perhaps because it seemed simpler. I'm good at imagining things. I told him about the Cambodian woman.

"She saw the soldiers slit the throats of her children and throw them in the river."

He murmured something as he wrote out the prescription.

"What operation do they have for taking away a piece of somebody's fate?" I asked him.

"I'm glad I'm an old man," he said. "World War II was enough for me. I was there as the Germans retreated from Auschwitz."

"I take her for walks in the park. I describe the flowers for her, and dogs and children. She likes the walks. But there is nothing in the world she wants to see any more."

He handed me the prescription. "One at night and in the morning," he said. "And it wouldn't hurt to get in a massage once a week. Very relaxing—soothing." He shook my hand.

Many stories, had little Florrie heard. But had never really been put to the test, as they say. Extremes, you're speaking of. Aren't we, forgive my presumption, being a little dramatic? Stretching things? The blind woman from Cambodia—why should she become? The Test? How many now have seen, experienced horrors and continued to look at the world? So argued the Florrie with the harder head.

Her blindness was not in her eyes, but in her desire. When you do not want to see the world or discover anything new in it after what you have seen. Eyes weeping and weeping, then seeing no more. What then? Being led like a child. So little Florrie led her all about—all through the park. The pansies in this bed, blue and purple with yellow inside, so many shades of—if only you could see them. Evoking, teasing. Describing dogs and children and babies in strollers. Robins in the trees and the Western jay. And faces, human faces. Let her be rescuer and liberator. Let her be the agency of love, that moving powerfully through all things, would bring the world to light again. Oh fairy tale.

You see, I thought if there were enough love, nothing personal, you understand, but some overwhelming force flowing through you; that is, if you could open yourself to it and it happened, that flood, it could wash away all the scars and stains. Then my Cambodian woman would be cured. I thought that forgetting yourself, peeling everything away to the core, to that point of brightness would somehow create the transcendent moment . . . Perhaps I don't have enough love, or knowledge. The three monkeys of my childhood no longer sit on the mantel. But perhaps they offer sage advice to one who doesn't know any better.

I went from the doctor's office and bought myself the loveliest silk blouse. A blue so brilliant it flashed into splendor. But even before the salesgirl wrapped it up, I was having second thoughts. Covering up. Pretending there is nothing but that brilliance of sky and water to lift you beyond earthly things. Covering up your death.

COLD AND FEVER
January 16th

I feel the cold take up my body, trying to enter and make my death. It is at my fingertips, at my toes, with messages demanding surrender. Begin with the extremities to put the bite, the chilling touch as it tries to claim its territory, and if I'm not careful it will gather an army and move upward. Inside, the heat comes and goes, like one of those furnaces without a thermostat. A blast and it comes over me. It is when the heat grips me most intensely I feel the cold waiting, powerful in its waiting, as though the heat is taking me down and down to betray me to the cold. What will happen if my heart freezes first?

I want to put my faith into waiting, into a new time after the old has peeled away, into being carried onward towards spring, when I'll feel so good I'll leap into the air and rush down to the lake in the park to see if the ducks and swans have hatched their broods and the tulips are in bloom. I want to be heedless as air in the spring sun, but now I'm left to wrestle with fever and chill. I'm a battleground between them, for both claim me. At night inside my comforter, the heat seizes my forehead, I begin to sweat and I am one sensation. If I doze I see phantoms and they are so real to me, I'm not sure if they really happened:

I am walking to the bookshop, and I see it as I first saw it. In the center of one side of a little square. It is late spring, and the restaurants have their tables set outside, so that people can enjoy the open air. I have often sat at a cafe nearby and had a beer and a plate of herring. From the street you have to step down a step into the shop, and there to the left of the door is a table with publishers' overstocks and some sale books. I can almost read the titles as I stand there. Inside, I climb the circular staircase to the second floor to browse unhurriedly among the sections of psychology and social philosophy and history and politics. When I come outside again, light clouds float overhead, and the light lingers on till you think there is no ending.

❖

Florrie wanted badly to meet the Czech poet and listen to his reading. She was feeling better, though she still had her cough. Eric and Beryl, and Mrs. Erland as well, saw to it that she had food and company until she felt well enough to be up and around. Long periods of sleep helped restore her. Fortunately, Jimmy had some kind of job that took him out of the city. Helga she hoped to see at the reading.

That evening she dressed warmly in slacks and sweater, combed hair that had been neglected and put on lipstick. The mirror gave back her pallor. Leaving in time to meet Eric and the others for dinner, enfolded in hat, coat, scarf, and gloves, she went into the street and hailed a taxi to take her to the bookshop. Outdoors it was still January, and the cold invaded her.

Eric was pleased to see her. "So glad you feel up to being here," he said.

Koenig and the others greeted her warmly. She was pleased to see that Helga was back from her travels and hoped she'd have a chance to talk to her during the dinner they would all have together or before the reading. Jimmy came up and crushed her in a hug that sent her into a fit of coughing. She drew back and held up a hand as if to bar his approach. "Sorry, darling," he apologized, seizing her outstretched hand in both of his—"didn't mean to take your breath away," he said with a sly grin.

The jerk, she thought. Eric intervened, slipping a hand under her elbow when she had caught her breath and guiding her to where the guest poet was standing . He introduced her to a tall slender man with a small mustache—Karel Baros. As they shook hands, she told him how much she had been looking forward to meeting him and hearing his work. She had read an article about him, which mentioned that he had been a political prisoner, and that his family had been continually harassed. When the group gathered at the Italian restaurant close to the bookshop, where Eric had reserved tables, she was able to sit beside him and she and the others encouraged him to speak of his experiences and what had led to his arrest.

"It is a terrible life under a tyranny," he said. "Your rights are stripped away, and any suggestion of truth or decency." His voice took on an old anger. "After the Communist Party took over, the relations you took for granted disappeared. Suddenly you couldn't trust your neighbors, your friends, even members of your family. They might be spying on you, ready to betray you to the authorities for some kind of reward or a little bit of power."

"Did someone betray you," Helga asked.

"That's what I believe," he said, bitterly. "But I was already suspect. I taught at the university in Prague and was known for strong opinions. People with ideas are a threat to those in power. First I lost my job. Maybe somebody wanted it, or wanted to give it to a puppet."

"What happened then?"

"Economic hardship," he said. "For a long time I couldn't find any kind of job—then a little work tutoring a couple of army officers in English—secretly, because it was against the rules to learn English. But the officers were discreet and not afraid. I had to watch my step. My wife, Adriana, got a job cleaning an office building. Low pay and hard work. It was hard not to be depressed. You can't imagine the box we had to live in—no outside contacts, no sending off for books, no travel, no free expression. You could be sent off to prison for playing jazz." He described how some of his friends and colleagues were sabotaged in their careers—one in political science who was barred from going to conferences or receiving papers and books from his colleagues abroad. He couldn't keep up with his field and fell into a complete depression. His wife had to keep the family going—he couldn't do a thing.

"Such things happened to some of my friends," Koenig said. "One of them, a wonderful scholar in archeology wasn't allowed to correspond with others outside the country. He, too, sank into despair."

"Of course," said the poet, "there was no mental illness in our country. It was legislated out of existence."

"Not to mention the harassment, continually being hauled up before the authorities and being questioned—you, your wife . . . That's to keep you in fear. And suddenly, on some pretext, agents arrive in broad daylight or the middle of the night and you find yourself behind bars—for months or years without a trial or any real sense of your crime."

"And so it caught you by surprise?"

"Not entirely. You never knew what to expect. Twice. Not to mention the harassment and persecution of my family and myself in between—and the hardship of just getting from one day to the next."

"When did you leave the country?" Eric asked.

"I was released from prison the second time right after the beginning of the Prague Spring," he said, "and immediately joined those who were trying to restore our rights."

He described how a group who created the Charter for Human Rights, Charter 77, as it was called, had been arrested as "traitors," for trying for greater freedom of speech and expression, the right to travel. Nothing in it was illegal or violated any rule or position of the Party. But they were denounced. Over a thousand people signed it, to their discredit. The main ones who created the charter, including Vaclav Havel, were sent to prison. "I was already suspect, so I landed there too, a few months after them. Adriana, my wife, and daughter went to live with Adriana's parents. When I finally got out, she urged me to try to leave the country and she would follow when she could. It was clear that I would cast a shadow over their lives".

His story continued as a kind of recital. No doubt he had told it many times. "I did what I could. I still had a friend in one of the government offices, though we kept away from one another. I knew

I was asking him to take a risk. But he somehow got papers and a passport for me under an assumed name. For a while I moved out of the city. Then some weeks later, I was his driver to a meeting in Germany.

"I was in Berlin for five years. I earned something of a living translating for various companies doing business with the Czechs. Every once in a while I translated medical texts into English.

"I got brief letters from my wife. She sent a photo of herself and Mara, which I still have. She hadn't been able to leave the country. Then a long gap. Nothing. I was worried sick. Then, finally, after many months, a long letter. She told me how terrible things had been. Her mother had been in failing health, then her father had died. She hadn't been able to leave them of course. Mara, she wrote, had been suffering from depression, but she hadn't been able to get help for her. She had been barely surviving, working as a maid cleaning offices in one of the public buildings. A man had surfaced in her life, someone who would take care of them. She was asking for some kind of arrangement whereby we would separate for good. In a couple of years I could be declared dead.

"It is shocking, of course, to be declared dead when you are alive, but what does being alive mean under such conditions?" He held out his open palms, as though asking what hung in the balance.

How would the world move just now, in this moment? Would it leap down like a tiger, tumble like a wall of bricks, leaving one crushed in a corner? The eyes moving from perhaps to perhaps. Even though the city of Copenhagen was solid enough. Or brooding: there was the past. And his eyes were fixed there for a moment. No, there was nothing to stay for, not even longing—the green fields were too far away. That was the impression Florrie got.

"Will you ever go back?" Florrie asked, "now that things have changed?"

"What would I go back to? My daughter is a grown woman. A stranger. What would we have to say to each other? I have seen photos of the north with its chemical plants, the air that cannot be breathed. Like the surface of the moon. No matter where I went or who I saw, I'd still be an exile."

"I know what you mean," Koenig said. "When you go back, it is only to your memories. There is nothing else, it is always too late. Everything has moved past you while you were away. And the things you think to have done—all that is a lifetime ago." So Koenig said.

"I think some people can go back and start over. Something is to be recovered," Karel said. "But for others old wounds are too deep and continue to fester. Old things that were never resolved."

"Yes," Koenig agreed. "They make the way back a very long way."

They seemed to Florrie to be speaking in riddles, alluding to things quite beyond her.

"I've thought at times of going back to see a few friends that have survived, see the villages where I spent so many happy days with relatives. Dare I go? I may have to—" Koenig said.

"So many things still to be wrestled with . . . ," Karel said.

When the waiter came to clear the plates, he had barely eaten anything. And Florrie had just picked at her food. His eyes haunted her.

It was curious. As they were walking back to the bookshop, Karel surprised her. After a comment about the cold, he began speaking about the wonderful springs he had known in the countryside during his boyhood. It was as though he couldn't keep from returning to the country he couldn't go back to. It was as though he were creating a painting filled with pink chestnut trees in bloom, and apple and pear trees blossoming. And flowers opening. Banks of rhododendrons, irises, and lilies. He spoke of walking the paths alongside the farmers' fields, along the river where he went fishing, the waterhole where he swam. She was entranced, as by a vision.

An audience awaited him. A varied group, of those familiar to her and those she'd never seen before. A few Danes who knew English and admired foreign writers. Some local artists and writers.

A journalist who'd write something for the newspaper. Several wanderers and exiles. Among them, some, she knew, like the poet, who carried a death within them. The Chileans, for instance, who'd come to the center there for the rehabilitation of victims of torture and who were now learning Danish, that hard northern language and who might never find a way back to the liquid vowels, the softer cadences, the gentler climate for the tongue they once took for granted

And, then, the American expatriates, who might never find a way back either. Henry and Yvonne, who'd bounced from one job to another and now kept themselves going by giving English lessons, doing a bit of translating for business firms and scholars. Florrie had been at parties with them. They still sought after everything American, gossiped about the country as if she were a disreputable old baggage going from scandal to scandal, but offering a vicarious thrill on the way. They sucked in all the little tidbits. You could see the yearning, for their own language, if nothing else.

She looked for Beryl, who said she would come. She'd kept a seat for her. Beryl, who stood apart and held her own. And, finally, herself, barely there. Not so far removed from home she couldn't go back. But something would be missing. And the missing part kept her here, against her better judgment.

The poet was sitting at the end of the front row of chairs, looking over the sheets in his folder. His leg moved restlessly, as they waited a few minutes for the latecomers to settle in.

Jimmy Caledonia's smile blurred across her vision. Then he got up and came over, Carla at his heels, the slow movement of her hips as elegant as a cat's. "Hey, gorgeous, how're you doing?" He bent down and kissed her on the forehead. Carla smiled down at her. Her eyes, such large eyes, indulged her: she had Jimmy.

"Hey, sweetheart, you feel all right? You're a little flushed."

He reached his hand toward her forehead, but she pushed it away. "It's the wine," she said flatly.

His hands were hard to dismiss. They were full of strength, the shape of the fingers long and clean. His hands flew when he spoke, as though to lift him like wings, to some fresh delight. He looked as if he could wrestle one into any of his convictions. "No, look, I'm fine—really." She did feel warm.

He let it go. "Hey, I'm working for a wine distributor now. I can get good stuff really cheap. Anytime you want something special, just let me know." The smile, the white teeth, the rather full lips. Moving towards her. She felt as though he might pin her to the floor. Ridiculous. Even his name: he'd chosen it because people thought it was Italian. She smiled warily. Wasn't Carla able to use him up? Was there always something left over for every other woman in the world? Oh, please, she thought, a little help here, and was relieved when he and Carla went to sit down.

"Is it warm in here?" she said to Koenig, sitting next to her.

He looked at her; he'd been speaking either Czech or German to the woman on the other side of him. "Do you feel ill? I'd be glad to see you home."

"No," she insisted. Perhaps the poet had something more for her to take away from the evening. She had yet to determine where her own experience met his. That would take a while.

Eric came forward to introduce the poet, who expressed his admiration for the bookshop and his pleasure in being there. Some of his poems had been translated into Danish by people there tonight, and his recent collection into English. "You cannot imagine how grateful I feel to have access to books again—all kinds of books. No more censorship and persecution for trying to speak the truth." He spoke of how these things deadened the mind and turned a culture into a whited sepulcher. Only in the free exchange of ideas could it be a living thing." He grew passionate—he came alive. "No one can imagine the deadly stuff that came out of the Writers' Union during those decades of censorship and repression."

He dedicated the reading to a poet killed by the Nazis, "a great poet and to those who had suffered under tyranny . . . those who have to lie down, for those who can't go through the Valley of Enchantment and whose lips grow bitter with unspoken words for those who have lost their way and can't shed their futile illusions."

A chill went through her. Koenig moved in his chair, resettled his feet, but his face was impassive. He often had such an expression, something impenetrable. She wanted to push away his silence out of sheer curiosity. She wondered at times if he made himself deliberately opaque just to be mysterious. She had a terrible curiosity, she had to admit. Very likely it would be her undoing. There were some experiences you were better off without. When she had her energy back, she thought, maybe she'd just cut her losses and leave. Her mind was beginning to blur. She tried to hold on to what the poet was reading: Learn to be a magician before it's too late. It seemed good advice if only she knew what it meant.

The rest she found it hard to concentrate on: a series of poems entitled "Claustrophobia," with images of halters, strait-jackets, narrow passages filled with the smell of urine. But at the end he read a love poem of such tenderness that tears sprang to her eyes.

THE BOOKSHOP

Her borrowed coat could have been warmer and she is glad to step into the bookshop. Eric has already put on the coffee and sits reading a *New York Times Book Review*. "Oh, hello," he says, putting it aside, getting up. "I'm glad you're here. I wasn't sure last night . . ." He gives her a hurried kiss and grabs his coat. "I've got to go out, can you keep things under control till I get back?"

She's moving in slow motion, and he's gone before she can think straight, react. She didn't think to ask him where he was going. She pours herself a cup of coffee and takes up the *Book Review* from where he has tossed it aside. Several people come in to browse, but otherwise it is a quiet morning. In one of the quiet spaces she dozes lightly, forgetting the coffee.

Then a gust of cold wind sweeps in from the door having been opened and swiftly shut. A man descends. "I'm trying to find Eric Anderson," he says, looking around as though expecting him to materialize. "He was supposed to meet me for breakfast." The look of dismay at finding him gone seems to settle on her like an accusation. His entry seems a bad omen.

"He left a short while ago," she tells him. "He didn't say when he would return."

He removes his gloves, takes out a letter, glances over it hastily, and stuffs it back into his pocket. He unbuttons his coat, wanders around the store inspecting the shelves, climbs the circular staircase and comes back down again, moves to the back and pulls open the curtain in front of the storeroom, Eric's sleeping quarters.

"Is there something I can help you with?" Florrie says, an edge to her voice.

"You have to look sharp to find this square," he says. "But it looks like people find their way here." It's something like a question, concluded by an odd snuffling laugh. "And with the right stuff, they'll find their way anywhere. Any nationality." He holds up a finger and wags it at her. "You can always smell herring." As soon as he says it, her nostrils are filled and she is overtaken with the stink of rotting fish, by a spell of coughing.

"Hey, you carrying some germs around? You got one helluva cough there."

"It's the coffin that carries you off," she tells him. An old, bad pun for his special benefit—he deserves it.

He gives her an odd look, takes off his coat and folds it over his arm. His suit is of a fine striped blue wool, creased over a firm, decisive midriff. He has kept himself in trim. He walks with determination, fist clenched, flexing an arm, as though carrying on his exercises, not wasting a minute. His eyes are fierce blue, inviting her to consider his sharply carved nose, square jaw, dark mustache, and silver- grey sideburns. What kind of scotch does he drink?—they should pay for his testimony. She could see the advertisement.

"Yes," he observes, "shelves for the books, tables for the magazines, the video tapes behind them."

He walks back and forth, trailing his shadow like a bat. She watches it expand and shrivel. The parts of his body do a strange dance: an arm expands until the fist touches the ceiling, the rest of him shrinks to nothing. Then a leg takes over, expands into a giant stump, the head a narrow little pin attached to a huge spike amid great shoulders.

"You've come to the wrong place," she tells him. "It's not for sale. The owner has changed his mind."

He turns, and everything—arms, legs, torso, privates—snaps back into place. "Is this some kind of joke? Listen, my time is money—I don't throw it into the dung heap."

"It's a misunderstanding," she insists, working now to get him out of the place before Eric barges in.

"Look," he says patiently, as if she were a child or a mental defective, " I read his ad in the Trib, okay? I'm looking for an investment, okay? I write, I get an answer, I make a special trip. And

I get this run-around from some—" He thought better of nailing the specific. "Now what is this and who the hell are you?"

"Get out of here," she snaps. She puts her hands up to her throbbing head. She bends over, closes her eyes till she hears the door open, feels the cold again. When she opens her eyes, as from a bad dream, she lets out a gasp. The intruder is gone, but standing in front of her is the poet.

"Are you all right?" he says.

"I was a little giddy." She straightens up. "But I'm fine now."

The poet stands in front of her as though shaping a thought. "I am getting ready to leave the country," he tells her. "Lots to do."

"Where are you escaping to now?" She reprimands herself for an irony at his expense. But she recognizes that she is looking into a different face, the face of a happy man. He isn't offended—it doesn't matter.

"I am going home," he announces.

"Why, that's wonderful."

Everything is different. Letters that had been held up for months have finally reached him. "You are no more astonished than I am."

His wife and her partner have separated amicably, he tells her, though they still share the same house. Pavel lives in the upstairs rooms, the smaller part, and Adriana and his daughter's family have the downstairs. They seldom see one another, though Pavel comes to dinner now and then. Fortunately, it's a big house. There is room for all of them, for him too. He now has two grandsons, one of them —named for him. His wife has asked his forgiveness for what she did to survive. He still loves her.

"Love is as much a curse as a blessing," he says. "In the beginning, it is a form of play, so tender and fresh, like floating on a dream, with parables for the future. Only to be betrayed."

"You should write that down," she tells him.

"I want to give you this," he says, moving off the subject. He holds out a notebook, a composition book such as students use in school.

"I'm delighted," Florrie says, thinking that it must contain some of his poems.

"I don't know this man," he says, handing her the notebook.

She is completely mystified.

"It was given to me. I went to a writers' meeting three, maybe, four years ago. And one of my countrymen said, 'Take it, maybe you can find someone to publish it.'"

"But whatever is it?"

"It came from a man, maybe an American or Brit, I don't know. It is written in English. They took him into Lubyanka—a spy for the West. How long ago no one knows. Maybe your people tried to get him out, maybe the Russians said he disappeared." He gives a shrug. "It has happened so often. He ended up in my country, in prison there. Maybe he is dead . . . People speak of him. His name comes up. When the fellow gave me this, he said, 'Maybe someone wants to know about him. Relatives somewhere. Friends who want to know where, when he disappeared.'" Again he shrugs. "Some things live on in strange ways. And who knows what to do with them." He strokes his chin thoughtfully. "It is a heavy burden. I know many exiles—refugees, people who have been in prison. I don't know what to do about them either."

She holds the notebook like a dangerous object.

"I don't understand," she says. "You want me to give this to Eric?"

He ignores the question. "I thought in your business you might know a small publisher. Since perhaps the prisoner is one of yours, a citizen. His name is Bauer—hard to tell the origin exactly." He takes out a little notebook, tears out a page and hands it to her. "They gave me this name also—a friend in Prague, a connection maybe. But how recent I don't know. That is all there is."

He is in a hurry, she can tell. It is a burden he no longer wants to carry, let the next fellow take it on. He wants to be on his way, it is his one impulse.

"But really—" She can't get her thoughts to coalesce. "If it's Eric you want to give it to . ."

"You'll figure out what to do," he insists, already on his way out. He pauses. "I have talked to our friend Koenig. He says it probably happened a long time ago. Very likely he is dead. You can do whatever you like."

"—I mean, who is responsible?"

He gives her a direct look. "That is the question." And he is gone. She is alone with the notebook and her curiosity. A curiosity that makes her wonder about herself.

THE PRISONER

A Slavic language I can somewhat understand. Some of them speak Russian, though not all. The train cranking along for hours, a slow train on ancient rails. I think they can't go faster without tearing up the track. Blindfolded. The clack of the train in my ears till I lose all sense of time. In the dark. Nothing outside. Trying to hold onto myself in spite of the trembling you take from that place. No one leaves without it, that's what the others say. From that labyrinth of horror. Your life will never be the same, even if they don't do anything to you. You want from that moment to speak only in a whisper, and you know you won't sleep again—you'll see strange things. Apparitions. After the interrogations, I wanted to leap through the window. I was always awake. Staring. Any hour they might come. I could only listen for their coming. Sometimes a scream would break into the glare of lights. I was blinded by light. How many days was I awake? Terror has a strategy. Here it is not so Asiatic, the atmosphere, that is, the specter of cruelty. The outlines are softer, but still recognizable. But I cannot think. It would be too much. I push it all away like ghosts.

"Eric here?"

Startled out of her concentration, she looked up to see Jimmy, in a hurry, for him. Flustered eve.

"He went out a while ago and isn't back."

"Damn—I got held up. Did he come—the guy he was looking for?"

She looked at him narrowly. "Yeah," she said. "He came and left."

"Damn," he said. "I was supposed to bring him over to the hotel for breakfast. Eric was coming after he saw the accountant. "

"Jimmy," she began sharply.

"Yeah, sweetheart."

"Tell me something—two things. Maybe three. You know him—he relies on you." Her throat caught. Was she reduced to that, to asking for an account of him from Jimmy—who was not to be trusted? "I wasn't supposed to know about this—right?"

"You mean he didn't tell you anything? The dirty dog," he said. "Christ, if I'd known . . ."

"Second—" She paused. It wouldn't work for her to confront him about the letter. Even if he'd sent it, he was too smart to give himself away. He was not the sort to be caught off guard. He didn't even have a typewriter, but he could have used the one in the store. She remembered he hadn't been there right before Eric left. He and Carla had gone skiing in Norway.

She changed course. "If I were ask you, Is there anybody around who'd really want to break Eric and me apart, is there somebody who'd come to mind?"

Of course she wanted to know. She had to know.

"Beryl," he said without pause. "She was pretty sweet on him until you came on the scene."

"And he?"

"There was a time he thought she was the cat's pajamas."

"How is it I didn't know? He acted as though they had never really been close friends. Was I so blind?" Eric had given Beryl a kiss when she came for the reading. But what did that mean?

"Maybe you had to be, sweetheart. Now your eyes are open."

She hated him for being there just then—for having revealed herself; for having asked him anything; for being ready to believe him.

"After all," he said, going at it lightly, "you come along, step in front of a man, and it's like lightning strikes. He's only a poor mortal after all. What do you expect?"

"I think I want to hit you. Come off it, Jimmy."

"You mean it? You think I'm jiving you?"

He stood there as though prepared to be ecstatic. "Hit me," he said. "Hit me hard. What pleasure—mine and yours."

"Go away, for God's sake. I can't talk anymore."

"Listen, sweetie," he said, about to put an arm around her, which she pushed away, "anytime you want me, I'm there for you. Right?"

"Look, it's okay," she said, digging in her heels. "I just want to go home and be left alone."

"You do that," he said. "I'll just take over."

She was glad to leave the shop to Jimmy. She had too much on her mind even to stay in its surroundings, though she had no desire to return to her apartment either. As she was putting on her coat and boots, it occurred to her to call Helga and see if she was free to have lunch with her. She hadn't had a chance to talk to her yet about her travels and what she might be investigating this round. "I've been meaning to call you," Helga said, after she answered the phone. "Why don't you come over to the apartment. I'll get a box of smorrebrodt at the cafe and some Carlsborg, and we can have lunch here. There are things I'd rather not talk about in a public place."

"That would be splendid," Florrie said, and slipped out of the bookshop while Jimmy was dealing with a customer. She was glad Eric hadn't appeared. She needed to put herself in a better frame of mind, and she knew that being with Helga would give her a chance to gather her resources.

Helga's apartment was her office and its main features were a large oak desk, with its padded chair, her German typewriter, the telephone on her desk, and a metal paper tray on top. It was flanked by a filing cabinet on one side and a tall bookcase on the other. She had a kitchen-dining room and a living room that accommodated a small sofa and two upholstered chairs. A colorful Turkish carpet that she had found on sale at an import store in the city covered the floor.

When Florrie arrived, Helga was putting together the dressing for the salad she had made. She invited Florrie to take off her coat and make herself at home. A tray of open-faced sandwiches was set in the middle of the table, that with their arrangement of salmon, roast beef, blue cheese and slices of pear with their various condiments, had a decorative effect.

"How lovely," Florrie said, sitting in the chair Helga pointed to. She poured a glass of beer for each of them and sat down herself.

"I remember you got up out of a sickbed to come to the reading," Helga said. "Are you all right now?'

"I think so," Florrie said. "Still a bit weak. "You know how such things drain you." She didn't want to talk about herself and Eric at the moment, so she asked Helga about her travels.

"I made a stop in Venice," Helga said, "to meet with some people whose names I'd been given. It's one of those flowers in the crannied wall," she said. "You pull one piece of the vine and find it connects with a string of others. I have the feeling the whole thing is going to erupt into a scandal. But I can't give you any details now. I have to be careful. Some toes will be stomped on before it's over. Do help yourself," she said, indicating the sandwiches.

"I made a trip up to northern Bohemia. You can't imagine the pollution. The Communist government, in its infinite wisdom, decided to put all the Czech petro-chemical plants up there— strung out all in one row for over a mile, belching out their smoke and poisons all the way to Poland and Germany. The workers get to breathe that—can you imagine? And the kids—they have to take them off for a couple of months to where they can breathe some clean air. And the forests—they're all dying. The land looks like the surface of the moon."

"That sounds really terrible," Florrie said, "especially for the children having to grow up there."

"It'll take years to restore the land and grow the trees," she said. "I'm discovering just how many are willing to take their profits by destroying the earth, without a care for those who live on it. But enough of that," Helga said fiercely.

When they'd finished their sandwiches, she took their plates to the sink, rinsed and dried them off, then brought them back with a little cake on each. A sweet to end the meal.

Then she gave Helga the news about Eric planning to sell the bookshop and go back to the States. She was trying to talk him out of it, but meanwhile things were up in the air. She didn't know, she said, whether she would stay in Copenhagen if Eric left. She didn't know what strands of her life to try to hold onto.

"Oh, I'm so sorry," Helga said, giving her a hug. "That is bad news for us all, you especially. I'd like to give you some help if I can."

"I can't think now," Forrie said. "I'm really taken aback. I'm not sure of anything, least of all myself."

"Do let me know what I can do. I'm supposed to leave again soon. Yes, this is awful. Ring me up anytime."

It was late in the afternoon when she returned to her apartment. Already getting dark with a suggestion of snow in the air. She was thinking about Helga, her dedication to the truth, her willingness to take risks. There was a comfort in being with her, of knowing what she stood for.

She was used up. She slipped out of her wraps and boots, put on her radio and found a music station to listen to.

She saw that Eric had left her a message that he wanted to talk to her. She supposed that he would come by after he wound things up at the shop—so that when the buzzer sounded, she responded automatically opening the door.

But it was Jimmy who stood in the doorway. "Hello, my sweet." He gave her a salute. "See this wine," he said, holding up a bottle wrapped in newspaper—really good stuff, but only four kroners a bottle. It was on special. Can you beat that? So I got some, and I kept thinking, who do I want to drink this with? Hell, why be alone when you can share a little joy elsewhere? Nothing in this world I'd rather do than drink this bottle with you."

His words came in an overflow of enthusiasm. But she wasn't letting him in. She was furious.

"Look, I'm tired. I don't want company. Now leave me alone and get out of here."

She tried to close the door, but he was too quick for her. He grabbed her up, planted a kiss on her mouth and shoved his way inside.

She was almost too angry to speak. "Goddamn you! Leave or I'll call the police—you've assaulting me."

"Don't make trouble for yourself. I've got my buddies down there and they owe me a few." It was clear he wasn't joking.

Her anger made her reckless. "What are you, some sort of snitch." He held up his hand as if to strike her, then let it drop. It was his turn for anger.

"That's a fine howdy-do," he said with quiet wrath. "I was worried about you. In the shop today you looked like a sick cat. At the last gasp. And this is the way you treat me. Just when I'm trying to do you a good turn—pick you up and put you back on your feet."

She was astonished. The tumult of her emotions suddenly gave way to a certain clarity. The exchange between them in the shop had left her utterly exposed. Now in Jimmy's view, they had come together with a kind of intimacy, an emotional bond, quite without her intention. It began with the New Year's party when he started kissing her.

It was as though some force kept heaving itself up from a dark unconscious source, trying to invade her life, take her over. His railing at her, after breaking in, storming her stricken heart. Demanding by rights a place for himself in it. It was unthinkable. She had to keep her head. It was her anger that aroused him, what was pulsing in her blood. And what was her defense?

"Who asked you?" she said coldly. Only coldness could deter him.

"You did—you're smarter than that."

"What! That's crazy ! Get out of here."

"I know how to make love to a woman," as though that was the question, "so she can enjoy herself, not feel like she has to owe me anything. Afterward they want to get up and dance."

He threw the bottle of wine on the couch and rushed toward her, arms open. When she tried to push him away, he grabbed her and pulled her into an embrace, pinning her arms to her sides.

She stood like a stone.

"I've been looking at you ever since you came," he said. "I've looked at you a lot."

"You were in Paris for two months," she reminded him. "And with Carla the rest of the time."

"A little frivolity. A passing flirtation. Listen, Florrie, there's something going on here, I know it for real. Your depth, your spirit. You go deep, I can tell. If we give ourselves to it, it can take us to the heights." He was kissing her neck, kissing her blindly, as though driven by something beyond him. "That great force—it's the greatest idea of the century. The true erotic. How we've betrayed it, yet what else can save us? I can help you become all you can be."

Her strength seemed to have ebbed away. She couldn't resist him physically, she was still weak from her illness.

"Please, Jimmy. You've got it wrong." It was a plea.

The buzzer sounded. Jimmy tried to pull her back, but in a burst of rage, she kicked him hard in the shin and yanked herself away. She pressed the button and pulled the door open.

"Eric," she cried. "Thank God you've come. Please tell Jimmy to get out. Please understand." she was trembling all over.

"Hi, man," Jimmy said, still wincing from the blow. "A little difference of opinion here. But we'll sort it out."

Eric looked from one to the other. "I see I've come at a bad time—I wanted to talk to you," he said to Florrie, " but I'll have time tomorrow. " His face was a blank.

"For God's sake, Eric, get Jimmy out of here. "

"Don't get in the way, man."

"Wait," she cried. "You don't understand."

"I think I get the message," he said, and as though he were moving in slow motion, she watched him turn, descend the step and walk away.

She felt as if she'd been struck by lightning. No matter what she said, it was the letter that he would believe. There had been only one reference to it. She'd told him that she'd read it, that someone who had a grudge against him or wanted to play a cruel prank must have written it. He hadn't yet read it. "I'll just tear it up," he said. But now she wondered.

She turned away from the door. The cold had caught her. She began coughing. Jimmy was standing there looking at her with a small satisfied smile, as though something had been proved in his favor.

What happened after Eric left her in the lurch she hardly knew. She made one furious effort to push Jimmy away, but he pulled her down on the carpet beside him, and though she tried to scream, no sound came from her. She felt herself sinking to her knees, down and down. She grew frantic, but whether with fear, loathing or desire it was impossible to say. "Come on," he whispered, "don't fight me anymore. You're only fighting yourself."

She was sure it was a lie, even as she was caught up in one sensation after another, all part of the same pulsation of being taken where she was certain she didn't want to go. A violation. She was undone. She sank away from it into numbed sleep.

The light finally found her still on the floor. Her bones ached. She woke to the smell of coffee and Jimmy singing in the kitchen. She closed her eyes again.

❖

"Oh, what a beautiful morning," he sang when he saw she was a awake. "The best of lovers. I mean it."

"What have I done?" she murmured.

"Don't get puritanical on me," he countered. "Impetuous is a damn sight higher in the cosmic scale than weepy, guilt-ridden little hypocrisies. I was trying to do something you'd appreciate."

"I have a doctor's appointment," she told Jimmy, "and Eric wants to see me. I'm having lunch with Beryl. And I want you out of here when I get back."

He shrugged, held his palms open.

"Look," he insisted, "don't you want a way out? You want to go on moping around like a broken-hearted onion the rest of your life? Face it—how many chances are you going to have?"

"Over the hill already—is that what you're saying?" she snapped. "A rescue for the old maid."

"Don't be stupid. You think I'd get trapped in those snares? The way a corrupt society tells you how to think." Clearly, she deserved his scorn. "How many chances does anybody get, I mean for the real thing? In this white man's world. Sterile as a tomb. Particularly with these tight-assed northerners. Waiting for the great glacial thaw. "

But now he had galloped in to offer her all the trophies. To one ragged and bereft of alternatives. How condescending of him. Yet she had sat there these past days unmoving, trying to put together the fragments from what had shattered—denying, avoiding. What was there but the long voyage home? Had sat there on her dung heap at the fag end of the day, when she usually gave out in a violent fit of coughing that left her spent, finished, without fresh ideas. It would have taken a whole new turn of mind to take her up and send her in some other direction. But she had neither will nor inspiration.

She could only clutch at the familiar, at the shadow of what had promised her both meat and drink. After the shop closed at seven, she had stayed a couple of times to eat supper with Eric. Dispirited hours in which they rehashed what had gone on during the day. Tiptoeing around the question that charged the air with tension. Surprisingly, he had wanted to make love on one of those occasions, and knowing better, she yielded to what, after a fumbling, almost apologetic, beginning, became mechanical. and finally, without zest. Afterwards she despised herself. As much as she did now.

"Where's Carla these days?" she asked, changing the subject. Had she simply fallen into a hole?

"Back in the States, I hope. She was here just for the semester."

"She was pretty keen on you."

"Is that so astonishing? I could give her what she wanted."

She found an affront everywhere she turned.

"Carla was a momentary diversion," he explained. "She's gone—it's over." He snapped his fingers. He paused, as though trying to find the right approach at this point. "I want to make you see I'm trying to offer you something. It's a pivotal moment," he said, his tone acknowledging a kind of uncertainty. "I'm having kind of a tough time right now—you could do me a tremendous favor."

"Look, Jimmy," she said, panic rising, "Really, you've got to go."

"At least hear me out. How did you know what I was going to ask?"

She'd heard rumors. There was the young girl whose apartment he'd lived in in Paris for two months, till she finally got her new boyfriend to throw him out. And then Elena, the lovely Greek girl in Samos he'd boasted of. She couldn't remember how Elena got rid of him.

"No, look—I had this apartment here I'd rented from a guy who was going to Belgrade for the winter. Only he turns up and wants it back. And right now I need to work; you see, I'm at a crucial place in what I'm working on, a masterpiece of erotica—all sorts of ideas, experiments . . ."

"Jimmy. The answer is no."

"And there's us—I mean we haven't gone all the way yet. I can take you, take us—" His eyes looked beyond her, "—to ecstasy."

"I thought, by all reports, we arrived there yesterday," she said dryly. "Are we behind schedule?"

He came toward her with a wounded, serious look and put his hands on her shoulders. "I swear we haven't even begun. Give me a chance, Florrie. You don't know what you're capable of. I wouldn't lie to you."

"Jimmy, things are all up in the air. I'm still—"

"—trying to cling to a shadow. At least let me stay here—just today. I've got to look for a place."

"But you'd be out all day anyway. You haven't moved out of your place yet, have you?"

"But if I can't find one, if I can't move in today—, even if I'm lucky enough to find a place."

Then God knows how long he'd be squatting there. She couldn't let him. Even if there was nothing further to be salvaged with Eric. She was sick over the amount of damage Jimmy could now do. And to get rid of him?

"You've got till 4:00 this afternoon," she said firmly. "You've got to be out of here when I get back."

He gave her a squeeze, pulled her to him for another kiss. "Oh, I know your hesitations," he said. "And that's all to the good. You're still testing me. But think it over—there's something between us. We've got to go on, build on what we have—to discover further possibilities."

The echo of something she remembered made her wonder who was imitating whom, or whether there was some underlying conspiracy. In what crazy territory had she been, and where was she now? Discovery? They had discovered that love, if it had been love, was a poor, thin sort of glue. Eric had become a wraith, a fleeting figure she had stumbled after into a trackless waste. Planted in front of her was a man far more solid: real flesh on the bones, power in the belly. She had to resist an attraction that pulled her toward him, even as it whispered of something despicable. So sure of himself, so clear about what he wanted and where he would go with it. A hockey player of the erotic. His conviction gave him a kind of dynamism, a charge that magnetized the pulsations of feeling and pulled them in his direction. And made him dangerous. Run while there is still time—that was her instinct speaking. And quickly.

She ate a piece of bread and butter to fortify herself, drank a glass of juice. She put on her hat and coat, put her gloves in the pocket and tried to gather her thoughts. Jimmy was taking a shower. She recalled something she'd meant to do: take the notebook. A long time ago, so it seemed now, she'd been trying to read it and decide what to do with it. It seemed important for her to go on with it. She'd take it to read while she waited in the doctor's office. Perhaps Beryl knew someone who could take it on. She slipped it into her handbag, then on a sudden impulse took her passport, bankbook and checkbook from her desk, put them in her bag as well, and left the apartment.

Outside, she gulped in the fresh air. The cold purity of it heightened a sense of loathing. Far more than the sour taste of the wine she'd forgotten she drank at some point. The cold air snapped her back to a clarity that widened the gap between the previous evening and the present moment, so threatened and precarious. What had she sunk to?

The task—put one foot in front of the other; one foot, then the other foot. She saw her bus pull in and hurried to the bus stop.

❖

When she walked into the doctor's office, it seemed she was being offered a return to rationality, an order to things, which she accepted gratefully. She sat looking at the photos hanging on the wall, scenes of the countryside.

You could create a convincing world, logical and orderly, and it might look substantial enough to fool you for a while, but a certain moment might turn everything inside out and you'd just fall through the sunny appearances of things and the beautiful logic had created them would disappear like the mirage it had been. Tricks of illusion. She wanted to draw back: it was too much to think about,

But the prisoner demanded her attention. She took out the notebook. Apparently this man had just such an experience. Left without rescue.

What was really known about this man? A few facts and a fog of speculations. She wasn't even certain of his name—Bauer—or nationality. American—yes, no. Caught by circumstances—like the Cambodian woman. Her responsibility? But why had she felt any need to take him on? What really could she do? She turned to one of the yellowed papers. She opened the notebook.

❖

Since I have landed here, I have lost all sense of time. It hangs heavy during the waking hours. Then the days drift away into darkness, and I lose all sense of weeks or months. If the lights are kept burning and I'm deprived of sleep, time turns inside out. I have no orientation. I try to engage my mind by creating designs from discolorations and marks on the walls. I have the notebook from a prisoner now dead. No doubt they will confiscate it any time.

I have never felt so alone, so stripped of my essential humanity, though human beings breathe all around me. It is not only a struggle simply to exist, but to want to. A world may exist outside, but what does it matter? All connections to it have been broken. We have in common our broken connections. A few words go back and forth now and then, and I'm glad of the sound of a human voice, that it exists, even though, for the most part, I don't know the language they murmur in.

Outside, there is sky and sun, weather, winter cold. You can't see them. Perhaps you recall times with your family, your mate or child or friends. But it is like a dream or a fantasy. Or if you try to remember what food really tastes like.

It doesn't matter if you were seized and sent here by mistake as a spy, as I was. Or are innocent of any crime. Any pretext will do when a government is a tyranny trying to maintain power. You are under suspicion until you can be charged. How easy to invent something. For power is deeply embedded in fear and paranoia and must keep arresting people right and left in order to intimidate its adversaries and to protect itself.

I have made confessions to I have forgotten exactly what. Confessions are easily extracted by torture. They can punish me any time it is convenient for them to make a point. Who knows when? It is all a monstrous perversion, not only of justice but of the vital force that makes us human. Torture is perverted sexuality, the pleasure in another's pain. It achieves nothing.

❖

She knew this was true as idea, but she was being asked to enter it as experience, an act of imagination. To take it in feelingly. it was what she could do.

She put away the notebook hastily when the nurse called her in. The doctor, a soft-spoken man grown old in the profession, greeted her warmly. He examined her head and chest, told her she'd made good progress , but not to overdo her activities. She told him about her coughing spells, and he gave her a prescription for a different cough syrup.

"Rest and good nutrition," he emphasized. "They do wonders."

She wanted to weep.

Seeing Eric was now uppermost in her mind. Somehow she had to reverse the mistaken ideas he must have come to after receiving the letter—though he said he wouldn't read it—and then seeing Jimmy with her in such questionable circumstances, whether or not he had read the letter. But how could she explain what happened when, in effect, the circumstances had only corroborated what the letter accused her of—unless she could say straight out that Jimmy had raped her. But where would that get her? Jimmy would simply argue that she had encouraged his advances. Which was almost always believed. Blaming the victim. Squirming out of any responsibility. Forget that he had forced his way into her apartment and forced her as well.

She headed in the direction of the bookshop because it was still there, and right now she had nowhere else to go.

Eric looked up from the pile of papers on his desk when the doorbell announced her entry. There was no one else in the shop.

"I'm glad you came by," he said, getting up. "I've got coffee on." He went to get some for her.

She sat down in the chair alongside the desk and accepted the cup gratefully. Eric always made excellent coffee. She would have been glad to lose herself in what it offered, the smell of it, the taste. It tasted good. But she forced herself on to the main thing.

"Listen, Eric, I've got to explain about last night."

"You don't owe me any explanations."

"I've got to tell you what happened—it's important," she insisted. "Jimmy forced his way in and I couldn't get him out. I didn't want him there—I would never want him there."

"Florrie, it doesn't matter."

"Does rape matter?"

"You can't mean it. Why that's . . . I can't believe it."

She didn't know whether that put matters on her side or what. "Yes," she said, "though he'll most likely claim I put out for him."

They sat for a moment in a silence underscored by shock waves. She took a deep breath. "Tell me then," she said in a low voice, "where are we now? Still giving things a chance?" Her hand trembled as she set down the cup.

"Florrie," he said, "she's been writing me—" He paused. "—almost every day."

"Of course. A powerful weapon, the written word. But remember what you used to tell me—how miserable you were, how she could always find some way to manipulate you." The tyranny of weakness, she thought. "How she always used the kid as a weapon." She knew she was merely spinning her wheels and wondered at her folly.

He shook his head. "An awful mess. She wanted to help out a jazz musician we both know. Another Charlie Parker. Really good. Got sent up for possession. Just out. Only he's on crack, and he sold everything of hers that wasn't nailed down. They need me, Florrie." It was an appeal.

"You think I don't?"

"I know I've done a terrible thing."

Don't disappear into the void. Come back to life. Life— "You haven't done it yet. There's still time.

Eric—listen. Whose voice is it that calls to a man or a man to a woman? The woman now, calling to her counterpart, her other mind and heart, her other animal. 'Come,' it says, 'don't play games. Time is growing short.' What if there were to be a child between us? For there's a woman who wants one to grow out of love and union. A child to carry that into the world." In spite of herself, she had gotten carried away.

"You're not pregnant, are you?"

"But if I were. . ?"

"Oh, thank God."

"Damn you, god-damn you to hell!" She was ready to throw the cup at him.

"I'm sorry," he said, putting his hands to his head. "How very stupid of me. Things have gotten so complicated. And now I've got to tell you—I've sold the shop. "

"That's hardly a surprise," she snapped. "You've made your choice." Her breath caught. "To that horrible man that came around?"

"No," he said, "To Yvonne and Henry. I never expected they could put up the cash or were able to take on the debt. I don't own the shop outright."

It was a small consolation, but something, at least, to be salvaged from the wreckage. Something would be preserved and carried on for those who cared for the things the bookshop represented.

He reached for her hand. "You deserve someone better than me. Can't you see that?"

He was switching the game on her. "Come off it," she said. "Don't be so damned self-deprecating. That's the problem, the excuse. You're capable of so much more. I thought you were opening a new chapter."

He gave a little smile, shrugged, but was not thrown off the track. "Really, you're quite special—your mind, your sense of things."

"Whatever I am, I've got to get rid of Jimmy. He's supposed to leave . . . . When you came around, I was hoping you'd get him out."

Eric frowned at the suggestion. "It looked like I was interfering."

"I wish." Suddenly everything else dropped away from what had been their relationship and only this remained between them.

"I couldn't get rid of him—I had to leave him there when I came here. He said he'd go looking for a place while I was gone . . ."

"Well, now he's found one. Don't you know how he works? That's his way of moving in. He's never gotten an apartment of his own."

"What'll I do? What if he's still there?"

"Why did you ever let him in?"

"I thought it was you. When the buzzer went off, I opened the door." He was trying to blame her. "I told him to leave and tried to close the door, but he forced his way in. Last night was pure hell, the way he just barged in and took over. Like I told you. What was I supposed to do? Why do you keep him around anyway? Why is he your buddy?"

"I could make use of him. When he needed a little extra cash, I put him to work. But he's a con man. He gloms onto a person, usually women, and you have the devil's own time getting rid of him."

She was trying to think straight, but things had gone all crooked. Now if Eric had to tangle with Jimmy, the two men brought to a fight neither wanted . . . And if Eric was afraid of him . . . So where did that leave her?

"Okay," he said. "If he's not out of there tomorrow, I'll come around and get him out. I'd rather not have to take him on . . . but I see you're in a bad way."

"Could you just go now and be done with it? I'm desperate. Or let me stay with you tonight?" She regretted the need to ask.

"It's a difficult business," he said slowly. "I have to think this through. And I've got to be alone right now, Florrie. This will make him an enemy and he can do damage. There's so much to do before I leave. So little time left." He opened his hands as though to hold it all. "Right now it's making me crazy."

"I understand," she said. She stood up to put on her coat. "I appreciate your standing by me." If only he could have made some commitment to doing just that—or at least could make it now. She wanted to get out of the shop as quickly as possible. She needed him to get rid of Jimmy. Beyond that, she had no desire ever to see him again. Not even to say goodbye. She put on her hat and scarf and grabbed up her handbag .

"Florrie, watch out for him, okay?"

"You think he'll kill me?"

"Of course not, but he has a strange power over women."

"Oh, I see." She was tempted toward sarcasm and had to hold herself in. She studied Eric's expression for a moment. "I'm counting on you," she said.

He nodded. "We'll see."

In the street she met the morning crowd of shoppers and those with their various packages and briefcases, on their way to somewhere. She had to look out where she was going, careful not to bump into people. She had a fair amount of time before she was to go to Beryl's and decided to have a cup of tea and a pastry at the bakery where she and Koenig had gone the fateful day Eric told her the news that separated before and after—that he was going back to the States.

When she stood inside the bakery looking over the selection of pastries in the glass case and on the top, trying to choose, it seemed to her the wheel had come full circle. She chose an apple tart and went to sit at a table by the window to sip the tea and try to regain her perspective.

If Jimmy was there when she got back, she'd throw a few things into a bag and go to a hotel. If Eric couldn't get him out, she'd simply leave. She had her passport and enough money for a ticket to the States if that was where she wanted to go. London, perhaps. She had a friend, Elizabeth there. She tried to reassure herself with these alternatives.

Now she could turn her attention to the prisoner. She took out the notebook, but somehow did not feel ready to encounter him. Instead she turned to the back of the notebook where there were still some blank pages and began to write:

At first he was only an eye staring into the darkness. And the eye too was dark, dark with waiting. It beckoned her toward recognition, down the long tunnel of the pupil grown large with trying to see in the dark, a black hole. Enter here and what do you see, what do you know? Emptiness. And in the silence: cries. The dank feel of stone, the coldness of iron. Time hanging like a drop of water unable to fall. An isolated sound, a clash of iron, a step in the corridor. What does it mean—are they coming for you or someone else? Let the footsteps pass along the corridor, echoing along the labyrinth. Let them come only for your release. But not into further uncertainty. They can't keep you forever; if nothing else you will move into death.

So it seemed, she had gone forward as well as she could to meet the prisoner, to try to put herself on similar ground, if only by means of imagination. An effort to enter his experience. At least she was ready to open the notebook:

> *The window is very high up, and you cannot see out. If they catch you standing on something trying to catch a glimpse of something beyond the walls, you go without food for who knows how long? Or else you're beaten and put in solitary. Things beyond the window remind you that you are alive and therefore a threat to the state.*
>
> *I think of what it is to feel the sun on my face or the cold or rain or the wind blowing through my hair. I would stand under the trees and breathe in the air, real air and listen to the birds singing. I try to imagine the river where I swam, the way it flowed over the rocks into eddies and pools—the willows along the banks. This was my childhood. Yet it is only the ordinary turned now into a fantastic dream that disappears like smoke.*

A page had been torn out and folded:

> *Dearest Miriam,*
> *If this ever reaches you, go to the authorities and tell them I've been detained here illegally. Sent here from Russia. A nightmare of confusions. They have mistaken me for someone else. And want to deny it. More, I suspect, a matter of having someone to persecute. But then, they can't admit to making a mistake. That would make them human and fallible. Better to make an example of me, call me a spy, accuse me of a plot. They insist I changed my name, that I'm working under cover.*

He wrote a name and address, telling Miriam to make contact with whoever it was. But the name had been crossed out, as well as the address. Perhaps he was afraid of implicating someone. The rest of the text was quite garbled with phrases that had little connection with one another, parts crossed out, repetitions, smeared words (wet by tears?) The letter itself spoke of desperation, if not a deteriorating mental state. How could his situation not prey upon him?

And why did it matter to her? Florrie wondered, after so many years? Perhaps because he had been robbed of his existence, made into a nameless ghost. What he had left behind was a testimony to his efforts to survive. The last part was a series of poems, memories. Publishing his work would at least give him a voice. Perhaps Yvonne and Henry would arrange their publication by subscription. Or perhaps she could ask Beryl, who knew a lot of people, some connected to the University.

She put the notebook away. It had offered her a chance to put aside her own situation for a time , ignoring everything around her except for the tea and pastry and one human being's anguish.

It was time for Beryl and she was presented with another set of concerns. She did not wish to confront Beryl directly, but she felt she had some justification in thinking she'd not been entirely straightforward. Or was it that she couldn't bear that a man she held in contempt should dump her for another woman? It was a puzzle. There was still the question of the letter.

And what was also significant, Florrie had to ask herself, what had the friendship meant? Actually, a great deal. They often met for lunch or dinner and enjoyed talking about books and films they'd read and seen, discussing what was going on at the Embassy and in the world, the actions and motives of people who interested them. If Beryl had indeed been in love with Eric, why had she taken her on as a friend? To stand back and savor her revenge? Did Eric mean so much to her? It seemed unlikely.

They were close enough to enjoy discussing various aspects of their own lives. They shared the same kind of fascination with the lives of those around them. Would Henry and Yvonne remain together in spite of the precarious economics that governed their lives? There was some disagreement here. Beryl was slow to grant that they loved one another. Jimmy she simply dismissed as a parasite with intellectual pretensions. Koenig she liked, though she found him hard to penetrate. Eric she said little about except that he was much too scattered, pulled in various directions.

Yet despite all they had in common, Beryl seemed to carry on a life Florrie had no part in. She had a sense of this once, she remembered, when Beryl let on to it with what appeared to be a boast.

"I've met the most interesting man—positively delicious." A foreign correspondent with Reuters. Deeply read in absolutely everything, and what was more, he adored the theater. "I think we'll go to the theater festival in Edinburgh this year. I've been dying to go, and I'm just going to take time off."

And then there was the theater to talk about, and films and art exhibits and books. For Beryl kept up with things. And the way things were different here—they talked a lot about that, what they liked and didn't like. Florrie wanted direction, longed to have those intimate, small revelations that went far beyond the immediate cause of her unhappiness. She wanted to exchange her ignorance for what she imagined as connections with place and culture Beryl had been so good at cultivating. She was convinced this was why it was important for her to be in Europe, for her to gain what she couldn't otherwise learn, not even from books. She required whatever would make her position less problematic and confused than the state she was in just now.

You could find in this small country a people who had a sense of history and direct experience of war and tyranny and peril. She wanted to graft a European consciousness onto her American stock, whatever that meant. The globe was shrinking all the time; you couldn't avoid looking in someone's backyard halfway round the world. but let that go for now. Let her get past what seemed critical in the moment.

Once Eric had mentioned that Beryl used to come round to the shop a lot more often. Florrie strained to remember what they'd said about one another, tried to find her way back to a moment not yet darkened by suspicion. Before the letter, before everything had taken on the complexion of a conspiracy against her. Now she simply wanted the truth. When everything else had fallen apart, suddenly truth was at a premium. As if it took on a value, became real only in the insistence that something must be rescued from the mess. If such a thing as truth existed . . . If the mind itself wasn't the source of all the distortions, including the one that insisted that there was a truth. An infinite headache.

It was impossible for her to ask Beryl about her relationship with Eric, too humiliating altogether. By now she must know that Florrie knew about her. In effect, they were both pretending to know less than they knew, were both compromised. At least they could talk about the prisoner.

And once she was sitting on Beryl's sofa in a room where the high ceilings, decorated with bas-reliefs of vine leaves and bunches of grapes, and the walls done in a handsome wainscoting, she felt she occupied a more ample space than usual. And with Thelonious Monk or Billy Holliday or Nielsen or Rachmaninoff or whatever else Beryl was into at the moment playing in the background; and all around her, arrangements of color and pattern, rich stuffs of carpet and wall hangings adding their appeal to the eye, she was invited to move into a sense of pleasure and harmony she had all but lost.

"It's so nice here," she said, as Beryl set down a plate of cheeses and Danish ham and herring and thin slices of rye bread.

"This'll hold us for a while," Beryl said, and then offered Florrie a glass of Chardonnay nicely chilled. They clinked glasses.

Beryl knew good wine and kept a stock of it. Jimmy could use a few lessons, Florrie thought.

"The most extraordinary thing happened," Florrie began.

"With Eric? You mean something extraordinary could happen with him?"

Florrie winced. "No, something else entirely." She told Beryl about the poet and the notebook. "He acted like he no longer wanted to be burdened with it," she said, but wanted to pass it off on the pretext that maybe it could be published. And I was there. But why me? There are publishers in the city, in other cities. He knows writers—it's really rather bizarre."

"Well, I wouldn't worry your head about it. If you want, you can just donate it to the library and I'll put it on the shelf." Berly thought for a moment. "There's Amnesty. Perhaps they could investigate—try to find out something about the man. That's another way to get shut of it."

Beryl had such a crisp way of dealing with things. Perhaps her job called for it.

For Florrie, it was as though a voice had assailed her:

Snap your fingers and it's done. Never enter the tunnel of the eye—it's dark down there. Let him go. Let Eric go. You loved him once, but that's all done. He's led you into a swamp. Now there is no tomorrow, only a doorway.

"If it were only that simple."

"Of course it's simple." Beryl was positive about it. "Whatever else did you have in mind?"

"I don't know . . . some sort of concern about his fate, I guess. Some sort of recognition of what he endured."

"Well, that's a different matter," she said with a shrug. "Such things happen all the time. What nonsense." Beryl took up a bit of bread and ham, layered a piece of cheese across the top. "It's unhealthy, that kind of thinking. And only lands you in somebody else's swamp. A foolish guilt, that we have to carry the world around on our poor little shoulders. The world gets along without us quite nicely, thank you. It always has. And what egotism to suppose we're going to make it any better. It's hard enough just to get through the day."

"Eastern Europe, the bombings in London. Russia. Jews and Gypsies. The old and sick, the children . . ." She was caught up in a rush of words. "In the States you never have to think about it, at least not very much unless it was your family or somebody close. You just read the newspapers and shrug and let it go at that."

"What are you supposed to do, may I ask?" Beryl demanded. "Exhume all the bodies? Count all the corpses? It was a nasty business. But now it's over and done with. And to my mind, it's best to sweep it aside and get on with it."

So Florrie could forget the South and the Civil War and Eric with the same snap of the fingers. Which is what Beryl had tried to do, Florrie thought. If you had loved, given yourself to love and been loved in return, then what had happened was betrayal. And here comes Florrie, a spectator of betrayal all unknowing. But there was no "Poor Beryl." Well, move over, dear. We're sisters under the skin.

"But you can't disavow what happened," Florrie protested "Not after such barbarism, such inhumanity. Maybe we can't even think about things in the same way."

"They," Beryl corrected her. "It's their mess, not mine. I don't want the mess at home, and I don't want their mess of the century here either. I've got one little life to live and that's all. Some people have just got to poke around in messes and screw up their minds and hearts and maybe even put themselves in danger. Helga is one of that sort. Not that I don't admire her guts. And maybe she'll expose some piece of ugliness or corruption that will get the newspaper readers excited enough to work up a buzz in the cafes for at least a week. Then something to bury in forgetfulness. Only she puts herself on the line, and if she makes herself too much of a nuisance to whatever little crowd of bloodsuckers feeding on the body politick, she might have more than she bargained for. And for what?"

"She seems to be in the midst of something—" Florrie paused. "—considerable." She wasn't certain she had the right word. Dangerous?—was that it?

"So much the worse," Beryl said. "She's done a lot of stuff on the environment, like our friend Anton. She likes to be on the cutting edge of the news, as she phrased it. Only that can be double edged and doubly sharp."

Beryl stood up and set aside her plate. "I'll just make some coffee," she said, and went into the kitchen.

She returned with two small cups of espresso. "You know," Beryl said, "I've been thinking. Koenig might be the one to give you some help with the notebook."

"Yes, that's a good idea."

"I'll have to go out after we finish this," she said, setting down the coffee. " I have a meeting over at the Embassy. But why don't you stay here and just relax. You could even give Koenig a call. I have his number if you don't."

"I've not seen him since the reading," Florrie said.

"Come to think of it, he's probably in Paris," Beryl said. "He has some refugee friends there."

Beryl looked at her closely. You look tired," she said. "Why don't you stay here while I'm gone. You can just relax during the afternoon, or if you like, there are all sorts of interesting things to read. I tell you what—I don't know how long this meeting will last. But I'll bring home something tasty for dinner and you can just spend the night—unless you have other plans."

"That's very kind of you," Florrie said with a rush of gratitude. She had no desire to go back to her apartment.

❖

"Now I want you to do justice to this," Beryl said, when she served the seafood medley she had prepared. "You hardly ate anything for lunch. You need to get your strength back."

Florrie appreciated Beryl's concern for her. And she'd done her best. The meal was quite delicious, down to the chocolate mousse Beryl brought for their dessert. And though she couldn't eat as much as her hostess might have desired, she felt satisfied. Her spirits had revived somewhat, but the efforts of the day had exhausted her. Fortunately Beryl kept their conversation going with news of the doings at the Embassy, which Florrie found interesting.

When the time came, and Florrie was comfortably settled on the sofa-bed Beryl had made up for her, she was certain she would fall asleep immediately. But as she lay there in the dark, every sound the night offered seemed magnified in her head, nor could she stop thinking. Beryl's self justifications kept repeating themselves in her head.

So you go looking for the evil . . . Most of the time you get no more than the surface finally, and the poking underneath isn't going to right the wrong, even if you find the truth. At best doubtful, and dredged up with a lot more grief.

"But then look what you've got. Cynicism and indifference. No one ever punished."

Is that what will satisfy you? Does it make the world any better? I'd prefer a different world certainly. But even if you catch somebody, it will seldom be the real culprits. Just a sop for the public outrage. And that's pretty short-lived. Surfaces don't bear a lot of looking under if you want to sleep at night, and quite frankly I do. For the rest, there are enough policemen to take care of the truly obnoxious and get them off the streets—fortunately. I don't want rage, it's bad for the digestion. I like my life.

As if no one else did. You didn't write the letter, Beryl. That's as clear as lightning. You'd never have to.

And yet Beryl had treated her with kindness just when she was at her most vulnerable. You've got to get back your strength.

Strength? Strength to go back to her apartment? Strength to get Eric to throw Jimmy out if he was still there? Strength to run back to daddy—who was no longer in the world. Strength to return to innocence in whatever tattered form? Without finding out exactly what? The truth? What was that these days—all the forms of betrayal?

Run back to the idea of safety? where was that? She had no one to run back to. The New World? New Beginnings? She could get her things, reserve a ticket first thing in the morning, then go without saying a word to anybody. A shameful retreat, but what else was there?

Beryl, she thought, had come out ahead. Yes, Europe had claimed her despite the Southern accent. When Beryl poured the wine, and they'd clinked glasses, she'd made a silent toast to those who had been betrayed.   For some reason, she included Helga.

❖

When she arrived at her apartment the next day, empty cartons and suitcases stood in the entryway just past the steps. And Jimmy had clearly settled in, though he hadn't quite finished rearranging her one closet to find a place for some of his clothes. A number of sweaters were lying over the backs of chairs and several pairs of shoes were in a little heap on the floor. And though she couldn't help being enraged, she was not really surprised

"It's all right," he told her when she walked in. "I've cleared it with the landlady. Nice woman. She and I had a good talk about her sex life."

Talk—with Kristen? Perhaps she'd told him her husband was away and she missed him. Jimmy could offer a substitute. "You were supposed to be out of here." She grabbed up a pair of his shoes and flung them out the door, then started for some of his clothes that were lying across a chair.

He grabbed the things from her. A shirt tore as she clutched it. "Don't do that." It sounded like a warning.

She couldn't stop. She seized a carton filled with his manuscript and felt him catch her shoulders; he swung her around and gripped her. For a moment they stood menacing one another. Then he let her go. "I love it when you look at me like that. God—" He wrested the box out of her hands, took it to her desk and set it down.

"Look, it's not like you think. I'm just trying to help you— honest. I know you've had a hard time being sick and all. You've not got your strength and the next couple of months are going to be really rough. Believe me, I know."

"That's my business, isn't it?"

"Eric's sold the shop." He stood arms akimbo with the announcement.

"Fine," she said. "Glad to hear it." She gave a scornful laugh. "Now, if you don't mind, since it appears you're not going to clear out, I am." She started toward her bedroom.

"Don't be ridiculous," he said, following her.

She reached up for her suitcase and took it to the bed.

"You're not going to do this, because I'm not going to let you." He stood in front of her.

"Get out of my way, goddammit."

"I'm here for you."

"Don't give me that bullshit. You're here to squat."

"And you want to run away in defeat. When all that passion is crying out—"

"It's crying out for you to leave. Either let me out or get out. Jimmy, I'm going to call the police."

"As I said before, you can spare yourself the trouble. They don't interfere with Americans, particularly when they think they're having a little—"

"Jimmy, do get out!"

"Cross my heart," he said, making the gesture, still blocking her path. "I'm not making anything up. If I didn't do right by you, I'd hate myself." He moved up, his chest against hers, and enclosed her in with his arms. "You think I don't know how it is. You've been burned and you want to flee. You're afraid to leap into the next great wave."

Finally he let go of her. "Let me help you get past all this. Let me be a bridge."

It was exhausting to listen to him go round in the same circle and futile to argue.

"How do you mean to do that?" she said derisively as she returned to what she had been doing.

The suitcase was still open on her bed, and she was emptying the drawers of her dresser. Jimmy wasn't interfering.

"The inheritors of the future," he was telling her, "must strip away the past, with all its broken promises and dead ends. They must breathe down to the living flame. And scrape away all the surface muck. The empty conventions. Loyalty is the main thing. They have the real power. They own themselves, and nobody owns

109

them." He landed a fist into his empty hand for emphasis. "It's wonderful to live that way. It's all you need."

And he was an example of this?

Apparently, she'd never lived that way, to put a fine point on it. Hadn't even come close. Probably been only half-awakened on her wedding night. Had never lived at all.

"Don't throw away the unity of flesh and spirit," he urged as he stood over her. "That's where it all starts."

"I'd just like to be alone, thank you."

"Only because you're scared. Because one day, no matter how hard all the golly-wonders try to keep it down, it all comes rising to the surface. Wham!" Once again, he struck his hand with his fist. "And breaks through—wham! Like a goddam lava flow. Burying all the old shit. And everything comes to life again. And those who try to stop it are destroyed." His voice kept rising until it carried the ring a prophecy. He could have been speaking to a throng.

"When does that happen?"

"After the old shells, all the hollow vessels are broken." he said in a low voice. "That has to come first.

❖

"I want to call Eric," she said, going to the telephone.

"Oh, he's been by. He wanted to know my plans. I told him about the crunch I was in and that I'd be in a good place soon. Told him I figured you'd let me crash here one more day."

"And that was all?"

"He said he'd check back with you later."

One more betrayal to add to the list. Check with her! About what? Packing a suitcase was a waste of time. Her only thought was to walk through the door and hasten into the street.

"Take off your coat and stay awhile," Jimmy suggested.

"No," she said, "I have errands to do."

"You're in no condition to go romping around the streets. Tell me what you want."

"I'm going out," she insisted, but he pushed her down on the sofa and stood over her.

"If you're heading for Eric's, you're wasting your time."

"I have no intention of going there."

"I need some money to go out and get us some food."

She clung to her purse and sat unmoving. And then she couldn't move at all.

"We're going to have a vacation," Jimmy said, "a vacation from worry and uncertainty, a return to the pleasure of the moment," he crooned.

And what led into it, she couldn't have said. For the first week or so, they walked around in a haze of wine and lovemaking. There was no world outside. At odd hours he went off to move cases of wine in the warehouse, to make deliveries. She didn't go out, for he have gone through her purse an taken her keys and locked her in.

"Stay cozy," he said, when he went out to do the shopping. He was very tender toward her. The days passed, melting one into the other, making it hard for her to tell morning from night. It didn't seem to matter; she fell into lethargy. If she tried to read, she was soon baffled by her lack of interest. She had a stack of things unread, including the prisoner's notebook. She couldn't concentrate on it, couldn't feel in his direction.

Meanwhile Jimmy cooked for her, poured wine for her, made love to her, even massaged her back.

His presence had taken over the apartment, There was nothing he hadn't touched, put his stamp on. When he went out, she hated to see him leave. She lived for the sensations he aroused, swept along, both dazed and compelled. She was unable to think of anything else, he so filled all her available mind.

She was being pushed beyond herself, taken somewhere she'd never been. And because she didn't know where it was, where it led, she couldn't question him: Jimmy, riding her to his own rhythm, till she found herself disoriented. Her body resisted, wanted to drop into its own little heap, as he grabbed at it, pummeled it, squeezed it until, finally, she began to cry out.

"Don't—" she protested. "I can't bear anymore. Why are you hurting me?"

"Christ, can't you understand anything? Think of the sun-dance ceremony. The Sioux. Gouging out pieces of their own flesh. And the saints—now there's passion."

"It's their way, not mine."

"So close the door without ever opening it? What d'you want, the ladies' magazine screw? Rape is better than that sort of warmed-over death. Give it a chance," he insisted. "You'll get used to it, even ask for it."

He kept on, attacking her, besieging her. "Only surrender," he insisted. "Your whole self. Don't hold anything back." Breathless himself, not letting her go until he was completely spent and she was a limp rag. "Let all the love of the universe flow through you."

Such magnitude? Was she somehow lacking? He moved on, eyes closed to her shrinking spirit, which left her feeling she would gladly abandon her body altogether if she could.

As for him, she seemed to drop away and leave him in the grip of a force that swept him past her. He used pain like the colors of a palette of sensations, plunging on like a maddened animal. When they opened their eyes, his grin showed all his teeth, but he was smiling not at her but in triumph. And he finished by whacking her so hard across the face her head seemed to split apart.

She screamed as tears stung her eyes.

"Oh, Christ!—what a fuck! I knew you had it in you."

"You've broken . . ."

"Don't give me that. You're not a piece of china. You're the real thing."

She felt her nose. Was it bleeding?

"I knew it. You couldn't bear to drown forever in bourgeois emptiness—that tepid bath. It's an indignity. Like swimming in warm piss."

She lay there in silence, unable to think beyond pain.

Her eyes closed. What was she living now—what sort of life? Unreal. Now going where? Caught between unrealities. But to lie apart, distant from all she knew, was unbearable. Utterly lonely, empty of possibility. She had to come back, find him there again. She ran her fingers through his hair. Tough, wiry hair. She pulled it, pulled it hard, till he reached up and pushed her hand away.

"You ought to be proud."

She looked at him dumbly.

"I mean it. Proud. You make me proud of my manhood. I want to shout it from the rooftops. How many men and women can make that claim these days? Here, wait a minute." Disengaging himself from her, getting up, he pranced around naked, found the wine, handed her a glass, then put on some African music. "To you," he said, toasting her when he sat down beside her. He seemed to glow in the dark. Ready to smash something. "The best of lovers."

She took a sip, set down the glass and lay back "Hey, come on, a little celebration here."

"Just leave me alone."

"It's because you're not used to it," he told her. "Just wait. You'll thrive on it, believe me. You won't be able to do without it. Wait and see if I'm right. Think of the pleasure. I had one lover—I can't tell you what she'd have me do. Beg me for it."

Yes, she knew about such things, had read about it in the literature. Some of her clients had spoken of their experiences. Episodes of violence that left them black and blue. And she had a sudden image of the prisoner. "It felt like—I was going under for the last time."

"Of course. That's just how it should be," he said excitedly. "Exactly."

"You didn't like having your hair pulled."

He laughed.

"It looks like a one-way street.

"Of course. You wouldn't know how to begin or where to go. You've got to get there first."

It seemed like a little imagination might close the gap.

He stretched himself alongside her and tenderly stroked her hair. "Everything's all out of whack. Men are wimps and women don't have anything to lean on. Perverted. The Erics of the world."

Yet what she had with Eric at its best, before it dropped into weakness and betrayal, had a human connection and warmth she had yet to find. Longing seized her. And a fear that she was approaching a deeper level of betrayal clawed at her.

"Birth pains," Jimmy said. He shaped something with his hands. "That exquisite pleasure. You can't get it any other way."

He sat up, reached for his glass. "When it's like that, it's like it's the last time. Like we're going to reach the last gasp together . . . . Us, the whole universe." He held the glass as though in the direction of that annihilation. "Then . . . " His eyes held the moment. "Then a new day will dawn." He smiled down at her. "Only you can't do it if you're only half a woman." he said. "The other half, that's what we're after now."

"What half is that?" she wanted to know. She frowned. Dubious, these outposts of new knowledge. New lunacies, they could very well be. And how could you tell them apart?

"Don't fight me now," he admonished her. "We're at the crucial moment. From here on, just trust me. Because it's in you—a whole new personality. In advance of the times. I saw it in you immediately. Just waiting to be born."

"And so you had to bust up Eric and me."

"It was going to happen anyway. I saw all the signs." And what could happen for you if you were freed of the burdens."

"What did you see?" she demanded.

"You'll know it, too, when you get there—it'll shout to the skies. You think you know everything just because you're a psychologist," he taunted her. "Did you ever think you might be a symptom of what you're trying to cure?" He laughed derisively. "You and all the others of that doubtful breed—pernicious. Feeding off all the sickness you claim to cure. You get your living out of it; you get to be superior to it."

"Wait a minute."

"It's a whole industry," he insisted. "And we cure them right back into the illness. What did you come here for, if not to do something else?"

And if my love leaves me, what shall I do?

"Only you took the wrong trolley," he said.

Run while there's still time.

"Trust me," he insisted urgently. "Remember, first it has to happen below the surface. A small group—pure, dedicated. But strong. Then little by little . . ."

His voice promised, cajoled, hypnotized. "But that's in the future, when we're ready."

"And first?"

"You have to give yourself to the experiment. Just like somebody has to be there to see what's got to be done. The whole personality has to be reshaped."

❖

"This is where we start," he announced. "You don't need all this stuff."

"That's crazy." She grabbed up the coffee, a jar of jam. "Since when is there a law against eating?"

"My and mine," he said, seizing them from her. "The first evil. The first thing everybody's trapped by."

"I don't want your goddamned experiments," she cried. "I'm still trying to get well. My doctor insisted I need good nourishment. Do get out of here. You forced your way in and took over. I've had enough."

He seized her then and whacked her hard across the head, across the face. "That's a failure of loyalty," he said, as he whacked her again. "Loyalty is the first requirement. Now say that," he demanded, continuing to strike her. "Say it."

"No," she yelled. "That's not what loyalty is."

"If anybody comes down here I'll tell them you've gone crazy. You look it too."

He would have much the best chance of being believed.

"Now I'll tell you what I want you to do. I'm going out to get what we need. And while I'm gone you're to write, 'Loyalty is the first requirement.' I need to carry out all this trash and get the things we need. It may take me a while and that's all you're to do—that is to write what I said. You understand? The door will be locked. Do not go near the window. Now sit down at your desk. Start writing."

He looked over her shoulder for several long moments. "You might have to write a thousand of them before you understand." He turned and left. She could hear the sound of the key turning in the lock.

She wrote for a few moments, but pain overcame her. Her hand shook and she had to lie down. She lay still until she could collect herself. Who would help her. She tried to call Beryl, but she wasn't at home. She didn't want to call Eric. She didn't know if he was still in the city, or would still try to help her if he were. Helga had already left on her travels.

She thought of her purse. She found it lying on the living room chair. When she opened it, she found everything still intact. Jimmy had not gotten around to this time, though he'd made her give him money before. She had taken her passport and checkbook with her to buy a ticket home, and now she wished she had done that. She'd also taken what little money she had left out of her account. She took her passport and hid it in a small drawer in her desk she could lock with a key, which she put in a box of sanitary napkins in a drawer in the bathroom. The money she left in her wallet and put the purse back on the chair.

Then she called Eric and begged him tearfully to come and help her. He said he would do what he could. He did not say when he would come.

❖

When Jimmy returned, he set down his various bundles and looked around suspiciously. It was already in the middle of the afternoon. She was weak with hunger and had gone to the bedroom to lie down. The paper she was supposed to fill with her statement lay on the desk.

"You were on the telephone, weren't you?" Jimmy said, storming in. "I know just how I left it. Who did you call? Eric—you called him, didn't you? I can tell. You fool! You think he cares?" He loomed over her as she stared at him blankly.

He grabbed her arm, pulled her up and dragged her to the phone. "Now dial his number. When he answers, I'll talk to him first. Then you tell him you're having a great time now, the best you've ever had. The first time you've been treated like a woman in a fulfilling relationship. Then you tell him you never want to see him again. You do it right," he told her. "Don't make me discipline you more than necessary."

She dialed the number and he took the receiver.

"Hi, Eric, how's it going? You got things all worked out? I figured you'd be leaving soon. We'll miss the place. Yeah, well, I'll probably get by, see you in the next few days. Yeah, Florrie wants to say a word. She got a little upset before—you know how it goes. But it's all okay now." He handed her the phone.

"Hi," she said, "Don't worry about a thing. I'm having a great time." She hoped her tone was unconvincing.

"What is this, Florrie? Let me in on the game."

"No, not a game." she said, hoping he'd understand. Jimmy gave her a poke, then pulled her free arm behind her back.

"I have a fulfilling relationship," Jimmy hissed behind her ear. She recited his words. "I never want to see you again," Jimmy prompted her again."

Her voice choked.

Jimmy grabbed the phone. "She doesn't want to see you again." Then he hung up.

"You almost blew it," he said. "I ought to punish you." He looked at her grimly. "The moment I turn my back, you call up a man who has dragged you through the dirt. That's your loyalty. That's the warped value you live by. No wonder you need me. You're still a child, hardly a woman."

"Leave me alone." She turned away.

"What cowardice! I was convinced you had the real stuff. And it's down there," he said. "We've just got to get it out." He studied her for a moment, then moved around the living room. "All this means I can't leave you alone. This will be a day of fasting and self-examination."

But that was all right—he was cheerful about it. It was good to begin with discipline. And there was still a lot to do. "May as well make a clean sweep at the beginning." He began pulling the prints from the walls.

"Why are you taking them down?" she cried.

He stood for a moment looking at her; then he threw first one, then another to the floor so that the glass shattered.

"What the hell are you doing? Where do you come off? They decorate the walls," she argued helplessly. "What have you got against beauty?"

"On whose backs do you get it?" he said as he continued the purge. "This phony art. Where do you find any passion? The last of it was probably Giotto. The rest is trash. Chagall!—God, all those self-indulgent, sentimental Jews. Klee—" He grimaced. "At least Picasso had some balls, something to say about the erotic. These!" he said as he smashed them, "—sugar and slop." More glass shattered as he tossed a print by a Danish artist into the heap. "These Danes," he said. "They do love their design. Precious utilitarianism. They get to make a work of art out of herring on a piece of rye bread. How's that for decadence?"

She huddled on the chair, grateful at least to be spared his attention. The walls were bare, cold. She was cold. Everything was being stripped away. She was tilting at the edges of her life. He'd started to work on the books, pulling them from the shelves. "The Ambassadors," he said with scorn, "All that wonderful effete, overblown sensibility," and threw it to the floor. "Isak Dinesen. Gothic schmaltz." It sailed into the pile. "Fear and Trembling. The Sickness unto Death. I hate all those Danish melancholiacs. They take all the joy out of things. They make me sick "

The floor was littered now with books and pictures, all her misbegotten preferences. Only the plants remained, the only honest things in her whole domain. There she was to take care of them. They were living things, and it was time for her to reunite her psyche with nature.

Then she'd know what belonged to her, what was excess. For the plants at least, she was grateful.

She sat still, her eyes on the plants. She wanted to devour them, to break off their leaves and feed them slowly to herself.

"Are you hungry?" he demanded.

He startled her. "You were thinking about food, weren't you? Meat, I'll bet." He whacked her across the head again. "The idea itself is the evil. This will help you get rid of it. You will see how easily I can strip things away from my life?"

She could have been hearing a sermon.

"No meat or prepared foods or pastries or jams. Break away from these lures and you were free. No coffee. Consider the state of the Brazilian rain forests, all in the name of greed." He, too, had been spoiled once, and it had taken strength and discipline to reach his present advantage. The past had to be broken down, all of it, the whole collection of false attitudes that had crippled and enslaved her.

"But you don't always live . . ." It was too much to hope that Eric would sense the coercion that lived behind her words, that he would at least send someone if he didn't come himself.

"Oh, there have been times," Jimmy said with a shrug. "I can see what you're thinking. That I only talk, that I don't live up to the idea. Believe me, my every thought and nerve and sinew is bound to it." Even when he dipped into other people's lives just to survive. He did it so he could get on with the book that would be there for others, a monument finally, to be their source and inspiration. Every great movement began with a text. As she watched his face, she could distinguish another play of expression beneath the surface. For a time, mistakenly, she had imagined easy sensuousness. But dark hollows lay beneath the eyes, shadows under the cheekbones. Now she saw a man who would indeed starve for an idea, strip himself down to its purity.

"I never allow myself to forget what I'm about."

Everything was directed to one aim and purpose. It was an important time for the book, he told her, and the little bourgeois chits who came his way helped him along. You took from them what you needed, and they thought they were getting the ultimate treatment. "They opened their legs for me and thought it was the kicks." He laughed. "Thought they were giving me the goods." He was smiling at her. That's as far as it went. They never fooled me—they weren't capable of sacrifice"

Then his expression composed itself, and he was smiling at her.

You couldn't call it practiced duplicity, she thought, the image he created for the sake of his ends. He was not to be questioned. The way his lips drew back and the hollows deepened in his cheeks, the way the dark fire came into his eyes—no, no questions allowed about what lay beneath. Eyes that held hers till the features began to shift and change, until he stood there not in the flesh, but as an image, a coalescing of her fears. Her mind pitched and reared. Then he face hardened into grimness.

What would catch him off guard? He knew everything beforehand, had an uncanny way of seeing into her mind, of knowing where it would go before she did herself. Any escape was blocked. Protest was useless: his ideas were to be her ideas, a color plate laid over the dim black and white drawing. That was what he meant by breaking things down. She had to hold on until deliverance came, if it did come, if it would ever come. She had somehow to get through the hours.

"Now we're ready for the real stuff. And don't worry," he assured her, "I won't let you starve."

The time dragged forward; Eric did not appear to respond to the significance of her phone call—a call for help.

"You're waiting for him, aren't you?" Jimmy taunted her, as they got ready for bed. "You really think he'd come? What a joke." He gave a scornful laugh. "He doesn't want any trouble, not now. He's going to leave the country and write this whole thing off."

She had to admit he knew with deeper insight than her wishful thinking.

Jimmy took her in his arms. "You've got me," he said. "He's the kind who've made the world the mess it is right now. We're going to make a whole new world, kid. Renew the fires. We're going to do it." He smoothed back her hair, kissed her forehead, her lips. "I love you," he said. "You're the jewel without price. And we're together, everything flowing between us, without boundaries—one person."

She lost all track of time. Hunger made her light-headed, and she took refuge in sleep. At some point of daylight during some nameless day, she found herself awake, Jimmy standing over her. He was going out to get food for them, and until he came back, she was to write. She was not to go out because she wasn't ready yet for the test of freedom. So the door would be locked. First she had to renounce the old patterns, surrender. She must resist the telephone. He could have cut the line or had it taken out, but he was going to leave it as proof he trusted her.

After he had gone, she sat in front of it trying to write the first principle. The telephone sat above her like a cat watching her every move. If she picked it up, he would be there, in that uncanny way he had of knowing exactly what she was doing, seeing into the workings of her mind. After a great effort, she lifted the receiver to listen for the dial tone and hastily put it back. Every second she wasted was a violation of loyalty. She wrote furiously, illegibly. The phone directory. She scrambled for it in the drawer, but couldn't find it. She turned quickly at what sounded like the door opening and was almost stifled as her breath caught.

She waited a moment and dialed the operator. "Please," she said, "Give me the American Embassy." Beryl—should she try her? How long would it take her to get through to someone who might help her? Beryl? She knew she looked terrible. He would tell them she'd been sick, was a little crazy. She put down the receiver. A strange lethargy overtook her; it was too much trouble for her to care about her life. Suppose she picked up a broom and pounded until Mrs. Erland appeared, or smashed a window and started screaming. If she moved, if she acted, what would be the outcome? It would require something of her. A belief that something mattered. She would have to move beyond a body that was a network of pain and a mind uncertain of its moorings. Surely it wasn't worth the effort. The woman sitting there, this strange creature she could barely call herself, could hardly be worth the trouble. Even to lift the receiver had taken an effort of will that left her exhausted.

Tears came to her eyes. Once Eric had loved her,—for being only herself—or so it seemed. And they had found joy. Now Eric would not save her, she wasn't worth his trouble. And Koenig was somehow out of reach, entirely abstract. Her predicament aroused her shame, as though she'd betrayed the idea he'd had of her, and she had no other to present him with. That left Jimmy, the only one for whom she had any real value. He could love her. And if she gave him her power, then she'd have some. Yet she wasn't sure of that.

She had a fleeting sense that she was letting go of something she might wish to keep, that some part of herself had dropped below a certain threshold and that rationality itself was somehow on a level above her, perhaps beyond her reach. Or at least what she'd trusted as being rational. But perhaps that, too, had played her false. What had taken over seemed real and certain. It flowed through her arms and legs, inexhaustible in its source. It knew. Its power held a great secret kept from her, but one that little by little would be revealed to her reconditioned mind. That was the promise. It knew her better than she could know herself. Could search out all the little hidden weaknesses she hoped to conceal. It knew and valued her. Had chosen her for some special mission.

She tried to remember all those who had crossed her path, who had made appointments and sat in her office, those who could no longer function. She'd been the one to know then, to peer down into their lives hoping to inspire them, to convince them of their power.

Now she was among them, her own life broken into pieces. And the power stood in front of her, beckoning her to be made anew. She needed to lie still and be without thought.

Yet she was filled with agony. He had taken all her money. She had turned over to Jimmy all her hidden cash and written out checks for all the money still in her bank account. They would live on that until another part-time job materialized for him. She had nothing of her own.

When he came back, she remained where she was, the lines she had written swimming before her eyes. She could feel him enter, feel the approach, almost catch his smell.

And with his field of force as it came near, the question arose, and would continue to arise, as to what his presence meant now, here in this moment, the only moment that seemed real to her.

Into it now he came with a sack of potatoes and a bag of dried white beans. "Protein and carbohydrate," he announced triumphantly. "A happy and nutritious marriage." There were beets, onions, and carrots, sometimes a cauliflower going brown or a limp bunch of broccoli. these he could buy cheaply at the end of the day when the stalls began to close up and the sellers were eager to get rid of the leftover they would otherwise throw away.

He had her put these together into a soup that would last for several days. Sometimes it turned out well enough that she would eat it without objection, though there was a dreary sameness to it. She knew that in many places people ate no better and often worse. She was often hungry. At night she dreamt of feasts with great rounds of cheese and hams as well as the various dishes her friends had served. They invited her to partake. She dreamt of the bakery and its wonderful smells and various pastries. Pecan-studded rolls and chocolate eclairs and apple tarts.

In her dreams she read cookbooks and was ready to cook something delectable. Her dreams became more real than the fog she woke to, and she would have happily settled for a piece of good bread and butter instead of the stale stuff he managed to find.

Now they spent long sessions during which Jimmy made her tell him episodes from her past life. He would interrupt her frequently to go over her mistakes and how they revealed wrong attitudes and a distorted sense of values.

"They trained you to mold conformists," he said, "all in the name of pseudo science. Symptoms of the disease, all right.

"When Eros came to London, he was met by little ladies who wanted to invite him to tea. Lawrence knew all about it."

When everything was broken down, the debris swept away, then and there the shining lake of the great and holy force would appear before her eyes. And true freedom. Celebration. Let people celebrate their bodies without trying to sell them to the media, parade them on billboards. Then they could build a true society, the New Jerusalem, a whole new world.

He kept repeating things like this over and over, one idea in all its guises. Their sessions lasted through most of the day, when Jimmy wasn't working, writing or doing errands. Or well into the night when he was. For Jimmy wanted to get past the fundamentals as quickly as possible. Often he would stop her in the midst of whatever she was doing and demand, "What are you thinking? What have you learned?"

And she would repeat some point of their previous exchange. In the afternoons she wrote down what they had done during the morning's session so that she could go over it, make it part of her. Then she could rest while he went off to the market.

The telephone never rang now. When anyone had called, Jimmy told whoever it was that Florrie was unable to see them and that they shouldn't call back. He told Beryl she had the wrong number. When she started to question him, "Jimmy What's happened to Florrie?" he told her she'd have to look elsewhere to sell her sophisticated cunt. Florrie had lost all interest in who called. If the phone rang, she didn't answer it. Certain people called Jimmy, perhaps those he had won to his cause.

Meanwhile she was making progress. "Don't you think I don't know your agony. Oh, I know it all too well. The terrible struggle to put aside all that's false and make the idea pure again."

She looked at him with the eyes of a terrible longing. Sometimes when he saw her expression, he smiled. "You're coming to it," he said. "It's moving you and you want me. Soon you'll want me more than anything."

"Yes," she agreed in a trembling voice.

"You're happy with me?"

"Yes," she said, as if it were a catechism she was reciting.

"You know now what is moving inside you."

When he struck her now, she didn't cry out. The pain made her feel alive. And it was necessary so that she could reach the place set for Eros, the holy place. Now she didn't want him to leave. When he left her alone to go to the market and now and then for some part-time work, she could hardly bear his absence. She begged him not to go. When he left, she was nothing, a blank, and she was overcome with terror.

One morning he told her she was free to go out now. But she didn't go. That afternoon he took her for a walk around the neighborhood. She saw that it was still winter. She was confused. Months and years had passed. The houses belonged to another place and time, and the mothers with their children, the various men and women she saw in the street, coming and going, walking, riding their bicycles, were such strange creatures she looked at them in wonder. They were solid, made from a different substance than she, and she felt shy in their presence. When their glance fell on her, they could look right through her. She didn't want to see anyone—she wanted to hide. Even stranger were the children, released from school, tumultuous and unrestrained. They ran along with their book sacks, throwing snowballs, laughing, making faces. She was certain they would turn on her, trap her against a wall, and set upon her with sticks.

"Let's go back," she whispered. She wanted to go indoors and sit as quietly as a stone while Jimmy went to her desk to work on his manuscript. She was content simply to watch him, let her eyes linger on the lines of his face, to take in his concentration while he was at work. He was simply there, with her. She didn't have to think.

He'd run out of paper, and she watched him rummaging in the drawer for another package. He came up with her journal and the prisoner's notebook. She was surprised to see them. Everything else had been thrown away—it hadn't occurred to her to wonder what had happened to them. "What's this?" he wanted to know.

"Throw them away," she said. "They're unimportant."

He took them into the kitchen and threw them into the trash. "I'm proud of you," he said when he came back.

Proud that she had given up everything that belonged to her, kept nothing back. And yet . . .

She waited until Jimmy went out again, then reclaimed them from the trash, the notebooks, hers and the prisoner's. For a time she sat without touching them, fearful of what might leap out if she looked beyond the covers.

But she felt a certain curiosity. What had she written last? She turned to the last page and read, *I have been invaded and I don't know what to do about it.* She didn't try to read any more of it.

She turned to the prisoner. She opened the notebook and found a sheet of paper on which some lines of what looked to be poetry were written:

. . . light and air.
You are trees budding.
You are earth, and water flowing.
All these miracles are you.
The memory of light teases me.
I could find the world in a single leaf
if only I could hold it in my hand.
The outside turns
into the inside,
and mind alone endures.
I am only what I hold in memory,
only that to tell me I lived once.

For a time she sat motionless. Yes, oh yes. Whatever had happened to the prisoner, he had survived and given her his experience. And there was hers. She opened her notebook again. She made a small mark, just that. And looked at it. Then she wrote, *I am alive.* The notebooks had to be preserved. She thought of Koenig. More than anything now, she wanted to put the prisoner's words into his hands. If she could get her freedom . . . The idea stirred her like a rush of air. A man's experience had been given to her. She had entered it so deeply she had almost forgotten about Jimmy. Hastily, she slid the notebooks under the sofa.

The idea that anything belonged to her, bore her stamp, was almost unimaginable. A momentary gleam, but it was hard to hold onto, like the notion of freedom.

Now the dark end of the afternoon, the time of waiting for Jimmy. Her waiting to learn that she was still alive. Yet it was different.

She pulled out her journal again, opened and read it, first silently, then aloud. The sound of her voice was both familiar and strange, as though she'd almost forgotten it belonged to her: whoever had written these words no longer existed. The creature she was now stood somewhere below the other, in a spot where words no longer mattered, but only the surge of her hungers, for whatever food would fill her craving: a touch, let him put his hand on her, even if he struck her. The worst thing was absence, silence—to be cut off completely.

Whatever Jimmy saw in her eyes, in those depths that descend and descend to the very sources of being, waited to open into some greater magnitude. Yet something called to her that was terrifying to remember, but that she could no longer deny.

Carefully, she slipped the notebook under the sofa.

That evening Jimmy returned with bread and cheese and herring. He brought wine. "To celebrate," he said.

She looked at the food joyfully, and when it was all spread out in front of her, her first impulse was to reach out greedily. But before she made a move, he caught hold of her hand. "Remember," he said, squeezing her fingers together until her knuckles reminded her of limits, "don't throw away all you've accomplished."

It was a test. She must take a little at a time, only a little. With discipline and without desire. And eat it slowly. And slowly drink the wine. He nodded his approval, then refilled her glass, once, a second time. Her head grew light and floated above her body. Her legs, when he led her from the table, did not connect her with the ground. And when he undressed her, slowly as he caressed her, so slowly that it was a torment, every square of her skin was raised to such heightened sensitivity she wanted to cry out. She would be consumed by her desire, lost in sensation.

And when he bound her hands together and then her feet, she did not resist. He had all the power, far beyond anything of hers; and she was to meet it with the power of her acquiescence. And with each caress her longing intensified, so that when he dug his nails into her flesh and took her, sometimes with caresses, sometimes blows, she did not cry out. Pain was the way to vision, to ecstasy, the necessary sacrifice. Only let it all mingle in a single sensation, a complete surrender of the self. They could go all the way towards that immolation the living god required. For now she held it all—it was all she knew—until she lost consciousness.

He was sure of her now. She could go anywhere, even back to her old haunts if she wanted. She thought of the bookshop.

"Yes, go back to the bookshop," he suggested. "You're beyond all that now." Yvonne and Henry had reopened the place and made various interesting arrangements. Eric was back in the States. "Good riddance," Jimmy said.

The idea of going off on her own terrified her, and she almost pleaded for Jimmy's company as he handed her a set of keys to the apartment. He didn't give her any money though, so it was clear hers was only a short tether. Then he left her for a new part-time job stacking boxes in a warehouse.

Tether—the word repeated itself in her mind.

She was alone to do what she would with her time. It was a

difficult moment. She was put in mind of some of the women she had worked with, abused by husbands or boyfriends, who could get out of the relationship only after two or three unsuccessful tries. And a couple had lost their lives in the process. It seemed a betrayal not to attempt it.

She thought again of Koenig and wondered if he was within reach. She could leave the notebook at the bookshop for him. And her own she'd take with her. It seemed important to have it in her possession. She retrieved both from under the sofa, then thought of her passport. She had put it in the desk when she gave Jimmy her money and was grateful to find it there. It was all she had to identify her when she stepped out of doors.

The streets were another world, though not yet released from winter. Even so, the movement and bustle around her, people rushing along, shocked her into a sense of time lost, unaccounted for. Though clad in her winter coat like everyone else, she'd been deprived of a sense of movement and vitality. She remembered how frightened she had been the first time she came outside for a walk with Jimmy, even though they hadn't gone where there were many people. She was surprised by the sound of laughter and the voices of children.

It was as though she had to discover the play of life once again, its various gestures. The turn of a head, a smile, different ways of walking. Now and then she tried to look into the faces she met, some smiling their eyes glancing in her direction.

Jimmy had told her to examine those smiles. Smug. Self-satisfied, he told her. She would see the ordinary for what it was. The lot so coarse in their desires and pleasures. Sunk into their unknowing. She'd see all of that now. They could only look on the surfaces of things, the obvious. Their eyes on shop windows and thoughts of the next meal. Or what had been made sensational for them to give them an emotional kick. They lived in the prison of such things.

She tried to see into their faces. "I want their expressions," Jimmy told her, as though she were there to collect them. "Look carefully. Now you are ready to see the world with new eyes and know people for what they are. Believe me, you will see more than they know about themselves."

But she had no desire for such knowledge. It took all her strength and will to carry her through the crowd of people, though it was cheering to take in the sunlight.

A sudden image came to mind from the past summer when she and Eric had shared such pleasure in being together in a little cafe. She'd been helping out in the bookshop then. After they closed up for the day, he would take her to a restaurant or cafe he was familiar with and suggest dishes she might like to try. She enjoyed the sense of discovery—she had discovered that evening a taste for eel. But it was ore than food that engaged her. It was a way of entering his world, furthering their intimacy as they lingered over their wine and conversation. A warmth enclosed them.

She shivered inside her coat as the wind gusted up, reminding here that it was not yet spring. She hoped that Yvonne and Henry were continuing the tradition of brewing a pot of coffee for those who stepped inside the shop, if nothing else to browse and chat awhile.

A couple of blocks from the bookshop, she saw that a crowd had gathered, or at least she saw that various people had paused on their way to their shopping. In the center of the space they made for him, she took in a peculiar figure, tall and rather emaciated, his face chalky with white makeup and his lips purplish rose. He wore a rusty-looking black tuxedo with a black top hat and white gloves and tennis shoes. His clothes were limp and soiled, though he wore a rose in his lapel. Perhaps artificial. He did a sort of dance—, stiff and mechanical, robotic, as though his limbs could move only by means of metal joints that held them together. He lifted his feet very slowly in contrast to the pulsating rhythm coming from an outfit behind him and he set them slowly down. The bystanders were applauding, but whether for his performance or out of sympathy for the performer, Florrie couldn't tell. She found something desperate in it. She had no coins to give him and turned away appalled.

She felt a sudden terror that she might have lost her face. She put her hand to her cheek to see if it was still there. When the faces around you become anonymous, do you become faceless as well?

To her surprise, she heard her name, looked up and saw the familiar face of Koenig. She felt a sudden joy and smiled to see him.

"Florrie!" he said, looking at her intently, "is that you? Oh, I'm very glad to see you."

For a moment she was unable to speak.

"How long has it been? I've been gone—off on a trip I had to make. Then when I called your number, there was a man—it sounded like Jimmy—who said you were unavailable and weren't taking calls."

"He said that?"

"Yes," he said, looking at her almost with alarm. "I couldn't imagine what had happened. Have you been ill?"

"I was," she said, "for a long while. But I'm better now. I was headed toward the bookshop. I hear it has reopened."

"I'm also going there. Would you be willing to take a short detour and have a coffee with me, perhaps a pastry?"

Once again he was offering her food. Coffee. Pastry. Tears sprang to her eyes. She looked at him as though it were beyond belief. "Yes," she said suddenly. "Oh yes, that would be lovely."

This time he led her to the bakery, but before she went inside, she paused in front of the window to look at the offerings. This was what it felt like to stand longingly in front of a window without a kroner in your pocket. Jimmy had given her only a tram ticket to take her back to what she'd left behind.

She trembled all over. Everything had been stripped away. She was left to pick up the frozen letters in the Snow Queen's domain, trying to put them together to spell her name while the rest of the world was skipping toward spring.

Inside, the smells of baked goods encircled her. "How good it is," she murmured.

"What would you like?" Koenig asked as the woman behind the counter smiled and waited for her to choose.

"I would like . . ." she tried—and halted, faced with choice. He was asking her—as if she existed.

". . . some thick slices of bread and butter," she said. "Something with seeds on it. And coffee. A nice pot with cream and sugar."

"Come," he said, when they had given their order, and led her back to a table.

"After the phone call," I was troubled about you," Koenig said, when they were seated across from one another. " I spoke to Eric before he left, and he told me you were tied up with somebody. I didn't want to interfere."

"Yes, he got that one right." She could see Eric shuffling from one foot to the other and then watched his face dissolve before her eyes. He meant nothing to her now.

"Please tell me what has been happening in your life, if you are willing, I don't mean to pry."

"I've been a prisoner," she said. "And I have in my keeping the notebook of a prisoner who somehow landed in Prague back in the seventies. An American perhaps, mistakenly arrested as a spy. Or English—who knows? The notebook was given to me by the poet who came to read at the bookshop. He thought I might know someone willing to publish it."

The bread and coffee appeared and an apricot pastry Koenig ordered for both of them, and Florrie expressed her thanks to the young woman who brought them. She looked at the bread appreciatively, buttered a slice, put sugar and cream in her coffee and began to eat. How good it was!

When she was ready to continue, she said, "When I read the notebook, I wanted to save the prisoner from oblivion. I felt it was a necessity. I wanted to rescue him, but I think he has rescued me. I don't think I could have escaped my prison without him."

"I see you have gone through a terrible ordeal," Koenig said. He looked at her questioningly as though some part of the story was still missing.

"Now the prisoner has brought me to you." She gave him a wan smile. "Beryl suggested that you might know someone who'd be interested in publishing what he left behind. It's too much to think of these injustices and losses," she said, putting her hands to her face. "When I first turned the cover and started reading, I felt I had to try to discover who he was, even if I couldn't find him. But now—" she said in a low voice, "—he has spoken to me."

"Ah." Koenig did not press her to explain.

"I still want to know if he could possibly have survived." Survival. Hanging on by a thread. It took so little to destroy the body, not to mention the soul. And the little light that kept it all going. How easy to snuff it out.

"Unfortunately not everyone survives. Many are forgotten, buried in the earth with no one to mark their graves," Koenig added.

"They are lost then, lost to history. Lost to themselves, lost to us."

"A terrible thing, I agree. And I don't know the answer. I will help you if I can."

"I think now of all the deaths, disappearances. I don't know," she said, wiping her eyes. "He is likely dead, there are so many dead." She had drunk some of her coffee, taken a bite or two of bread, but the sense of her own situation had taken over.

"Did you really want to take on such a burden?" he said with compassion. "It is hard to live with."

"I should never have raised the question. It's just too much, too complicated. But now—" She paused. In spite of herself something had happened, as though Koenig's presence had made something clear to her. She allowed her thought to catch up to her. "I can't go back to where I was," she said.

He did not ask her to explain. "I understand. I have been on an inquiry of my own. It has to do with Helga. She was in Venice. But I haven't heard from her." He looked worried. "She was supposed to be back by now. There is no answer when I phone. I've been at the airport, but she's not been on any flight.

"I've been trying to find out some clue as to her whereabouts. You pull a thread and find it attached to others. Confusing, mysterious. Liechtenstein, Germany, the States. She was in Venice, on her way back here, though she wanted to go on to Prague as well. Did something interfere?"

It was hard for her to listen. "I can't believe even this," she said. "This bread. And something in me rejoices." The body that refuses to be left out or denied. "But guiltily," she added.

"You've not been eating," Koenig observed. "Tell me—you can trust me—what happened to you? Is it something to do with that fellow? I never really knew him. Eric did tell me to look in on you. He sounded, well, evasive, I thought—though I didn't want to push him. None of my business really. But it did cross my mind that you might be in trouble. I didn't want to interfere if it was something you wanted."

"Oh," she let out suddenly.

Eric, Eric, I know you now. It was you all the time. You wrote the letter yourself—before you left. An easy getaway.

"It's like I was struck blind. One longing feeds on another until . . . And now I feel ashamed. I can't go back—believe me. The clothes, I'm wearing, what's in my purse, a notebook—these are all I possess."

She picked up the cup of coffee to take a sip, but had to set it down. "What you see is a broken object," she said. "Only I have done it to myself in some unfathomable way. I am in a nightmare. How will I ever come out?"

"I can see that. You must not blame yourself too much."

"It's unbearable," she said. "Everything broken. A great absence with only the wind howling through. It's hardly human."

He nodded, said nothing.

She looked down into the cup. "I have so longed for coffee—and this bread." She took up the cup again. "One can live on just the taste."

"They are good things."

The coffee warmed her, and she finished the bread, this time with the pleasure of not being hungry. But she could hardly sit in front of Koenig—he could see right through her—anyone could.

"The prisoner," she said. "He got to the point where only his dreams were real."

"Maybe that's how he survived. Would you like some more coffee?"

"Yes," she said. "Help me," she said. "Everything is chaos.

Help me to escape. I have to get out of here, out of this city. He'll follow me, I don't know how far or how long." Suddenly she knew something: Jimmy wouldn't give her up. In her own way she had enchained him as well. "This time I have to run. It is the only thing I can do to save myself."

"Then you'd better start right now."

II. Carnevale

The First Night

Spirit away the princess to where the century has landed in the lap of the past. Set her down, gently now, still rubbing her eyes from the gust of passage. Will she recognize the place? Is there anything she will recognize? Yes, of course: what hasn't tumbled down in ruins. And from travel posters be transposed into the midst of palaces and wonders.

Look about. A legacy of splendor in stone. All that gives the leap to the eye: arches and columns, spires and domes. The daring corvette, play of the arabesque in the peacock's eye. Dazzle of sun. There, there, there. Lavishness of stone: sun given back from the warm facades. And all sliding by, slipping into the shadow of the seen, the already forgotten. Look back, hold on: you can't, don't try. Go where the eye falls.

Water lapping the stone. Enter by water; by water enter, to be ferried along, lost in the tides: revelers, the press and stream of. Palaces and wonders, the edge, the surround of. Water lapping the edges of stone, lapping and stroking. The patience of water, wearing time away. The stain at the water line, the leaning and sinking. Look up.

She has escaped. Just barely, and for how long? Spirited away by the magician. Into the light, bright beyond February, leaning on the railing of the boat, hair blowing back from his face. Koenig, the magician, who has sent her forth in borrowed clothes. A magician. Nothing is her own except the moment. No piece of life. Everything cut loose from its moorings, afloat. For five nights she will try to lose herself, putting herself into costume and mask. To hide. That is her only thought. Disguise. Pretending to have a face. To follow the revelers through the streets, one more particle, to be lost among them, to throw off the pursuer. Love—no , the illusion of love—

brought me here. Love sent me fleeing. And where have I come? To depend on the bounty of strangers. I dare not look behind me.

"I'm hoping for something new," Koenig tells her. "A lead that will take me to some certainty. Our lodging is in the old Jewish ghetto. We'll rest there for a little while, then get a bite to eat and go on to my appointment."

He has his own project, and as long as he is there, she has something to moor herself to. How strange—she would eat and sleep as other people do. Pretending to be human. In a borrowed place. And for a price, always for a price. Only this time she cannot pay. Time is snagged here, in the notch of the moment. Nothing matters: money doesn't exist. A child lives this way. What is money?—coppers to play with, to buy candy with. Living outside necessity. No, just being oblivious to it. The iron gates are always there. Perhaps the child knows, as she does. There are things you can't help knowing.

At the moment, drop everything, give yourself to the motion of the boat. You are a stranger in a land of strangers. Who are the enchanted ones? Do not undertake to know the magician. Nor count on him. He has his own projects. Enough that he has spirited you away. Let him stand in his darkness, as though he is hoarding a secret; you have yours as well. Let him stand in the guise of a friend.

"How will I repay you?" She wants to know that. "I have nothing left."

"It's of no consequence."

"You've saved my life." She doesn't know what for.

"Maybe you'll do the same for me."

He doesn't mean it, of course. Smiling—a brief light in his eyes. He'd bought tickets to Berlin. There he'd bought tickets to Venice. He was doing all of it. He told no one where he was going. He didn't answer the phone.

Should she protest that he'd made a bad bargain after all? It didn't seem to matter. He'd made no promises of any sort. She could have asked to go back to the States. But that seemed too overwhelming an effort. All she could do was put one foot in front of the other.

Turn away again to watch the marriage of water and stone. The stone makes a place for the water. Solid, even if washed by the tides, everything leaning, sinking. The corpse of Empire, decaying in the glory of sun on stone. Tourists and revelers thronging on the streets now among the lingering beauties. What, still standing after all the centuries? Here to watch us come and go, if the century doesn't rear up in some new enormity. For the moment, you've escaped.

The boat jolts against the dock and the ropes are secured. They're caught in the flow of people down the ramp and along the quay, into the Piazzetta. Then into the great square of St. Mark, the campanile piercing the sky. Koenig ahead of her, carrying their luggage, certain of the way. Past the clock tower in front of the Cathedral. The columns rise, lifting the golden rounds: capturing the figures of time, rising into flourishes of stone, the four horses leaping out, booty from the temples at Delphi, and rising still, the domes above curving into an oriental splendor, to concoct a fantasy— that beauty rises from the earth, that all is light, airy. Real in its lightness. Yet solid.

Along the colonnades, reaching down the square, is a repetition of solidity: nothing can outlast this stone, this victory of a tower, these proofs and offerings. Now filled with people, walking underneath the flutter of pigeon wings. Amid sellers of balloons and corn for the pigeons. Sellers of souvenirs: postcards buttons hats film. Sellers of mask and costume. Throngs of people come to celebrate. Clusters of pigeons.

Carnevale: everything mixed up, pressed together. Faces— faces—faces.

The crowd parts suddenly as a robe, deep red, velvet embroidered with flowers, moves through. A gold mask. Gold above red velvet. On the shoulders, two faces, also gold, eyes closed beyond repose, rise into peaks of reddish gold, merge into a single cap. Rising as though from flowing lava. She cannot see into the closed eyes that pull the faces so far away, beyond the living. She reaches for Koenig. She doesn't know why she is aghast.

"What are they? I don't know what they are. Neither alive nor dead, man or woman." Faces. Have I lost my face?

141

"You see everything here," Koenig says, no doubt trying to distract her.

It does not assure her. It embarrasses her to cling. He is not there for revelry. Nor, for that matter, is she. His one thought is to set out to make contact with the man Helga knew, who had some connection with her. She really doesn't want to think about Helga—it is too much. She was plunged back into the conversation she had with Beryl. Nor the prisoner either, though she has taken him over until Koenig can turn his mind to him. That doesn't seem to protect her. But she'll have to let Koenig worry with the whole business. How tempting it was to sweep things under the surface and let them lie.

After they check in at the hotel, a small hotel on the canal, Koenig calls the fellow he wants to interview, asks directions to his shop. He is a maker of masks, one of the infinite number in the city, where Koenig tells her, it is almost impossible to find a plumber. On the way they will look for a cafe. Koenig spreads a map out on the bed, locates the whereabouts of the shop, folds the map, and puts it in his pocket.

Then they are in the streets again, turning from one into another. She cannot keep track of how they came and has no notion of how they'll get back. They burrow through the tunnel-like streets, across little bridges, around buildings. Up the many steps with the moving throng, across the Rialto Bridge and down into the market.

For a moment, she is stopped by the movement and color. Fruits and vegetables. Brilliance of fruit and flower. Stalks of gladiolus. Roses. Riches. Somehow she had forgotten such things. Pistachios and pecans, the brown wealth of nuts. Salamis and cheeses, olives and pickles. Then along to where the smell of fish takes over, from piles of shrimp and shellfish and the rest of the yield of the Adriatic: fish, great and small, pink meat and white over the delicate bones; the sheath of gray-silver scales, the white glistening bellies. She could linger bemused among the sheer variety: eels and octopuses, piles of snails.

They pause in a little trattoria for a plate of pasta and a glass of wine, quite hungry now from the boat ride, their trek through the streets. Koenig eats quickly, self-absorbed, as though eager to be on his way.

"You're thinking about her, aren't you?"

"Yes, pardon my bad manners." He wipes his mouth, sits back, contemplates the wine.

"There is no hurry, I suppose. All this has been going on for weeks, without any satisfactory information. I think I'm in a hurry to do something, when I know it is only my anger that drives me. And chances are everything will make me furious."

"You don't think you'll find anything?"

He shrugs. "More lies, I suspect. At first they tried to cover by saying there was a suicide. Even claimed to have a note in her handwriting. But when the police were asked to produce it, it had mysteriously disappeared. I keep wondering why they weren't clever enough to forge one. Do you think there were people who wanted— to kill her?" A chill goes through her.

"I think so. The articles she was writing."

"Mostly on the environment. She did a piece against the proposed Expo in Venice. It would have destroyed the city. And finally the plans were dropped. Preventing some people from making a lot of money."

"But the main thing she was onto was about the toxic waste being taken to Czechoslovakia from America, to be burned in factories there. Some kind of outfit with a base in Germany was behind it. She was beginning to turn things up."

She was too numbed by the situation even to cry.

"How extraordinary it is—knowing things, and how dangerous."

A parade of people passes by the window. All the young from everywhere, arms linked or thrown around one another, laughing, tipping back their heads to drink beer from the cans they carry, some with masks on or a piece of costume. And here she is sitting there, with Helga's disappearance and the prisoner's fate to think about. A journal with an individual voice speaking of the sufferings and evils of the world. And what is she supposed to do about them?

143

"What do you hope to uncover?"

"I don't know if there is any satisfaction in uncovering the scheme or those behind it if something has happened to Helga—such a bright light. Or even if those responsible are sent to prison." He drums his fingers on the table.

"You think she is dead," she asks hesitantly.

"I'm afraid so."

She remains silent, trying to hold onto her feelings. It is too much to hope for some other explanation or circumstance. I think Camillo just wanted me to drop the whole matter, stop being a nuisance and yet—I can't let go. Letting this just slide away under the surface would be a betrayal."

They are in the same boat, she acknowledges.

"Time rolls over such things—" Koenig says wearily. "There are so many wrong turns. This fellow, Camillo, has put me off a couple of times. And for some reason insisted that the best time for me to be here is during the carnival. 'Best to be wary,' he says, as though he faces some threat himself. Who knows? So it was arranged for me to be here now. Perhaps best for you as well. So I hope he will come up with something for me."

"At least your efforts have a meaning then," she says, almost as a question.

And mine? she asks herself.

"Of course. For the sake of what Helga lived and risked her life for. You can't just let such people sink to the bottom and be covered over by lies and indifference. Somehow we have an instinct for truth. It's a matter of our faith, yes, and our love."

She is struck by something in the tone of Koenig's voice she hasn't heard before—passion.

Outside, she sees everything sliding past, an endless parade of colors and shapes dancing before her eyes, a whirl of confetti, like the colors she got as a child rubbing her eyes before sleep.

"It is hard to be convinced," he says, solemnly. "Very hard. And hard not to think some principle works to snuff out any hint or intuition of truth. I don't know if that exists either." He gives a little laugh. "Neither God nor the devil. The squirming facts, what did your poet say? . . . exceed the squamous mind. A new word for me. " He looks around. "There are people waiting for this table." He has already paid for the food. "But come, this is Venice after all, and she doesn't let you sit with your questions. Anytime you sit down you have to pay for it in good time."

They pass shops full of glass, vases and figurines, beads in a thousand sparkling necklaces. Glass leaping into birds and animals, all the creatures. A whole creation real and fantastic, the play of artifice. And masks. Shops filled with them. She would prefer to stop immediately, seize hold of any one of them, to pull her face out of public scrutiny. She cannot help feeling that she is pursued, that Jimmy who knows the workings of her mind, knows exactly where she is. With a mask at least, she might be able to trick him. But Koenig hurries her on. He can't think about her now. He has his appointment and time is growing short.

"This is the place," Koenig says. For a moment they pause before the window of one more shop filled with masks. Indeed the sun has a face and so does the moon; the winds puff out their cheeks. Birds, red and blue and black and gilt, stare down at their prey, exult with great gilt beaks.

As they enter they are met with a whole cast of clowns and fools, lions and courtesans along the walls. Behind a counter a small sharp-faced woman finishes with a customer trying on a hat decorated with plumes and pearls. Satisfied, she pulls the veil down over her face and looks to her companions, a short plump woman and a tall man, for approval. Then she chooses a white mask with red lips. "Bella," they applaud her.

After they leave, Koenig presents his card. "I'm here to see Camillo. I spoke with him a little while ago.

"Yes, yes. A terrible thing about poor Helga," she says confidentially. "Yes, we are most sorry to hear. Camillo spoke to the authorities. He was the one—" She thinks better of it and breaks off. "But he will tell you himself. I will let him know you're here." She smiles at Florrie. "But you will enjoy the carnival, I hope. It will help to forget." She goes to the back. "Camillo," she calls.

There is a note to her voice, as of warning. Like the cry of a bird. Florrie is filled with apprehension. Forgetfulness, she thinks. Of what is too much to remember. It is encouraged here: things allowed to fall out of time. But can one afford to let them go? Something lingers at the edge that refuses to lie down under the confetti or the muck.

Camillo appears from the back, a tall, gaunt man, skeletal, but whose presence carries beyond his bones, as though a larger shadow fed the deep ridges and hollows of his face. Black hair and mustache, a certain dark look.

"Helga's friend, yes, Mr. Koenig. You are very welcome." Shaking of hands. "I'm sorry you are here on such a sad errand—when it is such a time of celebration. But you will receive hospitality—when we have done with this business. You must take away a good impression of our city."

He makes her shiver, this man. Under his words, he gives out a coldness that freezes the blood. While he and Koenig speak of Helga in low tones, Florrie wanders around the shop. The woman comes up to her. "I am Lucia," she says. "Do you by chance want a mask for the carnival?"

It is the one thing she wants. Her eye scans the array. "The fool, let her go as that. It would reveal her to the world even as it disguised her."

"But tonight you must go as lovers, you and your companion," Lucia tells her, bringing forward the mask of a beautiful woman.

As a lover? What would she know about that? Perhaps if she had the mask, she might discover what one is. And Jimmy—it might be he would never find her then. She is about to take it, to ask Koenig to buy it for her. She lingers at the edge of the conversation between the two men.

"There are certain people I have spoken to," Camillo says, but there is one more—he has been away. "Come back tomorrow. I may have something of importance then. The police here, I know them well. I know who investigated. But they did not tell me what they found. The report—we shall have a look at that tomorrow as well."

She cannot read Koenig's expression, though he expresses his appreciation for Camillo's help.

Camillo notices the mask in her hand. "No, that is not for you, my dear," he says, taking it from her. "I will have to show you. Lucia, give our friend here some coffee, while I show this lady our best offerings."

"Really, I'm quite—" she stammers. Koenig is impenetrable, quite willing to sit back and let her receive their attention.

And Camillo will not take her refusal. "I keep all the best things in the back." He lowers his voice as if it is a well-kept secret. "You will be astonished ."

I am not part of this. It is not for me to know. She does not trust this man. Let her not trust anyone. It is very strange. Why such bother? There is no one she wants to be really. Is it a good night for lovers? If she went as Eve, she would require no costume, no mask. But there is no garden any more in this bawdy world, or let us say, the garden is all unweeded, and the weeds kill everything else. Only labor, and the snake at the heel. Love? Something suitable for the winding narrow streets, for the beer-drinkers, buyers of postcards, camera freaks.

Through a narrow little doorway to the back, down a passageway. The light is dim as though they are entering another element. Denser, yet vaporous. Far from the warmth of the street, the sun on stones, the lapping water. Far from the taste of white clam sauce on pasta. Only a buzz of wine in her head. Will she be able to breathe? She cannot imagine love. There can be no love when everything must be kept hidden, nothing revealed to the light of day. What have you saved me for?

The lights leap on, sweep around the room, a ballroom itself, full of figures all in costume. She gasps in admiration. It is another world, its inhabitants seemingly more than real in their gowns of velvet and brocade, silk and lace; in their breeches and vests and ruffs and jackets. Strains of music, faint at first, insinuating, draw the figures into motion, and when she turns toward Camillo, he makes a slight bow. The figures turn and raise their arms, enter the dance. As in a great music box.

"How astonishing!" It is magical, and it plays upon her, tricks her into pleasure.

"Truly amazing!" She cannot hold back her admiration.

He acknowledges the compliment, his due. "Courtly society," he says. "All the ladies and their gentlemen. Ready for intrigue, the pageants of power. There is much to see."

"And a museum?" she says.

"No, no, a living artifact. Many come to study the parade of fashion—rooms of it. The costumes become part of the city collection," he tells her. "They give their spirit to the carnival, the dance. And you must choose."

"I? What would I choose?"

He gives a long laugh. "From among the lovers, the great bloom of desire. You know something about that, don't you? "

She bristles at his expression, almost a leer. She has chosen badly from among lovers. What she wants is disguise.

"All this—drapery and shadow." He waves his hand. "But the power. . ." He makes a punch with his fist. "A creation of the gods. From desire, a world comes into being. And continues. Leda and the Swan. The god swoops down and makes a world inside a woman."

Decoletage. Garters and black stockings. Cod pieces. The figures themselves seem to ogle and leer at one another. Queen and courtesan, advertising their wares. Buy, sell and trade.

The air is suffocating down there, and she has heard too many voices claiming to speak of love. They are a din in her head, and she is afraid she'll faint.

"Is there something the matter? I hope I haven't offended you." He is all attention. He takes her hand. She pulls away and turns to go upstairs.

"How foolish of me. I get carried away. I forgot the fan. Do forgive me. Let me offer you some wine."

He helps her up the stairs, then hastens off after they emerge. Koenig stands up, ready to leave, but Camillo and his wife will not hear of it. They must stay for wine and for something to eat. Wine to bring the blood to the lady's cheeks. They will drink to Carnevale. To friendship. To lovers, for this is their night. They will drink to the memory of their friend. And to love. Camillo has her hand again, raises it to his lips. "Such a lovely hand." The touch of his lips burns like a flame, and she holds down a cry.

He will poison them with his wine—she is convinced of it. Surely Koenig must know, but when she looks to him for help, she sees that he has grown amiable with these people. She is being tricked, but whether by Camillo or her own mind, it is difficult to say. He is there in front of her like a large black bird, his shadow filling the room. And she is afraid. Surely Koenig cannot trust this man. He was, Koenig said himself, one of the last to see Helga alive. And with his wine, he'll poison them, and call it suicide as well. Koenig gives no sign, but sits drinking the wine, apparently enjoying it. Finally, they are allowed to leave, with a time set for a meeting the next day.

"Here, keep hold of my hand," Koenig suggests, as they try to negotiate their way through the narrow street. "It is easy to get separated here." There in front of her he stands, with features capped by a black and silver hat, around his shoulders a black cape, and black tights. A single brilliant red tear is on his cheek. The lover. Something for Koenig to hide behind.

She puts a hand up to her own mask. A young girl for her. She remembers standing in front of a mirror, but how is it she has chosen? With three faces, a triad of faces. To replace the one she has lost? She is three in one. When she touches her hair, she finds a gathering of lace, a mantilla with a rose on top. One sleeve puffs up, flares out all in silver, a new moon sweeps across her shoulder; the other, black with a sprinkling of stars. A short flaring skirt of silver and black, and tights and silver shoes. She remembers Camillo handing her a fan, laughing lightly. "Tonight for youth and sentiment. It all begins with that."

It may be true for carnival, but she is no longer a a sweet young thing.

"I don't trust that man," she says to Koenig.

How long had they sat drinking wine, eating food that has miraculously appeared? Lucia, a sharp little bird sitting next to the great hawk who filled more than his share of space. And another presence: the young girl, Violetta, who served them, and who, by all rights, should be here now in her place in all the loveliness of youth. Hard to believe in a daughter of Camillo and Lucia presenting such innocence.

And then after the long stretch of conviviality that threw its haze over her, the costumes. When they bring them back, they can have others. And see how the masks are made. For these Camillo designs himself. What you become is what you see. You only have to get inside the mask and let the spirit of it come to visit. His family are all craftsmen, and theirs are the best masks in the city.

Everything to bring them pleasure. As though that is what they came for. A seduction into the delights of Carnevale. No, they cannot refuse. And Violetta will take them around the city, show them the churches, the paintings, all the beauties.

"You are quite right not to trust the old lecher," Koenig says. "I think it's all an elaborate ruse to throw us off the trail."

"Do you think he will tell you anything of value?"

"I think he'll try to confuse me with a mixture of lies and half-truths."

Musicians appear around them in the little square they are making their way across. Musicians in tights and short jackets and peaked caps, with drums and flutes and guitars. Yah la la—tri-o-la. Singing, spinning into their midst, a boy all golden curls. Cape round his shoulders flaring out, he spins to a stop, throws aside his cape. Stands, stripped to the waist. Holds up a mirror and paints his cheeks with rouge, as he listens and smiles, leans his head one way and another. A young girl running up, laughing, seizes the mirror and swings it around, peeks to one side and over it. She'll not let him see, but hides the mirror behind her back, while he reaches for it—furious. She tries to capture an arm, but he shakes her off. Then a young man pulls her away and slaps her, chases her down the street.

"How do you find out anything then? How do you know anything more than you knew before?" She cannot tell how he reacts behind his mask.

"Sometimes a word escapes. Already I guess he knows more than what he pretends. He mentioned the network she was investigating. And I have the feeling he's connected with it. I think he may be the sort who lets things slip because of a faulty memory. I listen carefully."

"Isn't that dangerous for you to know?" His hand feels cool even with hers in it. Their connections are very tenuous.

"I shall have to play along for a brief while. A little bluff on both sides. And that's a tricky business. I'm thinking the best thing might be to go on to Prague before he expects me to."

"Part of the bluff?"

"I'm not sure yet."

"You'd leave me behind?" She is troubled.

Merging, mingling figures. In a parade of figures, moving over bridges, across narrow canals, through the streets, making way for little clusters of people coming from the other direction, drifting under the lights. She is thrown into confusion and holds tightly to Koenig's hand.

Too many things are being thrown upon the senses. Taffeta and brocade: the sweep of skirts, the swell of sleeves and bustles; robes and pantaloons. White coiffures sweeping upward into velvet hats with plumes and feathers. Masks of red and gold. Mosaic masks. White masks. Masks on a stem, held to mask the masks. A procession gathering. Under and into a flowering of lights. Florrie and Koenig stand in the square to watch.

"Abandon you here? Of course not. I'm not certain yet of anything, but I'm certain of that."

She breathes out her relief, a whelming of gratitude. Camillo promises reports from the police. But what does that mean?"

"It's dangerous, isn't it, if the police, too, are involved?

"It may be. There may be a subtle threat in all of this. Camillo didn't refuse to talk to me; he acts as though he's quite as eager as I am to get to the bottom of this. That may be his ploy, his way of discovering how much of a threat I am to him."

"And your tactics?"

"To pretend I have many sources. He looked a little startled when I mentioned some connections in Prague and Germany."

"Would it be better if I stay—to throw him off the track?" She is trying to offer something of value—beyond fear, though she doesn't want to be alone.

He is silent for a moment. "No, I think that would be a poor idea."

Once again she is grateful.

"You're trembling all over."

"I thought I saw Jimmy."

"Impossible. He can't possibly know our whereabouts. And no one can recognize you. You have your mask."

She puts her hand up to her face—three faces. —Oh, she says. And something snaps back. Let her remind herself. The eyes, hollow—blind from love: aren't they the first things stolen? The face too, hers, taken away. Stolen as well. Sell it for a mask in some shop. Where x is ready to hunt her down. Koenig told no one they were leaving, and she had her passport—no complications there. But he sent her on the train ahead of him. Jimmy couldn't have known. Can't possibly know she is here? Even so— How will she find her way back out of all this madness? A madness that may have only begun.

"I'm glad the streets are marked," Koenig says. He points to the arrows and signs. "They don't let you get lost here."

That's what they think.

Second Night

Masks. They were everywhere. Lying in rows in the windows of the atelier where they're made, hanging from the ceiling, pinned along the walls at the back. The workshop is attached to the shop from which they're sold, and through the window from the side street you can see Camillo's two daughters-in-law at a long table, jars of various colors open in front of them as they sit painting. And Violetta, the youngest. Her two brothers as well, broad, heavy-set men, silent and unprepossessing, mixing the papier maché or dipping fine net into plaster of Paris, shaping the masks over the models, sanding the dried masks smooth, cutting and shaping. Masks in various stages lie all along a large table, a number piled at the end. The whole family worked as though they'd never catch up even if they gave themselves to it all day and night. Even though they work painstakingly, seemed without hurry, they acted as though gripped by an obsession: there would never be enough masks, never enough to capture all the seductions between good and evil, all the caprices on the way to joy or sorrow.

Violetta looks up from her work as Florrie and Koenig enter. She gives them a quick smile and turns back to her mask. She is painting flowers around the eyes, and golden eyebrows, a scarlet mouth. Florrie pauses to admire her steady hand and steps aside as Camillo beckons Koenig over to a corner of the room and shows him the police repot he has gotten hold of. He begins translating the details. There is no mention of a suicide note, only the details of a young woman's skull being crushed. Koenig listens solemnly. When Camillo finishes, he says he hopes that Koenig is now satisfied that everything possible has been done. There are no clues as to the killer, if there had been foul play.

If you aren't killed for knowing too much, you are put in prison.

And sometimes for not knowing enough. Perhaps they would leave now. She has had enough of the frolic, and no longer cares to watch the revels. She can see nothing in Koenig's face, neither belief nor suspicion.

"But I think it is not so much a question of who killed her," he is saying, "but who might have paid to have her killed."

"Yes, that is a question," Camillo concedes and appears to be considering it.

With that, Koenig thanks him for his efforts and is about to turn toward the door. Clearly, he has given up.

Camillo's manner, which has been aloof, though courteous, changes completely. "Please—" he entreats Koenig, "Do not be so impatient." They could not possibly leave, not when tonight there would be the pageant, one of the great events of the carnival. He himself has worked months in preparation. They can't miss it now that they're here. And who knows, perhaps if they wait, are a little patient, more news will surface. His tone is insinuating. Far more important information. He is trailing this lure in front of them. Florrie watches as the tension grows between the two men, Koenig moving toward the door, Camillo rushing up as though to restrain him bodily.

"I think we have accomplished all we can here," Koenig assures him. "But I appreciate your efforts on my behalf."

"My dear friend, I promise you won't regret a little more time. I think your leaving would be ill-advised in the extreme."

She reads something dark in his expression. Beneath his words, almost a growl, she hears a threat. Her breath draws tight. No, he hadn't poisoned them with the wine, but something dire waits in the wings.

The police would set upon them, hurry them off through the Bridge of Sighs behind walls of stone. They would never be heard from again. And who would know what happened to them? Like the prisoner. And no one in the crowd of revelers would think to look .

Koenig has turned in Camillo's direction. Their gazes lock. Florrie holds her breath: everything hangs in the balance. Let him not give in, oh let him not. It would be defeat.

She tries to persuade him with a look: don't you see? This is dangerous ground. But something resists her. From above, the masks grin at her, wink their hollow eyes and tease her away, break into a myriad of expressions and colors before her vision, distract her until she is sucked into fascination. Do you want to know this world? Everywhere they're present to you: masks and more masks. To leave you giddy from the spectacle of faces. Floating up from a sea of dreams, from waves of forgetfulness, from the bottom reaches of limbo . Upward from buried places, ghost gatherings, night terrors, from under the blanket of centuries, born from the gusts of old emotion. Lying there, detached, disembodied, as though waiting to be awakened. Hollow eyes, the turn of grins and grimaces, waiting to be filled. No, the prisoner is not forgotten; he is down here too, waiting . Waiting for the key. His image waits for an eternity, for new masks in which to show himself. For he will never disappear. And your face, the one you've lost, why not look for it down there too?

They sing and chant from their unseen depths, voices higher pitched and higher, winding round her brain, ululating, reaching past the pitch of reason till they hold her spellbound. Camillo smiles down at her, his eye burning the surface of her skin, as she waits for Koenig to free her, to free them and let them go on their way. Come, give me praise. See my power, she reads in Camillo's look. His pride is too great to take any rebuff from her. He is the designer, they are his masks, all the expressions captured by his art. Smiles, taunts, leers, grimaces, frowns—all the longings, affections, desires, given shape and color with papier maché, plaster and paint. With feathers and crowns and sequins and golden glitter. He had shaped them, the containers to be filled— with his power. And then it was done. "You have convinced me," Koenig says. "For Helga's sake, I don't want to leave anything undone."

"A good decision." A little approving shake of the head. But Florrie sees triumph—he has won. And her heart shrinks into an emptiness. But she knows what she wants: I want a mask that will take me through the world. A face that is a passport, an opener of doors. She receives a challenge, perhaps from one of the grinning masks: What is this—you don't want love anymore? No, love is a betrayer; it holds you in chains. Now let it be power.

As though Helga has now completely dropped from mind, Camillo is suddenly all full of plans. While they were standing bemused, he was scheming ahead of them.

"The pageant will begin in San Marco; then it will wind all along the canal like a great serpent. Empire. You will see. The greatness of Empire. I was called first to design the costume for Caesar. Then the chariot. My masterpiece. But of course the Triumphal Arch—I am told that surpasses everything. Now I want to give you a little map, so that you can find your way after the main event. Just in case . . . He does not explain. It's very easy once you reach Campo San Luca. All of it should be very interesting. By the time you reach Campo del Ghetto . . ."

He breaks off, comes over and puts a hand on her shoulder, giving Koenig a significant look, as though he'd chosen well. "My dear, you are a beauty and tonight you will have my best offering. Both of you, in fact. But for you, real gold in the fabric, gold in the necklaces and chains."

Gold. Lasciviously, he hands her the word. A joke, his idea of a joke. She remains silent. She sends a questioning look to Koenig, who remains impenetrable. Does he know he has been defeated?

The atelier is closed around them, the curtains lowered and the mid-day meal brought to the tables. The whole atmosphere changes, as the work is abandoned. Laughter and friendly banter fill the room, and Violetta makes herself so charming, Florrie can for the flash of a moment almost reconcile herself to the father.

But even the food and good humor can't disguise Camillo's impatience for the meal to end so that he can get on with what he really has on his mind. Finally, though the others would have lingered, he wipes his mouth, stands up and hurries into the adjoining room.

He returns under the weight of a shining cloud, the skirt dazzling with gold and silver. It catches the light and shoots it in all directions, drawing toward it all eyes, even the hollows of the masks.

"I can't think of wearing that," Florrie protests. She is no candidate for splendor. She would be weighted down by it.

"Of course you will," Camillo insists, as though offended. "It is an honor I confer. Each year I choose the one couple. It is a tradition. You cannot refuse."

Nor, apparently, did Koenig intend to. But with a slight smile, perhaps ironic, he looks over the parts of the costume the women have brought for him.

"Surely there are others more worthy," she contends, "who belong to this city. I am a stranger here. If something happens and it is damaged, it would cost a fortune."

As Camillo waves away her objections, she can see from Koenig's expression that she should acquiesce.

"Then I will own you," Camillo says with a laugh. "Of course you must wear this Think of all those who want to wear this finery, who have lusted from the beginning of time. Gold. Yes, the lust. Stronger than the lust for you, my sweet."

All this, she tells herself with a sweep of her hand, as though it might change before her, is not real. None of it is real. All fake surely—fake gold, fake gems. Nonetheless she is genuinely frightened.

"Fake perhaps," he says with a smile. "But nothing could be more real. It has always been so. At any rate," he says amiably, "I will be there when it all begins. I will keep an eye on you, and nothing will happen. It is the great event of the Carnival."

"It is a great honor," Koenig says.

Camillo nods—it is his due. "I have been looking for someone who will reflect its essence. And the two of you will come together, a Solomon for your Sheba."

His daughters-in-law agree in an enthusiastic chorus. Only Violetta, deep in her sewing, remaining at her table while the others gather around Florrie and Koenig to help them put on their costumes.

First, behind the curtain, Florrie must cast off her clothes and let the women slip over her head the hooped underskirt and the chemise, then the gold skirt decorated with silver sequins and pearls; the top, velvet with embroidery in gold thread and studded with blue, red, and amethyst-colored stones.

Fantasy , all fantasy: glass and paste into gems and pearls. Here everything is false. No more than the world is. Why should it matter? But it does—there must be something real, something true. Only because you are a fool. You can't run either: ignorance and folly have nailed you to the spot. I hate you, she says to the voices quarreling in her head. The Queen of Sheba was a dark beauty, one of the voices insinuates. What is that shadow you're trailing?

Meanwhile, Koenig is being transformed into Solomon, with, it appears, a certain equanimity, though, as far as Florrie is concerned, he has been betrayed, made Camillo's tool. He'd had to abandon his shirt and trousers, and looks a towering figure in a white robe embroidered all in gold. Solomon in all his glory. His gold caftan is brought together with a little fan of iridescent feathers round a single jewel.

She has virtually disappeared under her costume. But it is not finished yet. A wig of jet black hair is placed over her own. Then over her face a veil so fine it seems meant to capture the invisible. Her arms are enclosed in bracelets, her hands in rings with stones that strike fire.

"And now the crowning touch." Camillo takes up a tiara of diamonds, rubies and pearls, with a great diamond mounted in front and places it on her head.

"It was taken from Africa and since has made its way all across the continent east and west. Only in the hands of powerful men. Some would have given their kingdoms for it."

And that now, too, is his claim upon her, or so he would have her believe. The fantasy he weaves around them, out of the same cloth as their costumes, is a poison all the more numbing for its being only his suggestion.

"I saw it in a dream, so I knew where it was. And when I presented myself to the owner, a dying queen, I said, 'Come, I know your secret. You will not live long, and I am the next owner.' Of course, a certain sum changed hands. But I have my resources. As you can see. I'm a man of many enterprises. And this one—" he indicates the shop "—is my pet."

The man was mad. But then the world was mad. Now that she has been lifted from her moorings and set adrift, anything can be true. Facades swept away, gaping holes in yesterday that lead to unmarked passages. Blundering into these grotesqueries. A maggot in a brain gone whirring and whirling until this chimera appeared. She looks over at Koenig, now ready to receive his mask and sees a glint in his eye.

They exchange an understanding. No, he is not taken in. None of it is real; it was all an invention. And yet she knows that was too simple, too unwitting to account for what is happening.

But for the moment she holds fiercely to her conviction as a bustle is being attached, the cape put round her shoulders, as Camillo and the others turn her around, a porcelain doll to admire. She sees herself, a bedazzling image in mirrors, with Solomon beside her. Solomon and Sheba about to play out their song of songs. And then they are escorted out of the shop, where an admiring crowd presses around them to take pictures. Their progress to the square will be at a snail's pace, and by the time they arrive, Camillo will have waited for them impatiently in front of the cathedral, where they were to meet.

Florrie takes Koenig's arm and leans into his ear. "What will we do now?" she wants to know.

"He is counting on us not to leave the city. This is his way of keeping an eye on us. I went along with it because I thought he might try to prevent us if I were more obvious. He doesn't know yet how much I know. And he's nervous, I think. Not that we're exactly—"

"You think he has it in mind to—"

"I think he'd be willing to do anything that suits his purposes." Between what appear to be amorous whispers, they nod and smile to the crowd following them.

"A while before we came, I sent letters to friends in Prague, just to be on the safe side—if anything happened."

Safe side? When everything held the hint of danger. Of course

he had always known. As soon as you begin asking questions . . .
"Do you think we can get away—in these?" The whole thing was
ludicrous.

"It's like walking in a searchlight. We can't slip back to the hotel
and change in all this press of people—even if there was time to do
it. He has made us as visible in this crowd as a pair of elephants."
Koenig waves to a group of children dancing around them.

"He might not plan on having two people to follow. You're less
encumbered and more dangerous to him than I am. Just duck into
a bar and—"

"—make you into a hostage. I don't think so."

She has to seize on any scheme that comes to mind, even if it's
foolish.

"Take everything off and run for the water taxi to the train
station. I'll go on to the square, to whatever he has in mind. "

"I can't allow it. Even if it were possible."

"I can't without a loss of time. My clothes are hostage in the
shop."

"And you'll be if you stay here."

"I must stay and you must go. Really," she argues, turning to him.
"It's the only thing that's left to me. It's all I want to do now."

She has blundered into things, blundered in, and now she'd
never get out, maybe not even alive. This isn't even her affair. And
yet—But there is no going back in any case. They are at the Rialto.

"It may be the one and only chance. Go on, now before they
catch up to us. I'll say you weren't feeling well and went back to the
hotel. I'll say you'll join us as soon as you can."

"I'll see what I can arrange for both of us. I'll leave an envelope
with instructions at the desk. It will have a phone number and
address in Prague." He pulls out his wallet and gives her some
money. "Here is your passport. I'll try to arrange a flight for us. If I
go before you, I'll leave a message at the airport about your ticket."

"Don't think about it. That costume."

"I'll change at the hotel and leave it there. I don't want to leave him any pretext."

"Try to hurry."

They moved slowly through the crowd, and at the bridge Koenig falls behind her. She does not look around, but tries to lose herself in the crowd. He moves on, pushing his way through. "Good luck," she whispers, glad he did not say goodbye. He is gone, and she is left with whatever web of circumstance and intrigue she is walking into. It occurs to her that Camillo wanted Koenig to come during the carnival because it would be easier to get rid of him then, much more difficult for anyone looking for him to follow his path. Now there is no Solomon for her Sheba. She doesn't dare ask any question about what is left for her, or why she has insisted that he leave. For love? She is left only with the hope she might be visited by a few amazing suggestions.

She has to clear her mind, make room for clarity, find some place to stand. She has to resist whatever Camillo puts her way, pretend to an innocence she no longer has.

When she reaches San Marco, she sees that the Triumphal Arch has been erected with two great columns supporting horsemen brandishing spears, and Winged Victories holding the crown of laurel. A huge crowd has gathered, many in costume, filling the square, except for the path the officials hold against the throng for the pageant. The hubbub is a single blur of voices rising and falling over the heads of the crowd. The spectators stand waiting, filling space and killing time. Florrie finds her way to a spot in front of the Cathedral and a moment later, Camillo is at her side.

"Ciao," he greets her. "And where is your partner?"

"Not well," she tells him. " He went back to the room and sends his apologies."

Camillo does not seem at all perturbed. "A pity—he will miss the most amazing spectacle. But that means it will be my pleasant duty to accompany you."

From across the square comes a tattoo of drums, distant at first, then caroming across the space. Camillo seizes her arm and propels her through the throng so that they might see at closer hand. A hush settles over the crowd, and their heads turn as one. Through the arch a legion of Roman soldiers appears, moving in step, swords raised.

"First the sword," Camillo comments. "What would civilization be without the sword?"

She is not certain whether he is being ironic. The helmeted soldiers move on, eyes fixed on the space ahead; then a chariot drawn by white horses appears, bearing the great figure of Fortune holding a revolving wheel. Legions of soldiers follow, rank upon rank. Then comes the blast of a horn from a single trumpeter. Another takes up the signal, and another. A flourish of trumpets and the chariot of Caesar breaks upon them: white decorated with great golden eagles poised for flight, and drawn by two sphinxes—one black, the other white. The figure of Caesar, reins held in one hand, the other raised, holding out the palm of victory, moves slowly across the path as the crowds on both sides cheer and wave hats and flags. The chariot moves slowly, drawn by the two sphinxes, their great lion bodies pressing forward mechanically beneath their impassive human faces.

"My masterpiece," Camillo says..

It is indeed amazing. "And how did you do it?"

"My secret," he says offhandedly. He does not have to make any further effort to impress her. "Look now, more is coming."

Other chariots moved past them, the figures of Fortitude, Prudence and Renown, drawn by horses. "Not so interesting as my creation, you will admit."

Spectacle upon spectacle. The figure of Fortune appears again, this time holding up a golden florin and covered with coins. She stands astride as a Venetian galley on a float sails in front of them, followed by a train of Venetian nobles and their ladies in the velvet and brocades of past splendor.

"All the things that are Caesar's." Camillo waves his hand, as they turn to follow the procession around through the square.

Music— Lutes and violins, guitars and flutes. A troupe of gypsy dancers whirl about as she and Camillo move alongside the sequence as spectators toss flowers. She is exhausted. How long have they been there, Camillo, her unwelcome host, commenting on the procession, calling her attention here and there? She wonders if Koenig has been able to reach the airport, take a flight to Prague. Time was the only thing she had to give him, if that mattered at all.

Camillo seems to have abandoned all thought of Koenig, engrossed as he is in the festivities. But she knows better, and no matter what passes before her eyes, she must hold onto clarity.

A strand of melody plays through the throng, and Camillo draws her attention to a troupe of musicians and dancers ready to perform. The Venetian nobles lead their ladies into a set of courtly dances that unfold in the square. The faces of the dancers circle past her. Young faces. Florrie is drawn to what their faces suggest. That of a young man who can do all the steps with such a facile foot, such a beguiling expression, such an eye as to his chances, will prevail with any woman and break her heart. Florrie can see it immediately. And his partner, sweet and blank and innocent, her conventional eye turned toward him with adoration. Only she has to lose him to the next dancer. He flies around the circle to a girl who looks to Florrie to be pregnant. And perhaps knows only a little more than the other. She couldn't hold him either. Only one knows anything beyond what they have been told—knows far more, knows from some inner depth, but she doesn't know yet what she knows. So Florrie sees the story.

The dance ends, the dancers melting away as a group of senators and other nobles follow the figure of the doge along toward the Campo SS Apolstoli. Once again to music, the figures disappear, this time into one of the palazzos, the remainder of the crowd left now to twilight. It is growing cold.

"Beautiful," Florrie says, hoping now she might retreat to the hotel, remove her costume, and sleep.

"It is only the beginning," Camillo informs her, taking her arm.

Beginning. Look to beginnings in twilight. Forget before you remember— it's safer, no doubt. What, after all, can be dredged up from the depths? From fatigue and desperation, loss and anguish? Where am I now? Where have I got to? Can't you recognize the winds of change? They blow like trumpets down the centuries. Masks and more masks, like dead leaves blown aside. New faces filled with the sentiment of the moment. You are rising into another time and place. Don't you see things falling apart? The lingering pieces of empire here and there, along the coast that is not yet Yugoslavia, falling away from the Venetians. Turks and the Holy Roman Empire; the Austro-Hungarian goulash. Go back and farther back. You think nothing's older than America, older than your mind? You live in a nation without a history. All falling apart, without ever coming together. Nations rising, wars and revolutions—world war. That's the touch of experience for you.

"What will it be now that I've blundered in?"

Will it come out all right? For one always enters as a child, and the past settles down around your shoulders, falls down around your feet. You wear the past. Let me out, let me out. How can I hold together? It's a different world now. Still the pageant of Empire? You should know. Swords and coins. Sovereigns and swords.

"In a moment we'll have a little wine to warm you up inside," Camillo says. "But now a Solomon for your Sheba."

She stifles a cry. For approaching her from across the square is a figure identical to Koenig. Is it Koenig himself? It can't be. And yet it can't be to her advantage to act like it isn't. She brings herself to composure, as Camillo amiably joins her hand to the other's, all adorned with rings. A half mask hides the top of his face, and a beard the rest.

Inside the taverna where they go to drink wine, the place is filled with light and laughter. But Camillo doesn't let them linger. When they return to the street, it is already night. Florrie is weary to the bone. In the dark the old stone feels colder. The crowd has melted away with the light, the streets growing quieter as though they are closing down.

How dark it is! It must be November. Things being pushed toward their winter. But that is impossible Here, supposedly, they are emerging from winter and moving toward spring. November something insists, pulling her toward the idea, more than real.

The square is suddenly full of movement, uncertain in origin and direction, shadows moving and blending with the darkness. Then nothing. They take the pose of waiting. Camillo and her new partner stand with unconcern, as though knowing what they're waiting for. Workmen appear with lumber and hastily throw up some scaffolding. More people arrive, but in their workaday attire. In their golden glow, Solomon and Sheba are entirely out of place. She is still struck speechless by his presence.

How can he be here? It's all been lost, your Solomon too. And you must go wandering the world looking for an explanation. You can always find something to replace the real thing. Something phony. And bring out the prisoner too. Pretend that he is free.

Helga? That's another question.

Someone breathes foully into her face, brushes against her and makes an obscene gesture. A woman walks up and fingers the cloth of her skirt, gives a little tug. Florrie pulls away. The woman laughs, holds up a bit of sequin.

On the outer edge, a cluster of youths, who appear at first to be students with their jackets and rucksacks, standing around drinking beer, laughing, talking, singing raucously, start to move toward the workmen shouting taunts. Someone throws a rock, then another. There is a shattering of glass.

Menace grows on all sides of them. "Why are we here?" Florrie demands. Not a word from Solomon.

Something terrible is going to happen. And again she gasps. Camillo is no longer there. How can it be? Gone. Dissolved into the shadows. She doesn't know where she is, and she is left to a stranger there to mock her.

She must run, outrun the throng and the apparition at her back. She pulls off her robe even though it's cold and tries to slip away into a narrow street. Sounds of breaking glass echo all around. Shop windows crash and vases and glass animals explode into fragments. The air splinters with glass. At her back, her companion runs as if he too is afraid. They stand with their backs against the stone. whoever he is, he is not Koenig.

The side streets are choked with men, most of them young,

in uniform. They spill into the street and begin heaving rocks. An old woman runs for cover. A mother grabs her boy by the hand and pulls him indoors. There is nothing left but to move ahead, but everywhere they turn, they're met by another gang brandishing sticks and clubs. Windows shatter around them. When did this happen? Or is it always happening?

"What'll we do?—where can we go?"

There is no answer.

"He brought us here to betray us," she says.

The menace comes into the dark square, in the figures that move through and across, some holding torches. The sound of running boots over the stones echoes, along with shouts, cries and curses.

"Look, the Merchant of Venice!" "Grab him." "They've always got all the money, the filthy pigs." They're on them. Pulling away their robes, tearing at the silk, the embroidered vest, until the assailants have torn away all the stones. Tearing the rings off his hands. Then suddenly, as though at a signal, they bolt down the street and disappear. But not all. Hands grab her shoulders, reach up and tear off her bodice, rip away her slip, pin her back against the building. She tries to push away the heavy shadow, and in her frenzy gouges a face. Others beat at her face and arms. "Juden dreck! Where does it come from? Not from the Italians. Let them claim other barbarities. Who is the one who spits on them and throws her down?

She remains in a huddle until she can look out and see she is alone, then pushes herself up. She stands shakily, trying to collect her life, what's left of it. She cannot breathe or speak. Everything is allowed. She weeps, cowering in the doorway. She puts a hand to her face, feels for the bruises. The voices, the figures recede, but shouts, the sound of splintering glass and splitting wood reach her: shops being entered and looted. Shouts and cries. Then confusion.

Shivering in the chill air, weak and shaken, she moves in the direction of the hotel. Everything that happened seems to go on happening, rising up, putting on its mask. Even her companion has disappeared, as though he is a phantom.

How can she escape now? She does not want to meet anyone,

tries to keep to the smaller alleys to avoid people. She shrinks from light. Plunged into the crowd at San Marco, perhaps she'd be regarded only as an oddity. The costume of one robbed and beaten— more real than any fantasy. But how can she enter her hotel?

And then she sees them. Posted as though waiting.

She tries to turn away, but they stand there, blocking her in. And then condottieri surround and seize her.

She catches a glimpse of him on the edge, Camillo, speaking to one of the men. She does not call to him— it would do no good. There has been a robbery, right here in the midst of the carnival. He is there for her to see him and watch as he slips away, even as the handcuffs are snapped on her wrists. Now she is being marched away over the Bridge of Sighs.

I'll join you there, she says to the prisoner. We're one and the same.

The Third Night

"You will have to answer to the charges."

"And what might they be? For being robbed and beaten?"

"It does not matter for she is guilty."

This is the way it happens. As soon as you are charged, you are guilty. It matters only that you are accused—therefore you are guilty. Someone has spoken against you. They have the truth, and the truth is power.

You cannot speak for fear; you have no weapon; you drop into the void. Out of life, out of all structure and meaning. You have fallen through the crack, out of time, while the carnival races past, your voice lost in the revelry.

Let her protest, wave her arms. She has been a victim. A mistake, a terrible mistake has been made! Cause for laughter. Where has she seen all this before? Hear the chorus of voices. Behind them stands the logic of systems, the claims of justice. But down here in the murk what dark purpose moves words and actions? They dissolve before your eyes. Actions? Words? What are they anymore? Everything is turned upside down, ripped away. No mistake at all.

You were dressed for the masquerade. All the bright gems. Stolen now. Valuable jewels they claim. You're in with the gang that stole them. Anything can become the case. Where can you claim your innocence? You thought you had a disguise. There is no innocence. The case is waiting to make legitimate your exit from the masquerade. They'll cut your pictures out of all the history texts and encyclopedias and albums, obliterate your name and pretend you never existed. Trapped in all this. Blundering down the wrong alley. You're on your way to the prisoner, to share in the forgetfulness.

No one will tell you where you're going as you move unseen through the deserted streets where shadows lie and moonlight gleams in circling ripples on the water. No one passes, and the distant shouts of revelers, no doubt all very drunk, are totally beyond you. A different street, a different realm. The crash of a bottle being thrown. Through passages of darkness, along walls of stone. This is the Bridge of Sighs. Beyond that, stone and iron. You can go through in the daylight on a guided tour. But you cannot see the city from the windows of the prison. They put windows in a wall beyond the bars to tease your sight. It's cold there; stone is always cold. You can hear only the echo of your voice. And if you listen beyond hearing: the sighs collected by the centuries, mingled in a single suspiration.

Now the hours will pass into no-time, the world shrink into this space. Here where Casanova stood, one of the accused. Impiety, imposture, licentiousness. Charges by which to seize him from the masquerade. But he could escape with a monk who valued his skin like anybody else. Clever of him to get hold of a pike to lift the lead sheets from the roof and slip out under the cover of a night sky teeming with stars. And with ropes to lower himself. But he never said where he managed to come by the instruments of his freedom. Or the heart and strength to escape.

An adventure: with accidents that could have meant his death. Death as easy as falling off a roof. And you don't always make it, running for your life, hiding, trying to make it across borders, through tunnels, across seas and down sewers, guns and dogs at your back; sudden shifts of wind and tides and attention. Everyone, it seems, is trying to get somewhere else. And some fall by the wayside, into the realm of the forgotten. But Casanova stood on the roof of the prison, breathed deep, lowered himself into a casement window of the palace just as they do in the movies, and lived to tell about it.

❖

"Now I will own you," Camillo's face floats above her, the eyes hollow in the mask of his face, a slight smile across the lips. He does not overplay his game. "Robbed, were you? But you couldn't have been so innocent as that." He hovers over her whether she closes her eyes or opens them. Yes, in fact , she expected it. She knew that now. Expected even as she hoped for elusiveness. There should be a science of elusiveness, because power is always the same. She knows better than to be taken by surprise. Someone else to own her, as Jimmy would have owned her. Body mind and soul. Is there a soul? The word has gone to the trash heap along with the other tinsel. And taken the mind with it—and anything real? It all dissolves into particles anyway, dancing uncertainly through space.

When was there anything solid under her feet? Only an illusion after all? They swirled around her: masks with hollow eyes, mouths drinking shadows, dancing in closer. I see you, Solomon and Sheba, lords and ladies, monks and pilgrims, bandits and soldiers, black slaves and merchants, camel drivers and harlequins, tax collectors and hangmen, conquistadors and pimps, knights and gypsies, warlords and terrorists, guards and torturers. Yes, the whirling, swirling multitude.

Only now, now let her go deeper. The fear has played around and through her, till she is only her fear. Only now, let her enter it, descend into it, see if she can make her way, find her way to the prisoner, hear something out of his solitude. She thought once she heard him speak. Let him speak again. Is there, can there be anything beyond, some impulse living still beyond both words and silence—a spark, an incandescence that takes up all the fragments into a single flame—so that even forgetfulness no longer matters?

She is in the street again, her eyes hurt by sunlight. by daylight. Violetta stands there before her, the one image on the screen that seems to belong to a daylight world. In the darkness at the back of her mind, Florrie can still hear the jangle of keys, the clang of an iron door, the ticking off of centuries. She doesn't know what day it is, what night has preceded it. Weeks months could have been lost in an endless day-night. Huddling there in the dark, shivering under a blanket too thin to keep out the cold draped over her. Imprisoned in the flesh she could have been back in November.. Last night was a long December.

Violetta is waiting for Florrie in the lobby of the hotel the next morning, her face offering a light that seems almost a gift. Her eyes are glowing.

It is all very strange, what has happened during the night and what she can now expect. Her costume is gone. Violetta has brought her clothes for the day and a simple costume for the evening.

"Come with me. Come, dear lady."

Violetta takes her hand and leads her through a different part of the city. As they move along the streets, Violetta calls her attention to the various churches they pass, as though they have come like tourists to sightsee.

"This is a very beautiful one from the 15th century. The bell tower of San Zaccaria is from the 12th century."

She knows them all. Perhaps, Florrie decides, she can speak only of churches, oblivious to everything else. They slip through clusters of people without notice. When they reach St. Mark's, passing in front of the statue of Justice and alongside the Doge's palace, Florrie looks around her as though for the first time. Once again, she is in a city of strangers. How difficult to know where you are, where you have been.

If Violetta is her guide, she is also there to spy on her. Or use her somehow to draw Koenig back. She suspects everything. Trust nothing and no one. Survival lies in such readiness. As soon as you trust, you are vulnerable. Florrie tries to read what lies behind the engaging smile, the sympathetic gaze. One more mask. Violetta catches her intent look, perhaps the question in her stare, and blushes.

"So many things to see," she says innocuously. "Many beautiful churches, with paintings and statues of holy figures inside. I will show you some of these on another day."

She'll have to do better than that. Camillo needs to teach her a thing or two. A pretty face won't do it alone. Florrie's deepest desire is to leave the city quietly, to slip away if they will let her. Meanwhile what disguise will protect her—the desire to see churches?

"I remember Helga," Violetta says suddenly. "Does your friend think he'll find who killed her?"

She is taken aback by the directness of the question. A trap? "He was hoping your father might be able to help him. I know nothing about it." She is certain it's a trap. What does she know? It doesn't matter because Camillo can decide anything he wants to believe.

"My father was afraid it would happen. He was always laughing and joking with her when she came to see us. He was fond of her. And he warned her. He said to us, 'She better watch her step. She has enemies.'"

Florrie takes a deep breath. Ask too many questions and there you create a fate. A fatality. Now Florrie has stepped into the benighted circle. No doubt Violetta has been coached to scare her.

"It is all very shocking. And who killed her then?"

"So you suspect I know? Violetta says. "My father knows who killed her. And so do I. We both know. But we can't speak because we'll be killed. The name is in an envelope that will go to friends if anything happens to us. The rest of the family doesn't know. We must protect them."

Florrie doesn't know how to think or what to say. "You must live in great fear."

"No," Violetta protests. "It would do no good. And my father says the murderer will be exposed one day. Not this week or next or this month or next, but at the time it needs to be known."

Florrie is not sure what that means. "When it is to someone's advantage?" she offers.

"Yes." They walk for a moment in silence.

"But—"

"No more questions, please. I should not have spoken. But things have more than one side and can be turned this way and that till they are all out of shape. And I believe you need to know the truth. Perhaps it will ease your suffering And help your friend."

She is looking into Florrie's face. "If you can't believe me," she says in a low voice, "there is nothing for you to believe in."

❖

They visit several more churches, Violetta pointing out the special features of each one, inviting Florrie to appreciate their beauties.

Then she leads her toward the hotel, where she can change into the skirt and jacket Violetta has brought for her.

So the game goes on, with Violetta taking more of a part than Florrie expected. To disarm her perhaps.

"My father will meet you here to take you to the players," Violetta tells her.

"Will they rob and beat me?"

"There are many tricks to Carnevale," Violetta says imperturbably. "Are you afraid?"

"Shouldn't she be?" Will he destroy me? Because he can? Because he thinks I'm dangerous? What is more dangerous than innocence?

Camillo is waiting in front of the fireplace when she enters, and he steps forward to greet her as he had the first day they met, cordially, as though he has something special to offer. Indeed he does. This man who can take the odds and ends of the world as they come together in the gust of inspiration and shape them to his purposes, combine them in a swirl of color and design. His posture expresses a triumphant ease: prospects at his fingertips to be translated into the scheme of things, unlooked for possibilities lying behind the mask.

"The time is approaching," he says, handing her a cape of rough brown wool. "This is costume enough for tonight—it will be colder than you might expect. Come now."

"Really," she says, " I'd like to make my excuses. Stay here and rest a little."

"During carnival? What madness! No, no my dear. I cannot let you miss the best part."

He laughs silently, his lip pulling back to reveal the gold teeth at the side of his mouth. "You'll have time to sit back in the company of your friend. He abandoned you, but now he's in our care.»

Koenig! Was it really he, the figure who met her? Back in his costume, but reduced to silence? Or another in his place while he, kidnapped, sat anonymous in an unidentified bare room? She suppresses a cry, but Camillo ignores her loss of composure. A trifle. The game holds far more surprises yet to come.

"It would be an affront to hospitality on my part if you do not experience the best of what we have to offer, if you did not see all the show. He snaps his fingers. "And you would be the poorer for it. There are such subtleties. Only let me show you a bit of the cunning in the world of costume."

He holds up his cane to display an elaborately carved ivory handle.

"Only look. A little pressure on the Buddha's navel, and there you have it, a sword. And the tip. Look closely at this gem, especially the tip. A mere scratch with the poison, from a recipe that goes back to the Borgias. That's all it takes, the toxin is so deadly. A Yugoslavian exile in London knows all too well. A poisoned dagger in his case. See this ring." He shows her a handsome jade ring inset with a scarab that came from Malta—centuries old, he tells her. So delicate in conception. "One little prick— A skin's prick to eternity." He grins.

"It is more than clever," she acknowledges, willing to express the admiration he is waiting for.

"Power can't exist without it."

Indeed she is ready to take in anything.

"And with a few modern variations . . . Oh, but come. I only meant to show you. Think well of me. You will have your justice, your revenge, I promise you. And I'll have mine. Tonight it's your occasion. For we've been robbed, you and I, and you were abused by scoundrels. Your victimizers will receive their due. We seek justice on our own terms. It's carnival. Of course, you demand it. And must take your chance. And so must I. Even the law will help you."

Weaving mystification all around her—he is a master at it. Lies and deception. It is a grim joke. What can he do to her if she merely walks away? The prick of his ring stands between her and eternity, if that's the way he wants to play it . . .

"I see the mark of a master," she says, grimly amused.

"And you are the mistress of all a man could worship. Put on your cape, my beauty, and let's be off."

"And if I choose not to go?" she says, turning away.

"It is not your choice," he says, grabbing her arm.

She turns and slaps him hard across the face.

"She has spirit—indeed she does. We're well equipped to amuse each other. If only there were time—It is only a tribute to beauty that prevents me from . . . , though I don't mind being provoked now and then. But remember the one who thought to get away. Think of what he can be made to suffer." He purses his lips as though to kiss her.

Oh yes, let her not forget. A hostage or a ploy? She cannot know if Koenig has been trapped after all. If he were even alive . . . But she let herself be led from the hotel and in the direction of the Campo San Polo. Their lives are worth nothing, that much is clear. And there is small room for self-indulgence.

Once they are in the streets, Camillo's mood sharpens with anticipation; he will not cease his chatter: she will see marvels; indeed she will. She tries to ignore him.

"The purity of an idea," he says with the contempt of one who has seen it all. "Things keep rising to the purity of an idea. How glorious for a time—and it's all so stupid. The Roman Empire, the Crusades, all the big parades. And think of it, a master race of blond and blue-eyed giants. For a thousand years. And the great triumph of the proletariat and the return of Paradise!"

They weave their way through costumed figures moving towards them, whole families, and groups solely of men or of women, their costumes alike. A solemn entourage of men passes them, dressed in velvet capes and blue vests and trousers, their heads capped in blue, beaked, decorated with peacock feathers. She wonders what idea has drawn them to this guise. Birds of a feather and what is their prey? Elegant birds.

"And they're all so convinced of its purity."

He gives out a full, hearty laugh. "Even as I think of it, the absurdity overcomes me. How such things fill you up like helium till you're all inflated and rise like a balloon." He seems tickled by

175

the comparison, for he continues along with, every now and then, a little burst of laughter. "Even your Helga——"

"Some ideas are better than others," Florrie says, to be saying something. "Especially the idea of Helga alive."

He ignores her for his own line of thought, grows expansive with his mode of pursuit. "Only have your thread of illogic and you can find your way through the world. They're all convinced by an invincible logic."

He laughs and dismisses them with a toss of his hand. "The simplicity of it, the sheer reasonableness of making over this doomed world. And what will be the next bunch of fools to hatch, the next absurdity?"

They reach the square, where a scaffolding has been erected and a wooden stage mounted. To one side stands a group of statues, towering above the gathering spectators, but as yet hooded and anonymous. People have already congregated in front of the stage, and more continue to arrive, till half the square is filled.

"The old Comedia del Arte," Camillo tells her. "A great tradition. I'll tell you what's going on, since you don't know the language. But most of it will speak for itself."

The stage is concealed with a paper curtain hung from a wire. They wait as various movements go on behind it. Then the curtain is rolled up with a flourish of cornets, and each member of the cast, mostly youthful emerges in costume and sings a line or two of introduction. Those not immediately in the action descend the steps alongside and disappear into a wooden dressing room behind the stage, while those to appear wait on the steps.

At first three men in clown costume come on in white masks with thick-lipped smiles painted up to their ears. Between them they heft a great model of the globe, which they set down in the middle of the stage. Then they grab up saws, knives and hatchets, and set to work sawing and hacking parts out of it. Grueling work. They mop their brows with great handkerchiefs, certain national flags. Often they fall over each other's feet. One emerges from such a fall with a knife stuck through his head. Peals of laughter from the crowd.

"The world carvers," Camillo says gleefully. "There goes Ethiopia. They've got Czechoslovakia."

A small man with a black umbrella goes fleeing across the stage as one of the clowns gives out a long sustained yodel, meanwhile beating on his chest. Amid general laughter, he approaches the globe, pushes the others aside, and rips out a piece, which is snatched out of his hands, torn to shreds by the other figures, then stomped under their feet. Rising laughter.

"Poland. Everybody took some. Swallowed it down, threw it up. Ah, there goes the rest. France, Greece, Yugoslavia, the Low Countries. the Baltics."

Slices of territory are piled up here and there on the stage. From the interior of the globe stuffing falls out in all directions. Then two satyrs appear with army caps between their horns, with mustaches like paint brushes, and caper around, hitting at one another with huge phalluses made of bread sticks.

The crowd roars: "Give it to him." "Let me in there." "All you need is a big one." "Enough for a bastinado." "On the backside." "Give it to him." "Right on the bum."

The satyrs triumph with every stroke, strutting to the cheers of the audience, until their sticks lie about in pieces and crumbs . and they are finally chased off the stage by an eagle and a great brown bear, which tear at each other, one with a tin swastika, the other with a hammer in one hand, a sickle in the other, while the uproar of voices urges them on. They beat each other mercilessly till a gaggle of ragamuffins appears, rolling hoops and skipping rope, dodging the cavorting figures, sometimes caught underfoot, thrown down in the melee, yelling all the while. The lights dim as the eagle leaps up on the shoulders of the bear, takes his ear in his beak and digs in his claws. The squealing bear rushes around the stage, finally throwing off the eagle, and stomping all over him, much to the satisfaction of the crowd.

After his triumph, the bear strides toward the audience, menacing them, raging up and down. Taunts and jeers from the crowd.

Meanwhile, on a platform in front of the stage and below, another figure appears, huge, bloated, so that the pig's head it wears seems small by comparison. It strides forward triumphantly holding up a bundle of sticks , while voices behind it chant: "Il Eroe, Il Capo."

"If you can have only one to keep the airlines on schedule," Camillo says, "And make the rockets fall where they're aimed, then you have it. Civilization. The trains here were a scandal."

Ashes, ashes, all fall down.

Someone, Camillo is eager to point out, whether among the actors or the crowd it is hard to say, tries to yell above the crowd. At first the voice is lost in the din. But then somehow a cry finds its way: "I lost a father in Ethiopia!"

"Here is where the fun begins," Camillo says, translating for Florrie. "A scapegoat can be useful."

"And I, a husband."

"And so did I." "Traitor!" "Kill him!"

As though at a signal a throng rushes up on the stage, smashing away the bundle of sticks and dragging the hapless pig-headed figure, yelling and flailing, down the steps and into the center of the square. They make him dance with their blows.

"Go on," Camillo insists, giving Florrie a shove. "Go up and beat him too. It's your turn now."

Indeed the crowd is in a frenzy, rushing up to rain blows on the figure with the pig's head, to pull apart his clothes. Gold coins, gold teeth, gems spill from his pockets and roll into the street.

"They're mine, they're mine," Camillo shouts, as those closest root around in the confusion, grabbing up what they can make off with. Others, more intent on the man himself, are still striking at him in fury.

Camillo thrusts his cane into Florrie's hand. "Hit him, hit him like the others. He's the one. He stole from everybody."

She stands paralyzed, the crowd surging around her. Surrounded, cries and shouts in her ears as she is blocked by her fears that she will be trampled upon. Then suddenly there are blows on her back and shoulders, her head. Wildly, she lashes out with the cane beating back anyone who approaches.

"The sword!" Camillo yells. "Use that too."

Before she knows it, she is part of the frenzy, screaming and lashing out, sobbing in her fear. Finally, her arms sink to her sides. What am I doing, oh what have I become?

Their victim lies writhing at their feet until he is set upon with knives and turns into a pile of straw in the middle of the square. A figure considerably smaller than expected is raised up, exposed, everything torn away to the naked bleeding flesh. And that, too, seems threatened, but clowns and acrobats come plunging, tumbling into the crowd, drawing their attention. And the threatened one flees into the darkness as the pig's head lies underfoot in chunks. But the crowd seizes upon three they seem to know about, and in a moment these are trussed up in the square, left to hang upside down: dictator, mistress, and general.

"Justice," the crowd yells. "Justice!"

"Here now," Camillo says, rescuing Florrie, as she tries to free herself from the press of the throng. "The rascal tried to rob you, rob everybody, but now they've taken care of him." He takes the cane from Florrie. "You see, it feels better to have a weapon, even better, your own army. You soon learn what to do with it." His face looms over her as she stands panting. It is unclear to her just who is the target for her revenge.

Farther down the square, bodies struggle in the darkness, and Florrie hears the sound of machine gun fire. There is nowhere to turn—threat lies everywhere. Nearer at hand, groups of peasants with bundles on their backs work their slow way toward some unseen destination, looking as though they have lost everything and do not have the benefits of food or safety.

"The revelry can get a little dangerous," Camillo acknowledges, "but don't worry, you're safe for the moment. Watch now."

"Enough!" she cries.

"Come, come. There's always more. This you'll certainly appreciate. The abortive effort to seize the reins of history. A bold effort. A highly comic piece."

Up on stage the scene is being changed: a table, a black board, chairs brought in. A uniformed officer on the edge sits waiting, until he is joined by another.

First Officer: "Quick, he hasn't come up yet."

Second Officer: "But where will he sit? It's got to go beside his chair." He indicates the briefcase he is holding.

First Officer: "Where he usually sits. Closest to the stove."

Second Officer: "Watch out that no one comes." He steps into the room, looks around furtively, sets the briefcase next to a chair, then leaves.

A group of officers gathers and salutes as the Leader approaches.

Officers: "Hail, hail to our great leader."

The Leader, distinguished by a mustache of paintbrush bristles, enters the room, eyes everyone suspiciously, and sits in the chair next to the briefcase, then gets up and moves away to another chair. One of the officers gets up and moves as well. The Leader moves again.

Soon it is a movement around the table from one chair to another The Leader stands up as soon as someone sits down, and everyone watches for the next move, changing his position to sit next to the source. Everyone is moving and changing seats. Blundering in, a confused man with a top hat and umbrella, obviously lost, is asking how to get back to London. One of the officers pulls the top hat down over his eyes, pushes him off the stage. The Leader changes his seat again, crosses his legs, brings out a huge cigar. Three officers rush forward to light it, trip and fall against one another, become tangled in each other's legs and collapse in a heap on the stage.

The crowd is once again convulsed with laughter.

"They have to sit by rank too," Camillo explains "What would we do without protocol?"

Now all the officers are sitting, the Leader the farthest away from the chair with the briefcase beside it. Suddenly the briefcase explodes, and the officer in the chair next to it crumples to the floor. The Leader rises unscathed, yelling curses, a string of nonsense syllables imitating various languages and raging around the stage.

"Nice little ploy," Camillo says. "I'd love to have been on hand for the original and sat there as a fly on the wall. A pity it didn't work. It would have saved a lot of trouble. It only made the great Leader more suspicious than ever. And got lots of people tortured and killed—right before the end too. A great waste, but so it happens."

Somewhere in the background the sounds of fighting keep increasing, and finally the figure of the Leader appears, the same figure but in various multiplied, exaggerated poses. The crowd, now equipped with sledge hammers, sets upon them. An arm falls off, a head rolls to the pavement. Two men lift it and cart it away, bobbing over the heads of the revelers, followed by cheers. The smashing continues amid the frenzy—until various attempts succeed in restoring order. Groups of musicians appear and begin to play. The dancing starts. Wine bottles appear. Several are passed around. The revelers will dance till morning.

The Fourth Day

Just as Florrie finishes her breakfast of oranges, sweet rolls, and coffee, Violetta appears. She is wearing a white dress with lacy sleeves and white leather sandals, looking as though she is about to attend a confirmation or a wedding. Today her sleek hair is combed back into a chignon, which sets off her face becomingly. As before, her face carries a glow, as from an unseen source—a gift to the day. For outside the day is indifferent, overcast and gray, with a mist that points toward an intermittent drizzle. She is lovely: Florrie can't help admiring her. Moved, it seems, by some inner purpose that heightens her presence. She carries it unpretentiously like a secret dream. and she has come, as she promised, to show her incomparable art. For reasons she couldn't explain, Florrie finds herself wanting to trust her.

"I have been preparing for you," Violetta says. "Venice is a great city. More than just Carnevale. Now you will have the most beautiful things to see," Violetta assures her.

"Indeed I am certain of that," Florrie says. Whatever else is waiting for her at this moment, by way of trap or guile, at least she will see something rising toward beauty She has come this far.

Still she recognized a subtle coercion at her back. She wasn't so simple as not to recognize it, though she is less and less clear about its motive. She has no idea as to Koenig's fate, nor any sense of her own. It seems simpler to kill her than terrify her into silence.

Behind her stands the Knower, secure in his power, who can move through all the workings of the carnival. What power he has been given or has carved out for himself takes the greatest possible leap of imagination to guess at, in all its ins and outs, subtleties and connections—who has what on whom? what lies in hints and threats, what rewards are to be dangled, what insufficiencies punished, what one part means to any other? Things shifting into appearances like Camillo's changing colors before your eyes—how can you see beyond them? Behind him might stand greater powers, who know more than he does and are bent on greater mischief.

She has always been burdened by too much thought. A dangerous business, Koenig. We share that much. Is it better not to know than to know too much? Life is simpler if you look into the face of a Violetta and rhapsodize its purity? And never see beyond? For she has been sent in the service of that private ambition to lead her where she seems destined to go. A little diversion, if you will, before whatever this final night holds.

Well, she is going. They are off. She has reached a space beyond panic, a space where she can walk about, a small atom of composure, moving toward the finale of the carnival with its show of fireworks. And in a space there is some pleasure in the beat of blood, the feeling of the day, living it, taking in its sensations, even though it is a bit damp and chill. And if she moves through people oblivious to her, caught up in things that have nothing to do with her circumstances, she feels no dismay. She herself is clinging to the little life she has hold of.

That life connects with what is preserved in the Doge's palace with art promising a life beyond commerce and conquest. She gazes at Tintoretto's "Paradise," lifted beyond the moment.

"No matter how many times I see it . . ." Violetta says, continuing her gaze, unable to finish her sentence.

"Glorious," Florrie says.

Violetta knows the city and its art; if she were to be drawn anywhere, it would be on the wings of adoration, whatever dark wings were beating at her back. San Rocco and the Old and New Testament are her territory. And all the rest. The centuries left the churches behind for this young woman, while the city has grown loose and distracted around her, lost in revelry and dissolution. The ashes of the beginning of Lent are there to remind them, if they care to be reminded.

Those who have been drinking, it seems to Florrie, have been at it for days, but must continue beyond desire because it is still carnival. Daylight catches them like owls blinking in the light. Some of them, students perhaps, wobble around, voices louder than they need to be, insisting on their good time; or else they lie inert on their ruck-sacks in the squares, catching a little shut-eye before the next call to abandon. At various times during the day, they take their lagging energies around the points of interest, looking to their maps.

Lax and weary, the city is slowing down. Florrie and Violetta walk through its fumes of alcohol and cigarettes, the fag ends of revelry. The garbage bins are overflowing, bottles and beer cans lie where they've been tossed. The sky is boring, and the streets give off their exhaustion: they've seen all the costumes they can absorb. A surfeit. Nothing has escaped them, nothing that the revelers have brought, have hidden under their costumes. The shadows trailing at their backs have fallen into the street, connecting and mingling.

Florrie can tell, as she moves along with Violetta, that they are being followed.

Her antennae have become highly sensitive. The street singer standing outside the Doge's palace when they leave continues behind them as they walk along. He is dressed as a player, perhaps part of a company, and when they emerge, he is singing a ballad. His song follows them, at times thin and plaintive, as though they are hearing it at a distance—a plaint of love and longing, which, if they lose it momentarily, emerges again, as though the air will carry it even if no one is there to hear it. And then the tune changes, charged with a more robust sentiment.

He appears always to be in the street, not far away from whatever church they emerge from. If Violetta glances in his direction, her appraisal is cursory and without recognition. But his face has become emblazoned in memory as Florrie passes, a face that holds such intensity, such a spark in the eye, she is momentarily disconcerted. Violetta knows he is there; a certain consciousness is in her expression. They are lovers, Florrie is convinced of it. Something else: not everything is an eye to spy on her. Love has its own manifesto.

And does that make the girl vulnerable, open up a little place where knowledge or power has a gap? Florrie is suddenly become canny, sharpening her vision until it can reach a single focus: to catch them off guard in a moment when her presence is of no consequence. To make a hole she can slip through.

"Where is Camillo today?" she wants to know.

Violetta shrugs. "Very busy arranging things for the evening."

The final burst of celebration. He has already mentioned it. Then fireworks and the carnival is over. What then? She wonders.

"He is Master of Ceremonies," Violetta tells her.

"A man of many parts," Florrie says. "Everywhere at once."

"Yes, he tries to do too much, to be in too many places," Violetta comments. "But not here just now." She gives a slight smile.

And might she, Florrie wonders, the daughter, feel a certain relief as well to be away from the father?

They are silent for a time, catching bits of melody from the guitar, strains of a love song—it can be no other. The player sings, sometimes accompanying himself, at times singing a capella. His voice is a thread in a labyrinth that otherwise holds no clue. Only Camillo, it seems, knows how to move through the city, through all its devious turns and connections. Violetta is still a puzzle to her.

If he wants her to know he can threaten her in any way he likes, at any time, she is used to him now. He can't take away her agency, even if it fails. The truth, or even a lie, can always send you to the dungeon or out of this life. The inner secret of florins and swords.

"And what will you do after it's all over?" Florrie asks her.

"The shop will stay open only in the afternoons. My brothers will begin making some designs for next year's masks and costumes. We will go on vacation, taking turns."

"Where will you go?"

Violetta shrugs again, as though it is of no consequence. "Anywhere. My father travels everywhere on business."

"Europe?"

"France, Germany."

"The States?"

"Other places too. Iran, Tunisia. Turkey.

The singing has reached a pause, and Violetta glances behind her.

"We've come at last," she says, almost to herself. "To the best, the greatest of paintings. And do you also wish to see the foot of St. Catherine?"

Relics seem strange to her, such things made holy. It does belong to Violetta's world. Florrie is more taken up with the singer's continuing silence. Has he reached the fullest expression of his sentiments with this particular destination? Has he just disappeared, gone home without further need for contact ?

Making no real response when Florrie comments about the singer, Violetta leads her into the Church of the Friari to stand before "The Assumption." For a long time they do not move as they follow the triangle of red robed figures to where the Virgin gazes upward, beyond herself, borne aloft on a cloud, cherubim gathered around her. Splendor among splendors.

Then Violetta leaves her to continue admiring the painting and goes to one of the pews behind her to give herself to prayer. Florrie sits down as well, much too weary to visit the chapel where the foot is on display. Her own feet are tired of holding her up, and the holy foot is no compensation. Remember the body, the life that goes on in it. Abandoned finally. While the Virgin leaps toward her ultimate inspiration, leaving behind a less than perfect world with those reaching, trying to keep hold of a foot.

Below, in the side chapel, Christ still hangs on the cross, as he has done for centuries, once a prisoner Himself.

Did you, down there alone and abandoned, find your way to something deeper? Was there some place above or beneath the darkness where things converged? As above, so below? She couldn't ask any more.

It was there for any tourist who came to look: The Resurrection. Flower window and pillared arch, and the great pillar forming and

186

sustaining the wall and ceiling, combined their voices in a single message: up, look up, up and upward. In spite of everything, beyond the downward pull of stone and bone, corpse and desiccated foot. Rot. All that pulled and kept pulling. Bodies colliding in the dark. Propelled by the surge of instinct, the ambitions of power. In the clash of swords, glint of metal; clink of coins, glint of gold: the power of. Here in this home of all, womb of all. Bound by the logic of all.

Centuries it took for stones to rise, here, to rise into vaults. It took, what did it take to wait four hundred years? Not in my time, nor in my children's will the eye be allowed to soar. Wait beyond this life for stones to rise.

And still here, the throng all waiting on the ground. While Mary stands over the altar on her way up, hands below grasping at her, reaching, the faces turned up, still reaching, yearning after all the centuries. The stretch of fingertips to that receding holiness. Look up: into the spittle of jets catching the sun, writing their track across the sky; missiles shooting from the earth into the future, toward the vastness of galaxies. All the eye can see now.

She turns back to Violetta, perhaps aspiring there in her white dress, but the pew is empty. Empty? She can't believe it. Has Violetta gone to meet her lover? Has she in a burst of compassion left Florrie the space she needs to escape? In any event, she rushes from the church in a single movement.

Then she enters the movement of the street, trying not to call attention to herself. Faces rush past her, people in eager conversation. Some take her in, but with no particular notice. She means no more to this city than the pieces of confetti floating to the sidewalks. And yet . . . What is she guilty of, she or Helga, Koenig or the prisoner? What is anybody guilty of? She rushes away from threat, from the simple guilt of being alive. Let her claim that, dash on beyond this place, this city, in the direction of survival. That will suffice for now.

Let there be a hole for her to slip through. A boat at the Rialto, a train to Mestos.

She does not look behind her. Only in the direction of escape.

When she reaches the boat, she waits with the others to file on. She feels something near her foot, and moves to avoid stepping on a grinning mask.

The Key

Cross the threshold. This is the doorway. Praha, the threshold. Cross over now. Libuse, queen and patroness, awaits you. This is the point of time, the moment of the century on which everything turns.

Go past the cemetery, where the dead are lying in medieval silence under the tombstones, crowded, canted this way and that. There, the creator of the Golem that stalked the city. In the museum are the children's drawings from Treblinka: the butterfly flown and gone beyond the barbed wire. Continue down the street of the two moons, two clocks—two measuring lights. Pause for the chimes: time, time, time. The backward moving hands of the Hebrew-lettered clock. The houses sleep in the silence. Shadows merge into one another, pieces of dark geometry in the carved space. For this is the way to Kafka's house. A workman this morning was putting a new lock on the door.

But he did not know whose house it was.

So much has been pushed into forgetfulness, buried under the weight of the present. What will rise to the surface again? And what will happen if it does?

Would she find Koenig even? the ticket had been waiting for her at the airport, and she had boarded the plane. But even as she landed in the city, hours behind schedule, the flight delayed by engine trouble, she could not be certain of anything. The telephones were a frustration. He was not to be reached by telephone. She, alone, getting past the customs inspectors, taken by taxi into the city as it was getting dark, could only hope that the directions she had would take her to where he was.

.

He, too, must be found, located in his shadowy origins. It is hard to imagine real flesh and blood, sunlight on his face. She thinks of pale creatures in caves, that have never seen the light, having lost use of their eyes because they no longer need them. She is afraid to find him there in the dark, afraid of what might be expected of her. Perhaps they will float like shadows, unable to do anything for one another, separate and alone.

❖

"You've come," Koenig says, opening the door of the flat, answering to her knock, the motor of the taxi throbbing in the street. Found after the dark turnings in the streets in a city she can barely see. She wants to throw her arms around him, cling to him. But something in his face prevents her, even though he smiles and clasps her hand. They are strangers still, and both of them might melt into shadows. They confront one another with their separate amazements. Then he goes to pay for the taxi.

"You're here now," he says, as if he still can't believe it. She doesn't know if he means that as welcome. Perhaps he did not believe she would come. "Can I bring you something—tea, a glass of wine, something to eat?"

She had eaten on the plane, but not enough to satisfy her during the hours without food after breakfast. A hot drink would be welcome to relieve the chill the night air has given her. She is thoroughly tired, but not ready to sleep. She is experiencing the physical weariness as well as the confusion and the anxiety of travel hardly knows what to do first.

"Something hot to drink would be good." The night air has left her chilled.

And he seems to be in some confusion about which of her needs he can satisfy immediately. "You must be exhausted. I can take you to a hotel, if you like. Here, I have only the sofa you're sitting on to offer you. My bed is not at all comfortable."

She doesn't want to move. "The sofa will do nicely." Once again,

she has to depend on him for everything—an awkward situation .
But right now she can't dwell on her discomfort.

"If you're not too tired, there is something you might enjoy.
There are some good places to eat not far from here. We can pick
one of those. I often have my meals over there. And you can see
something of the city by night."

"I would like that."

The tea he made for her warmed her pleasantly, and she feels her
energy returning. Then they set out for the restaurant. They step
into the street, where there are still people going about—a group
of casually dressed youths, smoking, joking, laughing; an old man
walking a large white dog that strains in their direction; a small girl
chatting away as she walks between her parents, holding a hand of
each.

Florrie takes a deep breath. How extraordinary it is for her to be
walking out like this without suspicion or a sense of threat.

A nearly full moon casts its light above them, superior to the
street lights and the remaining lights of cafes and shops. They are
not far from Wenceslas Square. "Do you like Indian food?" he asks
her. "There is a wonderful Indian restaurant here."

"Splendid. I love Indian food." He leads her to the restaurant.
Once there, they enter a spacious room, the walls decorated with
figures from the Indian epics along with various animals and birds.

Florrie is delighted. "Such colors. I hope the food is to match."

"You'll see."

The waiter, a slender young man named Andres from Kerala, he
tells them in response to their questions, leads them to a table in the
almost empty room. He recommends the lamb. A man sitting across
from them says, "The chicken curry is delicious," and indicates his
plate of food. They'll have one of each and divide their choices. And,
oh yes, nans and Indian beer.

And how does he find things here since his return? Florrie asks
him after she tells her story, and he has assured her he wasn't the
Solomon for her Sheba.

"I was afraid you'd been captured."

"Finally," Koenig says, "I don't think we were worth the trouble. A few threats, playing on fear and seeing us run off. "

"Camillo has a way of making people into puppets."

"He is in a position to do that," Koenig suggests. "As for being back in Prague," he says, "in many ways it is quite wonderful. Havel is an amazing man. The way he let all the prisoners go free—just let them go—without even making a plan for them. Nobody thought that would work. But it did, except for a small number—almost negligible. 'We didn't want to shame our president,' one of them told me."

"How extraordinary!"

When Andres brings them their food, they divide the portions and take in the wonderful smell of spices and begin to eat.

How pleasant it is, Florrie thinks, to be here in this moment, savoring what is before her, being together, sharing both the food and their experience. They had done this before, and that had been part of what had connected her to Eric. Something special in the past is being repeated

"Yes," Koenig says, continuing the story of the prisoners. "they went off, found help, found shelter and friends. Many good things have happened," he goes on to say. "Just having the freedom of expression. No more censorship and repression. No more prison terms for speaking out," he says. "No more Party to leap on your back. Though it's still there and not to be trusted. You can print any book you want. Only now," he adds, "you get all the junk too, and that's what people want to read. So a new day has dawned. We're much better off by far. But in some ways poorer too." She can tell by the ironic turn of his assessment that he must have a lot more to say.

He was about to tell her some of the deplorable conditions that remained, but stops himself. "We are here together," he says, "and with this food, it would be a shame to spoil the occasion. Revolutions can accomplish only so much even as the struggle goes on. Politics! Dirty work! No, you can't expect a revolution to keep its purity. No revolution ever has, and some change things very little." He drinks the rest of his beer slowly, pays the check. They smile and thank the waiter as they take their leave.

The moon is starting its downward journey when they step back into the street, warmed by their food and the pleasure of each other's company. The moonlight lends a quality to the night that is almost magical. Florrie has almost forgotten her long hours of travel as they walk toward the Vtalva.

The streets are nearly empty now, and those who walk appear engaged in their own solitude. Yet it seems to Florrie they are not alone but that voices linger and speak to them out of the breeze, out of the river, taking them past fatigue, past sleep, into a night of whatever the moon allows to be revealed.

Proceed to the square, then into the heart of the city, where the cathedral rises into its towers and the astrological clock measures out the hours with a parade of Christ and the Apostles, followed by the Turk, the miser, the old man who clings to this life, and finally, Death with his scythe. The cock crows over all: over the death that waits for all. The death they push against.

A dark shape on the hill across the river, lights sparkling: the castle. Guards stand watch over its labyrinth of rooms. The castle stands always just over your shoulder. A watching shape, a hidden eye.

On the Hebrew clock, Koenig shows her, the hands move backwards, Time circling around itself. Ghosts move along the echoing streets. Look at the clock. It approaches midnight. The stars are still out, though the sky will close again. It is starting to snow. The hours will turn: their time here, hers and Koenig's, a book of hours. To the old stones belong the story, the story woven of the hours. Hers and Koenig's. And will she find the key?

So you're here now, and you've still got your question. So does everybody these days. Should my life turn inward or outward? should I be looking upward or down to earth? The air is filled with voices. Will they give me an answer?

—*Well, you might have a word with Kepler. He can tell you a few things.*

She cannot really see this stranger who seems to know what she is thinking.

Kepler? wasn't he some sort of scientist?

Koenig knows about him. —He jolted a few good souls and a number of churchmen who thought God put us at the center of things. then along came Kepler, who discovered the paths of the planets. And the earth was just one more of them

—*Bad news for the box makers and the keepers of thresholds. But don't worry, the two old guys, him and Tycho Brahe, are still hanging on. Warming the Chair of Galaxy Gazing. Watching the stars run away into the universe. Better than stoking furnaces, eh friends?*

—*Mostly watching Red stars, wouldn't you say?* *Another voice chimes in. Oh, we watched red stars for a long time.*

—*And where do we go to find Kepler.*

—*In the Cathedral. You'll find the two of them.*

—*The Cathedral?*

The exterior of the cathedral is covered with scaffolding, and none can enter. But when they try the handle, tentatively, the door gives, unlocked. A creaking when they pull it forward, as though it hasn't been opened for centuries, but then in the quiet street any noise seems imagined. Koenig enters first. Inside, it is profoundly silent, the walls draped with shadows, layers of shadow lying over the pews, the dark pipes of the organ, the altar, the unregarded Christ still on the cross. Like thieves they steal into this space, shine their lights into the interior, disturbing dust and saints, and move through the door at the side. The stairs spiral above them.

—What do you think?

—I think it'll be a long climb in the dark even with our flashlights.

—You think we can make it?-

—Well, the batteries were made in the USSR. You can't see a thing in Russia either.

With the light of their beams, they ascend on stone steps into the tower. Echoes resound in the surrounding vault, in the entombed air of the centuries. Colder as they mount the stairs, narrow, spiraling around until there is barely space for one climber. Breathless, they reach a landing and peer ahead. A light perhaps— they can't be certain—winking at them as they move forward. Ahead a short flight of steps promises a threshold. And when they climb these, they see off to the side yet another set of steps and a figure somewhat elevated. A telescope is mounted on one side that can be reached only by a final set of steps, and to see out of it, one must stand on a stool. The figure turns toward them.

—Visitors! Well, well. Haven't been any visitors here since they dragged us in for questioning the last time— Let me see . . .

(He shakes his head.) —The fact is unimportant. He doesn't appear annoyed to have been interrupted, but climbs down, gives a hand to each in turn. A robust man with a long mustache and a thick beard. Behind him a small lamp burns at the center of a heavy wooden table. Charts cover the walls, filled with lines and pins, various equations. He scrutinizes the visitors closely.

(To Florrie.) —You look a bit done in. Quite a climb—isn't it? Takes the wind out of your sails and the light out of your head. Light-headed. A pun, forgive me. A contradiction. Just don't forget your name. . . . (He laughs)— or who you are. Mine's Tycho Brahe. Nobody knows who I am anymore. I invented the lens. (He gestures toward the telescope.) — And remember, you haven't seen me. You can dissolve into nothing here if you're clever and if they're content to forget you. (He shifts ground.) —You're enterprising to climb all the way up. It's all I can do to get Kepler to go down for sausages. Forgive me for babbling.

American? You found us—me, that is. Kepler's gone for the beer and sausages—it's his turn. You'll get to hear him groan all the way back up. Claims it's his arthritis. Bad back. But it's mostly for sympathy, trying to get out of his turn. He likes to groan. Makes him feel alive. Here's a bench to sit on. We stole it from down below. God knows how we got it up here.

"You're up here—all the time?," Florrie says with some surprise.

—Where else would we be? (He leans over confidentially.) — We're custodians.

"Of the cathedral?" Koenig asks.

—Of just about anything. The cathedral? It gave us a hard time once. But now, since we're here, they've forgotten they kicked us out of the university. And the place is boarded up. You might say that of the past. Or even the future—who can say? Or even speak of sausages and beer.

(Florrie looks at Koenig and they exchange glances.) —But the telescope. Have you discovered anything new about the universe? Some new stars on the horizon?"

—Sshh. Not so loud. The walls have ears, as they say. It's still secret. They don't even know who is up here, if they think about us at all. We're subversive, you see. A new regime—it's hard to know about it. Even so, you have to be careful. They still think we work for G.O.L.E.M.

—GOLEM G. Stars rising and falling meanwhile. Who's in— who's who's out And when? It doesn't matter what the bureau's called—it all adds up to the same letters. Voted it in in 1948. Supposedly. While the Ruskies stood over our shoulder, fingering the putsch underneath the ballot box. The star system. We've been star-gazing ever since. They rise, they fall out of history as well— into the dust bin.

(Florrie is bemused by this recital. She sees that Koenig is nodding.) —And what do the letters stand for?

—The Global Ontological Logistical Emergency Map. It's a mouthful all right, and I've never figured out what that's supposed to mean. I'd agree that we're in some kind of questionable state. They're fond of those initials that go to make a word. There's a word for that too—only I've forgotten what it is. Words, words. It's a secret organization.

—You said they didn't know you were here.

—Depends on the they you're talking about. But mostly they thought we were here to sweep the floors. Only we're waiting . . .

—What for?

They hear a moaning echoing from below. At first it sounds far away and mournful, but as it comes nearer it sounds more like a chant sung in various registers.

—Ah, Kepler's back. Sounds like he's in better humor than usual. Sometimes when he gets to the top he tries to strangle me.

The three of them sit listening to the approaching voice. Tycho Brahe stands up and moves to the doorway, holds out a hand to pull a man up. A short, broad man, bent and crippled. His hands are gnarled. His face holds the strain of the climb. He, too, has a long, two-pronged mustache and a sizeable beard . Florrie notices his curly hair.

—Hooray for sausages and beer. You've not got extras, I suppose. We have guests. Here give us a look.

—I'm hungrier than two Russian bears.

(Kepler regards them closely, then shakes hands.)

—It's snowing out. Suddenly colder and snowing. I was looking at the snowflakes on the sleeve of my coat on the way back. six-sided every one of them and each one different.

—Is that what took you so long? My God! (Brahe has already bitten into a sausage. He remembers himself and offers one to the guests, who explain that they have eaten already.) Kepler is in no hurry to eat. He stands bemused.

—Have you ever wondered why snowflakes have six sides? They still don't know—not after all this time. Why six? Why not five, as with flowers? But crystals, you see, are often six, or formed in octahedrons. And when you look at crystals, you wait for something to arise, a correspondence.—

Brahe holds up a sausage, and Kepler reaches for it absently.

—But what I think is that it comes from the heart of nature—a formative principle. Snowflakes, crystals, flowers. And it's done in play. Nature is one to play in the passing moment—.

(Brahe, clearly impatient): —For the sake of your stomach and brain, there is nothing worse than a cold sausage. Besides our guests want to know what we're waiting for? (To Florrie) You've come here expecting something, haven't you? And not just entertainment.

(Florrie, fascinated) —Both planets and snowflakes—great and small, high and low. Do you think, down there where nature is at play, making geodes with crystals inside them and other things. . . . (She breaks off.) This man, too, goes looking for a key. If you

199

descend far enough . . .

—When you're buried under three centuries and forty years of idiocy—is that far enough for you?

(Koenig offers a question.) —What are you waiting for?

—For news from the farthest reaches of space. Of some life beyond this sphere.

Koenig (ironically): —Isn't the revolution enough for you.?

—Yes, of course. You've read the papers. A thing of beauty. Now we're waiting for the stars to turn backwards. The galaxies streaming toward us—that will make a new revolution. A greater coziness. Time turning back. Only see what we could mine from the past, even as we turn in the direction of another dimension. What a play for the imagination—that's what it will take.

—And before the stars come clashing in the mightiest bang and we all have to jump into space . . . (Brahe breaks into a laugh.)

—If only there were a voice, just a voice, no matter what it said. Even if we couldn't understand it. A hallo from out there, traveling down the light years. We might feel less alone. I tell you it's very quiet here.

—Indeed one can die of waiting, we prisoners of waiting. we're glad of your visit—.

—Meanwhile we're counting the stars. You see all these pins—

—Meanwhile we get paid in sausages and beer. But would you mind giving me a cigarette. You see, if we spend all our time counting, we can't be dangerous, can we?—

—Unless, of course, there is something there so extraordinary that it might change the whole perspective . . . (Kepler goes up to the telescope.)

—What's the sky doing?—

—It's snowing hard . You can't see a thing.—

—Better here than looking at the economy. Everything's doubled in price—gas, meat, milk. But don't worry —with the pollution it isn't safe to eat anything anyway. The old regime is in the soil.

(Koenig (bitterly): —And the new springs out of the old. The forests are dying, and nothing can be done to save them. And there are the children. Blighted in the womb.—

—Careful of what you're saying.

—But it's the truth—.

—Always truth too hard for the telling—is that it?—

Brahe points to where Kepler still stands: —We occupy this Chair, you see. Kepler's chair. His place. We keep it warm for him, have a little beer, a little sausage in his honor. As I told you, he got kicked out of the university. All those years ago now. But we've been keeping the chair warm. Only now we're getting old. Our eyes aren't what they used to be. It's getting hard to see through a telescope.—

Maybe we can try the other end. We've made things too big anyway. Now they're out of hand, out of time, out of tune.

Brahe (interrupting): You see these pins. All the red stars. That was '68. Now they've fallen out of the sky and are hiding in the woodwork. Now a brighter constellation. Certain others sent off prisons, but in their returning brilliance they still hold a menace.

—It's always the same story. The poor Hussites beaten to pieces and everything forced back into the same old boxes. Three centuries ago now—and they still push people out of windows. They tried to force the sky back too, into the old safeties. But we're holding on. The planets still make their orbits—elliptically. The earth won't stand still

(Kepler continues.) I finally got my mother out of that hell-hole of a prison. She's dead now.

—Your mother in prison? Why her?

—Why not? They read my book all wrong, the fools. They thought the spirit of knowledge was a devil, and because of a little playful reference, they decided she was his familiar the usual stuff. (In a different tone.) But it's out there, my dream. Somnium. the trip to the moon I envisioned—and it has happened. Perhaps instead of voices coming to us, we can go outward to different worlds, full of discoveries. Perhaps something awaits us. If I could imagine that . . .

Florrie: —So looking up . . . And when you dig down into the debris, can you ever dig far enough?

—For what? For truth? Kepler comes down from the telescope. (He gives a little shrug.) Things take a curious turn. Even that dream of mine, traveling to the moon—

—I was told of a prisoner. I have his journal. No one seems to know anything of him.

—And I've been here trying to find out how a journalist was murdered. Even now it's difficult to ask questions. So much buried. People searching in the debris. Relatives, friends—property confiscated, who owns what. And yet, how else can one continue?— (Koenig looks from one to the other.)

—A vexing business all the way around. (To Florrie.) You at least can go to the window and look out, look up.

Kepler (objecting): Much too cruel.

—But she'll have to go there eventually if she wants to learn anything—.

—Send her to Libussa. Who knows what she knows? She might have something for them both.

Brahe (grudgingly): —She's at the factory where the other crazies are.—

—They don't believe in madness here—they just create it. That's not a joke.—

—And in such variety. Every year new factories, new bureaus. It's gotten so you have to order them years in advance, the demand is so great. And the backlog. They wanted to raise oranges here and cotton. (Brahe gives a long melancholy laugh.)—

—You'll have to get past Libussa's raven first. Canny bird—it can smell an official a mile away. But you shouldn't have any difficulty.

Florrie (uncertainly): —Go at this time of night? Where is this place? And can we find it ?

—You'll have no trouble, let me assure you. Just say the name Libussa in the street and listen for the echoes—.

And then you must go to the Opera and see the performance— the Castle, of course. (To Koenig) And you'll want to see some of your old friends.

Koenig (with a shrug): — If there are any. Some of —Some of

them betrayed their friends, even members of their families.

—Betrayal, yes. Even I know something of that.

Brahe (drawing a finger up to his lips): And find news of the Golem. There are still pieces of it in the attic of the old synagogue. Someone keeps sneaking up there and bringing it back to life. A dangerous creature, though some say it is miraculous—.

Koenig: And I must go up north to see that country once again.

Kepler (sadly): —I wouldn't go there if I were you. Let me take you on a journey to the moon instead. I planned the trip three centuries ago . . .

(Brahe shakes his head) —. You're always eager to get off. It's not that easy when everything's so unsettled. And you're wedded to your beer and sausages.—

—But it's not just the moon, you see—it's a journey to another realm. Perhaps a place for new beginnings.—

Brahe (countering him): Or old nightmares. what the moon hides. The dead don't stay dead, but enter the parade of the living. They won't rest; won't be forgotten or appeased.—

Kepler: —but a trip to the moon, think of it. One day someone will step on that ground.

The Factory

After asking for directions, Florrie and Koenig find themselves in the street in front of an abandoned factory near the gasworks. Some of the windows are broken out and boarded up, and the fumes from the gasworks hang in the air. As they move toward the doorway, they discover a raven, head tucked down, asleep on the stoop. It ruffles up when they approach and caws loudly. A bustling can be heard from above, then silence; they have the sense of being watched. The raven parades slowly in front of them, cocking its head. Then it moves behind them, cocks its head again, stands for a moment in front of Koenig, turning its eye towards him, parades to the other side and settles on the stoop.

Koenig: (unsettled) —Why should it look at you as if it suspects something suspicious of you?

From behind the door, the metallic sounds of chains clashing and a key being turned in a lock. What appears to Florrie as a small hunchbacked boy opens the door. Looking more closely, she sees that he is older, of indeterminate age. The skin on his face is very smooth. Behind him a man in a cap and workman's clothes holds a lantern.

—You're not supposed to come this late. (The hunchback speaks in a gravelly voice.) — It's long past midnight. It's always the wrong time unless you're entering a bedroom.

—Kepler sent us here. We've lost all track of time.

—No excuse, no excuse. He sent you here, did he? Well then, come in. Jiri will lead you upstairs. You'll have to see Libussa. No one gets past her. It's her raven.

Florrie (in a low voice) — They told us she was mad. Is that a thing one ought to say?—

The hunchback (laughing uproariously) —Who pays any

attention to that? There's always enough madness to go around.

Jiri, who has given an occasional grunt of assent to whatever the hunchback has been saying, leads them to one side of a dark open floor that houses complicated machinery. In the dark it is difficult to know its function. The forms occupy the floor solidly, but with pipes and other appendages rising up and extending in various directions, so that they all appear interconnected. The great hunks of machinery sit inert in the silence, giving off a smell of metal, machine oil, and dust. At the side, Jiri pushes open a door onto a stairway, then plays the flashlight along the wall to a panel of buttons and levers. He presses one of the buttons twice and a whistle like that of a tea kettle rises with earsplitting urgency and subsides. Other noises mingle with it, then voices, and from above come the sounds of mirth, the clink of glasses.

—You always have to keep an eye out. (The hunchback takes Florrie familiarly by the arm to lead her up the stairs.) — Even now. One day they'll kick us all out.—

—This is a huge place. What was it used for?

The hunchback (with a little snort of laughter): —It was never used. They built it for a cotton gin. The Hungarians were forced to grow cotton. Cotton and oranges. They were going to change the course of agriculture. Re-program nature. Forgot what the old Mother had in mind. (Panting a little from the stairs): Then they thought they could change it into a shoe factory. After that, they tried to forget it. Maybe now when they remember it, they can make it into a hotel for Japanese business men.

(General laughter.)

—Jiri (from behind) :— Paradise he calls it. Paradise.—

—Of course. Here it's paradise. We hid away, and nobody came for us. When you've fallen far enough through the cracks, you land here. We have saints and martyrs, including jazz musicians. Even a plumber—try finding one of them—.

— Do you come out now that you can?—

—We go out, but we come back. Bohumil plays sax down in the park. But nobody wants to leave here—.

They have arrived now in an upper section of the building, perhaps designed for a warehouse. They are met by voices and cigarette smoke, the sounds of conviviality. Against one wall runs a counter, bottles of wine behind it at the back; to one side along the walls kegs of beer are mounted horizontally on stands. A bar girl runs back and forth among the dozen or so customers seated at the small wooden tables.

—Who belongs to Paradise?

The hunchback (squeezing Florrie's hand): —Anybody for whom it's a state of mind. Here, I'll take you to the one who knows it best. Libussa, our queen.—

The hunchback, who has never revealed his name, leads them to a table on the far side of the room, where a woman sits on a man's lap with her arms around his neck—voluble, laughing raucously, joined by various men and women around her. Some are sitting with her, some standing—on their way to other tables. She is a big-boned but elegant woman, her thick hair plaited into a long braid down her back.

—Visitors here. They've been talking to Kepler.

Libussa scrutinizes them carefully, blows a long reflective puff of smoke, then a series of smoke rings through the first, while they watch with some fascination. Everyone around her remains silent, though the man whose lap she occupies continues to blow in her ear. She ignores him.

—They've been approved—officially?—

—The bird's given them the eye.—

—Well then, they must have some wine, a little hospitality. Quick now, and bring them something tasty. We've never been known to turn away one of us . Here, make a place for them. (With a gesture she invites them to the table). —Sit down, please.— (The talk and laughter resume.) —You've come to hear about my love, isn't that the case?

The others sitting at her table, rise and give place to the newcomers, while those flocked around her wander off. The man whose lap she occupies, lifts her aside, rises up, tall and gaunt, then bends down to kiss her on the cheek. Koenig and Florrie gesture for the others to stay, but Libussa waves them off.

—They've heard the story ten dozen times. Whenever there are lovers, they want to hear the story. I'm the source and reference book. You are lovers, I can tell—and you want to know because of that. No, don't protest. It doesn't matter. It's a story you have to hear whether you want to or not.

The barmaid brings them a bottle of red wine and glasses and sets them in front of each. A plate of ham and a basket of bread appear. Libussa, rummaging through her clothes, keeps pulling out slips of paper. Some she examines closely; others she tosses aside without looking at them. One she reads, her lips moving, fingers tapping out a rhythm—apparently with satisfaction.

Florrie (leaning forward and touching her on the arm with one finger): —They say you're mad—.

—Of course. Lovers are always mad to begin with. Did you ever hear of such an absurdity as love; in this mad world it's always mad to love. That's the first thing to know. Here, let me show you. I write a poem every day. I will never run out. (Reading aloud):

> *My beloved*
> *Small is our knowledge of love,*
> *For I am separated from you*
> *By eight union officers,*
> *four passport controllers*
> *and by an iron door:*
> *Distance*
> *That would not be distance,*
> *Were it not for politics.*

Another one? Florrie (leaning forward eagerly): He was in prison?

Slowly various people have moved over to listen. Florrie has not noticed them before, so raptly has she been watching Libussa, who ends her poem with her hand outstretched. One of those gathered, a heavy-set man with a thick reddish mustache, having waited for Libussa to finish her poem, interrupts before she can continue. He sways, first one way, then the other, catches himself

—A toast. A toast to love. A glass to open up the reaches of the heart, to travel deep into the eye. Love's country—all the sights. Love, I say. Let's drink to that. (He waves his arms so that some of the wine spills; but he doesn't appear to notice.) See, over in that corner are lovers. A different music. Another language. Passion and yearning. At first, the flesh in the first sizzle. Ah, don't forget that. Then the melting. (He tilts dangerously to one side, returns briefly to equilibrium and sings:

> *I had her in the parlor*
> *I had her in the hall*
> *But when I turned and tried to run*
> *She had me all.—*

—Come, come on—you're ruining the story.—
—We've heard it a zillion times. Listen I've got a dozen songs.
—We've heard those a zillion times too.—
One of the men claps him on the back, then drags him off to the counter, signals for a glass of beer. He seizes it up, pulls away and drags his companion back to Libussa's table. Confronting the visitors, he breaks into Libusse's speech:

—Her lover died in prison—yes, yes, we know it all. She's the one who gets to talk about him. To be crazy over his memory. It's all right—she can tell the story. I've heard it fourteen million times, but it's okay. I'll hear it again.

The little group of people gathered around to listen start to murmur: —Let her tell it then. You know she tells it to all who come. It's the way into Paradise.—

Libussa (waving her hand): —Let madness be for love. I have my madness. Moonstruck madness. And every night, I drink wine to go mad again. I ask only, let me be mad. I'm free, and that's my paradise. That's why I'm here. I can rub my eyes, see colors, hear voices in my head. But outside. . Please, another glass.

The barmaid (filling the glasses all around): —She never goes out—.

Libussa (motioning the barmaid to silence): —Why speak of it? What is there to see? What I lived in three days is more than all of that.—

(A young girl comes up to Libussa, takes her hand and turns it palm up): See, her hands are clean. No one has hands so white as hers.—

—Don't speak of it. No, I never betrayed anybody. I minded my business. (Looking sharply at Koenig, then speaking in a low voice): —I remember you.—

Koenig (giving her a melancholy smile): —Some people are best forgotten.—

Florrie looks with puzzlement from one to the other. Her thoughts come in a rush. Of course, having lived here he might be remembered. For what? For things that can never be forgotten?—

— Speak out. It is too much otherwise.

Libussa, singing:

> *I have known the fools of darkness*
> *Blinded by the light.*
> *And if the world grows colder,*
> *Do not lose your sight.*

Two drunken men come reeling into the room. An unkempt man in a thin gray coat: —It's so cold out there our urine will freeze as we piss. His companion, in a torn military coat: (roars with laughter) The wine will warm the frozen parts.

— I met my love on the train. My first trip, setting out on my way to Paris to work as an au pair. He was sitting across from me, a fellow with a shock of wild hair and a crooked smile, not at all handsome. There was a liveliness in his expression. He kept smiling at me, and I didn't know what to do except give a little smile back and turn and look out the window. When I turned back, he leaned over and offered me an apple. A woman sitting next to him cleared her throat and pulled in her neck and chin, as though she disapproved. And maybe because she did, I accepted it and said, "How very nice. I do love apples." That opened a whole conversation. He was a musician going to study violin with a master in Paris. He wanted to compose music.

There was a delay caused by a dead cow on the track, and for a while, we got off the train with the other passengers and stood around talking and smoking. Life in Prague had gotten very worrying, he told me, and he hoped things might be better in Paris. He looked at me as though he was trying to tell me something.

Florrie: —How young you must have been. And with all that was happening in the world.

Libassa laughs wryly. —I have never been that young again. (To Koenig): —You were young once too.

—We all were. And it's a very long time ago—.

The drunken man begins to sing again:

> *When we are young,*
> *Love is our wrack and ruin.*
> *A glance is a thorn,*
> *A smile is a knife.*
> *OOO let me love again.*
> *Awaken a fractured heart.*

—I loved so many and you loved only one. Libussa, why did you buy your madness so cheap?-

—Once is enough if the moment is right. By the end of the train ride, he wanted not to let me go. And I—I had fallen head over heels in love.—

Florrie: It was that simple?

—It was a long train ride. And parts of it were very slow. You know the quality of the rails here, and the trains. The engines were old, the tracks in poor condition. We had time to tell each other our whole life's story. And to throw in the family history to boot. Mine was very brief. I was a girl from the village. A poor girl with only a little schooling, though I read a lot on my own. Oh, how happy I was, my heart all afire. Oh, my poor Daniel.—

Florrie: —Do you have a photograph?

—No, there are no pictures. He was not a handsome man to remember, but what does that matter? A German, a musician, off to study with a master. A Jew—that was the worst of it—for him. That was what he was trying to tell me. (She sinks into what she is remembering, forgetting her listeners.) —All the time he was in Paris he was at my side when he wasn't practicing. Do I have to tell you the rest—?

Week to week, you never know what you might get. And if you're caught, you'll get something you hadn't bargained for.

They fill the glasses and drink a toast all around.

Florrie (still deep in thought): I still don't understand why they wouldn't let him go home.

—He was a German and a Jew. They wanted only to kill him.

The drunken man (explaining): She stuffs them in the windows to keep out the cold. and in her mattress where the springs have fallen in. (She rummages in her pockets.) —These pockets are all lined with poems.

—And her shoes where there are holes—.

—I sleep on poetry, I walk on poetry. That's all it's good for.

—No, forgive me, dear Libussa. I drink to your poetry, and to love, and the wine that makes the pool of the eye deeper. You see, I am a romantic at heart.—

—Love. We were together for a few weeks. You could say married. At least we said so. And I lost my Daniel—my star, my bird. What is love for but to let us sing about our grief.

—Or stuff our shoes.

(To Koenig, pointing a finger at him.) And I know who you are. You've come back. I remember when your name was everywhere, and you smiled from all the papers. The rising star. The new Paradise.

Around Koenig voices rise in accusation: —A traitor and a spy!—

—No, only a civil servant, a bureaucrat. Trying for something better—

—And landing something worse. A Party member—how about that—?

—In name only. . Others had the power.—

—Now I remember—you had to get out—

Koenig (holding up his hand): Who is to decide whose hands are clean? The President's are the cleanest. He always put himself on the line. There were a few more like that and those who chose exile. As for the rest, there were many betrayals. That's what we did to ourselves. (To Florrie.) You see, we are not innocent. And I— who fled— What do you call me? what do you call madness? —

The drunken man (holding up his hands for inspection) — Wherever I've been they've put me in prison. Do you see—look. (Pulling up his shirt and showing his back.) Scars. I wish I could see them. I'd look only at them—day and night.

Libassa (holding up a crumpled paper) —A poem.

Madness to think you can escape
The cymbals crashing in your head . . .
The musicians begin to play an improvisation.

—Go now. You have so little time—it would be a pity to miss the opera. You'll have a hard time with the tickets even so. Maybe you'll be in time for the returns.

(Koenig steps forward and kisses Libussa's hand.)

Libassa turns over her hand and considers her palm . — Hands— what we do with them. Now we must try for something else. She kisses Koenig on the cheek.

—You must find again who and what you love. That is all there is.—

Koenig shakes hands with several of her companions.

(The drunken man takes Florrie's hand and kisses it.) —When you get to the bottom, you have to turn and go the other way. Otherwise you might split your brain all the way to infinity without any light getting in.— (Whirls his finger next to his head.)

—Here least you can live. (Laughs.) . . . if we're here ourselves. Who knows from one day to the next?

Florrie: —But if things are mad already, can you find a place to lay your head?—

The Drunken Man: —Just keep a keg to tap. Libussa will show you how to write poems. You're always welcome.—

Florrie loses the words as the wail of the saxophone fills the space followed by the bass fiddle, which finally accedes to the drums. The music wraps around them, pushes her back into silence, into dissolving space. She momentarily loses her balance as she feels the ground slipping away, and grabs Koenig's arm. He staggers backward.

The Opera

They stand in line at the box office, which has not yet opened, but where a cluster of people has already gathered to wait for last minute returns. The vestibule of the opera house is beginning to fill with the regular subscribers, men in suits and ties, and women in a variety of evening dresses, some decorated with sequins and embroidery, and wraps of fur and velvet. Florrie studies the poster announcing a performance of "Tosca." When she returns to Koenig, he tells her there is very little chance of their getting a ticket. His source of information is a young man standing to one side of the box office. He comes up to them, gives Florrie his greeting, while Koenig goes to stand in line.

—I do hope there are tickets. I've never seen "Tosca."

—I have seen it six times, though it is not among my favorite operas, the young man tells her.

—Six times—what are your favorites?

—"Don Giovanni"—I have seen that twelve times. And "Madame Butterfly" and "Carmen"—fourteen times. "The Magic Flute"—sixteen times. I live only a few blocks from here. Opera's the only thing I've found to get me by. When there's nothing else, there's always what they're pleased to call culture. And the gallery is cheap, if you have the stamina to stand all through the performance.—

Someone approaches with two tickets, which are eagerly snapped up by one of the waiting couples. The box office opens, and several receive the last available seats. Koenig comes away from the ticket window empty-handed.

—I'm afraid there is nothing else available the young man tells Florrie, unless someone comes forward with another set of tickets. Then he indicates a gray-haired woman with a maroon vest and black skirt. —Ask the chief usher. Sometimes she can find a place.—

He leads them toward her, explains the situation. She appears sympathetic.

—Come to me just after the performance begins. I will have seats for you. Meanwhile you can visit the exhibit—over there in the salon—.

After thanking her and their companion, Florrie and Koenig enter a doorway to the left. Inside they discover an exhibit of sculptures. Gestures of various parts of the body captured in stone: hands pointing and beckoning, in attitudes of acquiescence and supplication; arms brandishing unseen weapons. A single muscular foot poised ready to take flight. A torso without limbs or head. Another that appears to be falling backwards. A woman's figure. Heads, marble and bronze: faces caught in horror or surprise, a few in repose. An ear listening. Florrie pauses before a pair of clasped hands.

Hands. More hands. And feet. And the rest—all fragments. In the flesh the effect would be unspeakable. But here a hand is its gesture; a face, its expression. Only fragments, but they seem like more.

They view the exhibit in silence. Then Florrie, not knowing what to make of the voices lifted against Koenig, finds herself asking, — Do you think you have been wrongly accused?—

Koenig (turning away): —I suppose now that the whole nightmare has finally collapsed, the recriminations will burst out for a long time. It's only human. And I got some dirt on my hands.—

—But you feel unjustly blamed?—

He answers with raised shoulders and open palms, then moves to a classical figure of a woman's torso rescued from the infinite number of fleeting things. A broken object. (In a low voice.) — A testimony, do you think? Does it speak anything to the streets?—

—What sort of testimony?—

(Indicating the torso.) —To some expression of beauty we can never have again.

They stand for a moment without speaking. Koenig follows a curve of the torso with his hand.

—I don't know, Florrie says —Maybe it has always been a dream. A dream carved in stone. Things are always falling apart. At least now musicians can play jazz in the square.

—Yes, they can have their youth. But two generations have been sacrificed to madness—what about them?—

When they hear the overture they head toward the lobby and moments later they see the usher beckoning them. Soon they are seated along with others who have been waiting.

The tale of love, torment, torture, sacrifice, betrayal, and death unfolds in a drama of political intrigue. On stage as they watch, the tyrant Scarpia tries to convince Tosca to betray the whereabouts of their friend Angelotti by torturing her lover. Scarpia will agree to allow her lover, Canvadosi, his political enemy, to escape if she will yield to his advances. The bargain made, the arrangements carried out, Koenig and Florrie, held by the intensity of the music and voices watch as Tosca reveals a knife.

The usher is at the end of their row beckoning. Koenig rises, but she indicates that it is Florrie she is summoning. The intrusion at such a moment generates a series of angry whispers around them.

Florrie follows the usher outside, who then leads her away from the vestibule, past the cloak room and in the direction of the toilets, then down a corridor with several doors leading off. She holds one open.

—In here. Then she adds, —You can come back to the opera tomorrow.

—I don't understand, Florrie says, miffed to have lost the most dramatic moment.

—It doesn't matter—they want you to see the rehearsal. It's part of the new play. You've come to be in it, haven't you? Hurry now.

She enters a room bare except for a desk and chair, a filing cabinet, an official-looking portrait on the wall. A man of middle age with a fringe of graying hair circling a bald crown that gives off a shine from the ceiling light rises from behind a desk. His glasses, too, give back the harsh glint of fluorescent ceiling light. His jaw is set—his eye is sullen. He paces back and forth. A small, dark-haired subordinate enters with a sheaf of papers, then stands with a diffident slump of the shoulders, observing him, waiting to speak. From a small radio on the shelf against the back wall come strains of music. It sounds to Florrie like a continuation of the opera. The official and his underling take no notice of her presence. She stands there uneasily, then looks down at the chair next to her

OFFICIAL:

(mumbling): No gratitude. No sense of history. Years of service. (Looking at Florrie, slamming his fist on the desk.) No one sits until I give permission. (She continues to stand, shifting uneasily from one foot to the other.)

SUBORDINATE:

Sir, if you'll excuse me, there's a little matter of business. They continue as though Florrie is no longer present.

OFFICIAL:

But don't you see—such waste. (Giving a sweeping gesture.) — Everything we've learned. All the techniques of interrogation we've perfected. Hauling them in after days without sleep. The smile, with just the right shade of friendly concern as you offer them a cigarette, and all the while the light glaring directly in the eyes. So simple, so effective in breaking down the resistance.

SUBORDINATE:

(Buttering him up) Everything I know, I learned from you, sir (still flattering unctuously) You were a master of the game. Such wit and subtlety at the right moments. Such ferocity in striking terror. I've heard from others how the most stubborn cases shatter like glass.

OFFICIAL:

And in that moment I have wept, yes wept and called a man my brother. My tears have mingled with his. His cries have been my own. Knowing that I, the instrument—

SUBORDINATE:

(getting impatient): Sir, you've been more than dedicated.

OFFICIAL:
The one truth— And now they blast it, throw the country into the trash heap, the scum.

SUBORDINATE:

But people can't hold onto freedom. They get careless. They don't want to be bothered. They close their eyes to abuses. They seek pleasure and indulge themselves. They become lazy and corrupt. (In a low voice) I think there will still be a place for us.

OFFICIAL:

I think you may have some special talents to bring to the service.

SUBORDINATE:

Tell me about your methods. I have a lot to learn.

OFFICIAL:

The arrest is most important. Entering the house at night when people can be rudely awakened gives you great advantage. Hurrying them off before they can get to their friends or lawyers. Not giving them a chance to dress. Letting them spend the night in a cell before being questioned. Before anyone knows where they are.

(The subordinate is making notes.)

OFFICIAL:

During the day can work well too. First you go after the pets. If there is a dog or cat on hand , you simply take out your gun and shoot it. The kids will blubber and the mother will be all upset trying to comfort them. A real advantage.

(Florrie tries to stifle a cry, but they pay no attention)

OFFICIAL:

(reciting automatically) —The confession is extremely important, especially if there is to be a trial. Days without sleep, hours under the glaring lights. Listening to the cries of loved ones being tortured. You know all that. And you know it doesn't matter what they're accused of.

(Subordinate, taking notes, tries to keep up, but it is almost more than he can do. He runs out of paper, looks around frantically for more.)

OFFICIAL:

—The sessions, will all be different—that's a must. Most at night but some during the day. Surprise is the element. And meanwhile, threaten those at home—the wife, the children. Constant surveillance of course.

But the confession is the key thing—for the good of those you serve. (Closing his eyes, extending his palms. Almost ecstatic.) As it flows from the lips of the accused, all the crimes against the state even only in thought are revealed and undone. Oh the purity of that moment. A child restored to a much-wronged mother. Then you hit the prisoner with a powerful light. (Opening his eyes) Oh, it's the moment I live for—the moment he's confronted by the truth—naked unspeakable, relentless. It's like a conversion, if we can borrow that word from an outworn superstition.

SUBORDINATE:

You have made the whole process into a true art. I'm sure your work will not be in vain.

OFFICIAL:

(Gets up and begins pacing.) (Eagerly)—You think so? Meanwhile all their eyes are on us. They listen to you sneeze. Every way you turn. Seizing our passports. scrutinizing our bank accounts. To tell the truth, I've put away a little stockpile in Switzerland. Just for emergencies, you understand . . . (He pulls out a cigarette and lighter, but his hands shake too much to light the cigarette.)

SUBORDINATE:

(Stepping forward to light it for him.) Now that the new regime . . .

OFFICIAL:

Yes, Yes, and we're put to the trouble of trying to trace those who should be forgotten. (Finally noticing Florrie) —You may sit down now.

FLORRIE

(Still standing.) Please sir, I've come in regard to—just such a person.

SUBORDINATE:

(Interupting.) —This folder contains files of those claiming property here, some from exiles and relatives of those still missing.

(Florrie is seized by a fit of coughing, and the official takes notice of her as if for the first time.)

OFFICIAL:

(To Florrie) —No doubt you are on one of those missions.

FLORRIE

—I am trying to find some information about a prisoner, an American perhaps who was arrested by mistake and sent to prison here in this city. His name is Bauer, what happened to him is unknown.

OFFICIAL:

I face these annoyances every day. Impossible situations. People can't let go of the past. (To Florrie) —You'll have to go to the Bureau. Though you have nothing to go on. They've set aside space in the Castle for just such wild goose chases.

(Turning to the Subordinate and speaking as Florrie leaves) — In the old days you were rewarded. I enjoyed many invitations to the countryside, wonderful hunting parties with the Big-wigs and afterwards, feasts of wild game and the best imported wines and cognac . . . we lived like . . . (His voice fades.)

The Bureau

On stage the set of an official building is indicated by three floors and rows of windows. A Czech flag flies outside. After climbing the wide steps, Florrie enters alone into a large central hall set about with grilled windows. Some of the offices are open, some not. People are standing in line in front of certain windows, waiting for those closed to open. Petitioners hold various documents. Some stand impatiently; others study the papers in deep concentration, as though making still one more effort at comprehension. Florrie, intimidated by all she sees, tries to ask directions. One woman stares at her blankly. Another points towards the other side of the hall. But when she reaches it, she discovers the door is locked. She addresses a uniformed guard and is directed towards a set of stairs at the corner. At the upper level she finds herself in a large room. It is virtually empty, with only an elderly man and woman in front of a bulletin board reading the notices. Every once in a while, an office door opens, and a purposeful-looking man strides across the room to another office. Sometimes the sound of conversation and laughter can be heard from behind a glass door. A janitor is sweeping at one end of the room.

Florrie finds her way to a window, uncertain it is the one she requires. At the moment no one is standing in front of it. Behind it a slender young man is stamping papers. He looks up as though glad for a release from his apparent boredom, adjusts his glasses, and regards her with interest.

Florrie (uncertain how to begin): —I'm looking for someone. A prisoner. I have only a surname, rather common. His name may have been forgotten.—

—Nearly all the prisoners were released—.

—Is there no way of finding him? If I make the attempt. I don't know if he's dead or what may have happened to him. (She shows him the notebook.)

He goes to a filing cabinet, removes one of the files and sorts through the contents.

(Returning to the window.) — There's no Bauer listed here, but we can make an inquiry. And you say this belonged to him. Was he your husband, brother, or father?

—No, he is a man I never knew.

—What is he to you then?

(She hesitates) —My obligation, perhaps, my burden. His countryman gave me his notebook when he couldn't think what to do with it. He thought it might be published. And I didn't want to let this man be forgotten. He is my predicament and has shown me my ignorance. This notebook, you see—it's a piece of his existence, what he lived and suffered here in this place. And—

(Interrupting her.) —Without more information it will be almost impossible to find him. Officially, he doesn't exist.

(Making one last effort):—He was last known to be here.

A rather disheveled man, whose coat is unevenly buttoned to cover places where the buttons are missing, has come up and stands just behind, peering over her shoulder, trying to see what's going on. He cocks his head, keeps listening.

(Disconcerted, Florrie looks in his direction. She can tell from his breath he has been drinking, but decides to ignore him and steps aside.)

But once he did exist, she wants to insist. He has become part of my life, my fate. —This notebook—perhaps a former prisoner might recognize it, someone who knew him—.

—But notebooks weren't allowed. Hard to say where it came from. I'm sorry that we have so little to go on. It's difficult to look for someone without a clear identity.

The man who has been breathing down her neck interrupts.

—Maybe he's undergone a metamorphosis. Look down among the cockroaches. Or up into the stars. Ask the Golem, with Truth and Death on its forehead. Petition the saints on the bridge. Consult the swans on the river—have you ever seen so many? Look into the shadows flitting along the byways. (After each suggestion, he laughs and slaps his sides.) Don't you know we'll spend the rest of the century with questions falling on our heads like meteors? Yes, I see them now.

(The young man at the window, who has been prevented from speaking): —I hope you find some other source of information. (Moves back into the office.)

(Florrie starts to turn away, but pauses.) —This room. I keep hearing voices. It's very odd.

(The man still behind her lets out a melancholy laugh): —They're gathering now. It may be the window will be open. See, over there.—

Florrie looks across the room to where she has been before. A group has gathered there. She did not see them come in. Women mostly, of all ages, though several old men with canes are clustered there waiting for the window to open. They stand in a wash of pale yellow light that gives them a kind of transparency.

(A man just behind her begins speaking out in a ringing voice): —Looking for names, uncovering graves, poring over deeds and claims. Who owns the houses, who has disappeared. Think of the court cases. All night I see hands holding out papers, certificates, deeds. Thrusting them under my nose. I work all night, every night, and I'll never be done. Can't you see them, the petitioners? Can't you hear their voices? Each time they wait differently. But there is always waiting. They spend their lives in waiting—that's what their bodies tell you. Waiting first for the knock at the door, fear's first stroke, waiting to be summoned or searched. Now waiting here.—

(The man, pointing with his hand.) —That window is open only until noon, and not every day. Often they don't know when the window will be open, though the hours are posted. Some days the window never opens. Now it's closed

Florrie can see forms moving behind the glass, someone is there. An old man says,— It's time, why don't you open? The door next to the little office is flung open, and an official strides out and looks up and down the line. Everyone pretends nothing has been said. The official's eyes move from one face to another:

(Yelling) —There is a counter-revolutionary in the line, and I want to know who it is!—

(The old man steps out and draws himself up.) —I said, It's time, why don't you open?—

There is silence up and down the line.

(To Florrie) —I will tell you what happens here. Over and over. You see—now that scoundrel is telling us all to go home.—

Florrie watches as the official summons the old man inside the office. A haggard woman indicates that the window will not open now. Nor tomorrow. On the third day—she counts with her fingers—the window perhaps will open for an hour after the officially posted time.

Most of the people have already left the line. Only those remain who'd achieved the perfection of waiting: waiting as a state in and of itself.

But somehow it is determined that they can say, It's time—I wonder when they will open. Or, It's time: perhaps they will open now. Whether or not they have given those behind the window some incentive to respond is impossible to judge.

So it is only a repetition of what has happened many times before. And she will not be able to go to the window herself. But the group is still standing there. It is eerily silent, as they stand, they watch the window slowly opening.

Florrie and her informant move closer. When it opens, the women as well as the husbands or brothers or elderly fathers press forward eagerly to ask for news and to try to send packages. Voices arise from those at the window.

—My husband says it's very damp there and he is sick. There are clothes in this package.

(Florrie's informant, now at her side):—The walls are always damp. The floors are concrete—always cold.

They are always sick there. They never have enough heat. They don't get fresh air—the food is terrible. They are worked like cattle.—

—My brother wrote he didn't get the package. Please, can you give me a receipt for this one?—

—We die of waiting while they are dying. Two halves of a nothing, and that is called life.

—Wait, wait—you can't close the window! It took me an hour to get here.—

—Tell us what's happening. At least give us a bit of news.—

—This is the package I sent before—it wasn't delivered? And this? Died December 18th? It can't be.

—His name is— His identification number is—

—Wait, wait, you can't close the window

—Get your hands out of the way. Animals—all of you.—

—It isn't even time to close.—

Florrie watches as hands reach toward the window and muffled voices protest and finally, those present disappearing, the yellow light fading. Echoes linger for a few moments. Even the man who had lingered so long in her company is gone. She stands for a moment listening to the last echoes of voices. Then music and singing.

Tosca is hastening to the battlements of the fortress to join her lover and escape from Scarpia's men, only to find she has been betrayed and that her lover is dead.

Morto! Morto!
O Mario! Morto? Tu? Cosi? Finire.

The end comes with her leap from the battlements. The performance is over. Tosca and Cavaradossi appear to thunderous applause. Then Scarpia, for a performance received with wild enthusiasm. The whole cast appears on stage. A young woman brings out a bouquet of roses for Tosca. Another round of applause. The audience rises, drifts out of the opera house, fills the salon and overflows into the street.

Florrie turns to leave and to find Koenig in the crowd. Carefully she puts the prisoner's notebook into her handbag. Perhaps Koenig can still find a publisher. At the moment, as she thinks of him, she hopes that the page of the notebook expressing the prisoner's love for his wife allowed him a moment when the walls of the cell shrank away and the window he could not reach opened to the sky.

Outside, the clock chimes: time, time, time.

The Quarry

As if there were explanations . . . As if in the wake of events, History threw out a net of logic and causality. As if there were words for what had happened to all those millions of lives during a century of war and struggle. As if one might speak for the dead, knowing what visited them in their deaths and could try to capture something to light the way into the future. No wonder the task required the inspiration of a muse: Clio, the teller. And what do you make of it all?

"My ears are still full of echoes," Florrie said to Koenig. "I can't get rid of them."

She had the sense that he couldn't either, that he was haunted perhaps more than she. He seemed more remote than ever, lost in abstraction. And quite as obsessed.

They had gone down to Wenceslas Square for a political rally. The atmosphere was one of celebration, as crowds of visitors and Czechs, no longer kept by fear from speaking to foreigners, mingled freely for the first time in years. The square was filled with musicians and campaigners. All during the day speakers rallied the crowd to vote for one of the innumerable parties that had sprung up, including a Beer Party. But the real battle was between the Civic Forum and the Communists, who had changed their emblem to a bunch of cherries.

Florrie had been standing with Koenig in the crowd listening to the Communists offering their new set of justifications and promises. They were not far from the circular flower bed where candles burned continually in front of portraits of Jan Palach and others who had died resisting the Russian invasion. As Koenig stood absorbed in the speeches, his face working through various registers of disgust, Florrie watched two small boys scraping away wax from the candles and molding it into little figures. No one appeared to mind. In the vicinity several groups were gathering names for petitions, one of which Florrie had also signed, and circulating literature about political exiles or warnings about those who would betray the new openness.

Suddenly her eye was caught by a great head in a truck moving along one side of the square. She nudged Koenig and they both watched as a head of Stalin, removed from some statue, was being carted away.

"It's true—the people get their revenge at some point. Sometimes violently," Koenig said. "But there were, and maybe still are, those who could never believe Stalin was really dead."

They had walked past all the old horrors on the avenue leading from the square. After passing under a banner that flew with the words, Where is my home? words of the Czech national anthem, one encountered cardboard figures of Stalin and Gotwaldt, Kadar— the whole Communist entourage, more than life size, standing along the street in their gestures of power. And reproductions of old newspapers were posted around the pillars, their headlines speaking of those political events that had shaped the national fate, while in the shop windows, television monitors replayed events from the past forty years, events that caught Jan Palach in his agony and the failed liberation of the Prague Spring. The past, long suppressed, had now caught up to the present. And everything was up for grabs.

"Let's go," Koenig said at last, pulling away from the harangue. "Enough of that slime."

"What are they saying?"

"That they've changed their spots. That they now have a new face and are promising a new future."

"What do you think?"

He looked angry. "I think they can't just brush aside the old nightmare. It's hard to forget what they did, how they've ruined the country. Killed the forests, polluted air and water. Generated sick mothers and babies born with birth defects." He paused. "That's what they don't want to talk about—the ways they used to make people betray one another, spy on one another. Plus the radioactive waste being burned in the stacks—sent there from America."

Everyone had a hand in it, it seemed. The secret Helga had been foolish enough to try to expose.

Florrie noticed tears in his eyes. Her tears came too—she took hold of his hand.

"A stupid unworkable system," he said, "fueled by greed and the lust for power. Twenty years of coasting on the legacy of the past, then twenty more of robbing the future. Now everything is sucked dry."

No, she had little to offer him. No more than she'd had to give her patient who'd lost her children to the Khmer Rouge. Or the prisoner. Only memory, only recognition—if that counted for anything.

He gave her a little smile. "Forgive me for ranting. We're in a different moment and must look to that. But not be taken in."

Indeed the jubilance in the square was infectious, with groups of musicians playing for all they were worth, and the political parties broadcasting their new ideas.

As they walked away from the square, he said, "I remember that you told me once about your father, and his discoveries. Mine had his discoveries too."

"What were they?"

"He had a little shop. He'd been an electrician and invented a light bulb that could last on very little power. He was doing well. Then the government took over his shop He was a bitter man—all his work gone for nothing. Every chance he got he spoke out with contempt for the new system. It's a wonder he wasn't sent to prison."

He walked along in silence. "I had absolutely no sympathy for him," he said finally. "I thought he was simply an obstacle in the way of progress, the social good. Me with my engineering degree, all hot and eager . . . " He broke off, then said, "I feel very bad about all that now."

"What happened to him?" she said, after a time.

"He died."

He wasn't going to tell her any more. "And now," she said, not wanting silence between them, "what's going to happen?"

"They have a lot of power. After all, they're the only party with a real organization, and experience. The whole bag of dirty tricks. They're desperate, you know. The habit of power isn't let go of easily. But Havel is very popular. I think the Civic Forum can pull it off."

"Oh, I do hope so." Florrie said, wanting to yield to the celebration around her and watch a new day dawn.

"The people in the countryside are satisfied enough. Here was the only place where the collective farm was a success. They don't want change. All you can do is hold your breath."

So the days of the campaigning went on in the still continuing mood of celebration, but Koenig didn't go down to listen to more of the speeches. A curious indifference had settled over him. Though he'd said he wanted to travel north to see the damage that had been done there, he seemed to have abandoned the idea. If he continued on the track Helga had marked, he no longer spoke of it, or else mumbled something evasive if Florrie asked about the subject.

They sat indoors over coffee, Florrie trying to lose herself in a novel she'd found in one of the book shops—one of a few titles in English. When the day brightened in the afternoon, they went out for lunch. Afterwards, as though it were a program or a duty, they visited cathedrals and museums, wandered through the grounds and gardens of the castle. Or else they explored the little streets ascending the hill.

Florrie noticed that his efforts to do some writing did not hold his attention. Even when he sat over his books and papers for a stretch of time and sometimes spoke of the articles he'd set out to do, he didn't appear to be making much headway.

Sometimes he arranged to see people he had known in his youth, but he returned from these encounters more silent and uncommunicative than ever. When she asked him once who these people were, he said only, "They were the ones who stayed. Some people," he added, "kept their heads. Made the right choices."

His homecoming was tearing him in two, that was easy to see.

And now he was sinking into apathy. He did rouse himself during the afternoons to take her to some point of interest in the city. Mornings tended to be overcast, with a drizzle in the air. No pattern emerged in these wanderings; at times Koenig gave her the impression he was looking for something. Every once in a while he'd startle her by coming to a halt in the middle of a street as though listening for a voice. He would run his hand along a wall, pause and look intently at a certain house-front or turn expectantly into some narrow alley and look around confused. In the midst of one of these walks, she saw him become suddenly agitated. His face paled, and for a moment she thought he might be ill.

"What's the matter?" she asked him. "Are you all right?"

She saw him will himself into calm. "Nothing," he insisted, with a slight smile. And they left the section of the city, descended to the park along the river. They bought some bread and spent the rest of the afternoon feeding the swans that gathered there or idly studying the flow of the river.

"We could buy some bread and cheese and bring our own lunch here one day," Florrie suggested.

Koenig murmured something out of his self-absorption that wasn't either yes or no.

She let it go. Clearly he wanted to ignore her. She stood up and wandered along the path where several women were chatting as their children played on the swings.

Nothing more, is that it? No real life for her to build upon life here after all. His demons were his own. How did you speak to despair, and what, if anything lay beyond it? She'd made an effort to put herself together enough to go back to the States, take up what exactly she wasn't sure. The career she'd all but thrown away? Perhaps she could still put bread and butter on the plate. It would be a life of sorts. Out of cowardice, if nothing else.

That evening they went to a Moravian restaurant, where they had a dish of pork cooked with apples and a good red wine. They spent some time talking to a young fellow who was trying to learn English—he could do that now and was eager to share his wine with them for a few new words. They helped him with his numbers. He was a mechanic, eager to improve things for himself.

After they returned to the flat, Florrie said, "I think I should leave you now. Go back to the States."

Koenig looked at her and nodded. "I can understand that," he said.

"As soon as I get a job again, I'll pay you back—for everything."

He gave a little impatient wave of the hand. "Don't think of it."

She didn't argue. She was tired and wanted simply to go to bed. She took off her coat and stood for a moment avoiding her image in the mirror as he hung both of their coats in the closet. "Florrie—" he said, and paused.

"I thank you for all you've done," she said.

He waved away her gratitude. "It hasn't been all that much." He was still holding her with something left unspoken. He was sorry he had nothing further to offer her—was that what he was trying to say—or more accurately, that they had nothing to offer each other?

"Before you go," he said in a low voice, "there is one more place I'd like to take you to."

"All right," she said, letting it go at that. It didn't matter where or what he had in mind.

For the next few days she saw very little of Koenig. He was going to order her ticket, he promised her, but apparently in his own good time, and she was waiting to find out when she'd be leaving. But he was altogether preoccupied, taken up with his own purposes. In the mornings he slept late and now she left the apartment before he got up. She didn't mind. She had seen whatever of the city he was going to take her to, and she was quite content to go out alone in the afternoons to walk where she would. She knew which trams to take and could find her way around now so that she didn't need a map to wander through the old parts of the city. She ate by herself these nights and came back to find herself alone. If Koenig returned to the flat at all during these intervals he gave no sign. Usually she went to bed before Koenig came back from his own wanderings. She had no idea where he went, but once she'd been awakened by noise in the street, and looking out, had seen a very young man and two older ones, close to Koenig's age. They had been drinking. She heard bursts of raucous laughter that accompanied some difficulty getting up the stairs. A certain clatter and banging announced Koenig's entrance, and then moments later she heard loud singing that gradually subsided into the distance.

Alone one evening, she had a sudden impulse to take out her diary, and glance through its pages. She hadn't written anything in it since she had fled from Copenhagen. What she had written then sounded like the voice of a stranger. A prisoner of that moment; yes, she could call herself that—if that's what illusion meant. She held her pen poised but did not write: to do so would be to reveal herself, risk discovery, even though life had pushed her forward, into the chaos of the unexpressed: where, though it was hard to remain, it was even more difficult to begin something new..

Suppose she did try to write something. Even if she was the same person, her life before and her life now—how would she connect them? Connect two halves of a geode falling apart in her hands. Impossible. Tell about herself, as a character in another person's story? Make it up as she went along? Surely, out of all the stories she'd listened to, it was possible for her to have one of her own. But her story could be anyone's, just as the prisoner's was. And not just one, but all the stories— Stories of victims and tormentors and those who'd escaped one way or another, very likely with some part of themselves missing were variations on a familiar theme. All the creations of every era, bound up with who held power and who had none.

Invented at the mercy of those not allowed to speak, their voices suppressed, their freedom stolen, their lives dashed to pieces. But there was always the thing that kept heaving up no matter how often and how brutally it was beaten down. Under the illusion of those trying to put things into a dozen boxes instead of two hundred or two thousand or maybe an unimaginable number waiting to be discovered. With innocence abetting the keepers of cells and torture chambers.

She closed the journal and laid it away. There was no telling when Koenig would shamble home; once he'd flopped down without bothering to take off his clothes. But as she undressed, put on her gown and robe, went to brush her teeth, she felt the pull of something unfinished. Then as she stood in front of the mirror, a sentence entered her mind as though it had been spoken by someone else:

Once there was a man who was born blind . . . Somehow she recognized him, as the sentence echoed and repeated itself in her mind. Quickly she went for pen and notebook. Perhaps if she listened, she would know how to tell what had happened to him and what might be his fate. She wrote the first sentence and then wrote it again, made a number of repetitions before she was able to go on:

Once there was a man who was born blind. The world was beyond his knowing, except for what he could hear and touch or smell and taste. But he did not know it. Everything was a sound. When he spoke the word bell, the sound made a shape in his mind, and the objects he touched filled in the sensations of hard and soft, smooth and rough. So that stones and trees and everything he could hear or put his hand to filled the corners of his life.

He could not go far, but he knew the things around him, the familiar voices. They were real enough.

So he had his familiar world, could make his way around in it. And that should have satisfied him. But somehow it never does. Very likely his condition seemed an indignity. And he was pushed by some unfathomable yearning or curiosity: for those that won't

235

leave well enough alone. Or maybe he was simply bored:

But once he heard a voice from far away. As he listened, it seemed to call his name like one chosen; calling so sweetly he could not resist some promise that lay within the melody, a suggestion beyond himself and all the life he knew. He had to find it, or at least set out in its direction. He left his home secretly one night with only his dog to guide him.

The voice kept luring him on, over mountain and dale, until he arrived in a strange country. Still the voice lingered in his ear, cooing, drawing him, soothing his weariness, and wooed him toward a joy he had only dimly surmised.

But as soon as he crossed some mysterious border, he was seized, beaten to within an inch of his life and left on the pavement, helpless and bleeding. All his money had been stolen, along with his identification papers. As he lay there in the depths of his pain and anguish, he strained to hear the voice that had betrayed him. But he could no longer hear it.

Only now he heard a strange accent. He couldn't tell if it was a quality of the voice itself, or a different voice. As he strained to hear, he was told he had broken all the laws of the country and was a menace to society. Without his papers he couldn't prove he wasn't a spy.

But since it was his first offense and he was a stranger, he would be treated mercifully and set free. Thereafter, he would have to beg for his food and live on the streets, for, after all, he could only be an outcast.

She paused, unsure how to go forward. For once you got to a place like that, there was, unquestionably, no going back—even though she was doing that—going back across the Atlantic. A geographical movement. She did not know what to think about what she had written or what she was planning to do.

It was getting late. By the time she finally went to bed, Koenig still hadn't returned. That night he didn't come back at all. She waited around for him all the next day, but he didn't appear, nor did he return that night either. Frightened for him, she debated whether or not to call the police. She didn't want to make trouble for him.

A strange thing happened to him, he told her that afternoon, when he appeared looking thoroughly tired and somewhat at a loss. He was quite sober. He'd been walking along the street, quite casually, and at a certain instant it seemed to him he'd fallen out of time. Just that. The present had dropped away and all the years, and he found himself back so far he might have been walking into the world for the first time.

"I was just walking along the street," he said, "and I heard my mother call, Karel. I haven't had that name for years. I left with forged papers, and I never wanted to be called by my real name. All that was past. But when I heard that—Karel— I was there again."

It lasted only a moment, and he'd continued down the street. But when he passed a cafe, he caught the odor of a dish his mother used to cook, a beef dish with wine and prunes and apricots. He shook his head: he hadn't got over it yet.

"And what did you do then?" Florrie asked him, jarred by his strange mood. It was odd that they were brought together in this moment of unexpected intimacy now, just as she was on the verge of leaving. She felt a curious kind of suspense as well as interest.

"I realized I was back in the old neighborhood," he said. "—where I grew up, after we moved into the city."

"Did you find it the same?"

"Oh, no. It's long gone. I thought a certain street felt familiar, after I turned off the Mala Strana. But then I lost that sense. I had the curious feeling my feet could take me there. But no such luck." He shook his head. "Funny how you get caught up in such romantic

237

nonsense."

But it was clear, despite the appeal to the rational mind, he couldn't shake off the mood that had seized hold of him. She was certain of that much.

"Did you look for a street name?"

"Many of them have been changed. The new regime," he said ironically, "has tried to get rid of certain offensive reminders of the past. Not that I blame them. Or maybe it's a burst of commercial progress. The street, alley really, probably no longer even exists. And who knows what has been torn down in the interim? Not to mention what has been thrown up. There are apartments, official buildings—it's been over forty years since the end of the war."

"What you were looking for—is that the place you were going to take me?"

He looked puzzled, was making an effort to remember.

"Have you forgotten? You were going to order my ticket, but you said—"

"Forgive me," he said, interrupting her.

"You've forgotten?" She couldn't believe it.

He didn't say anything for a moment. "I put it out of my mind. I was distracted."

"You haven't ordered my ticket?"

"No," he admitted, pausing. "I can't really believe you're leaving."

"I thought you wanted me to go."

"By no means," he said, getting up, going to her. "Only it's not right to keep you here when I can't give you what you need."

"Oh," she lamented and turned away. "Is it so much?"

"I think you deserve far more than I can offer."

She was reminded that these were the same words that underlined Eric's excuse to leave her. This time she was equally at a loss. The words seemed to represent such a failure of nerve, or else such a mask for self-interest. Both seemed true of Eric. But Koenig had depths that were unknown to her, and she was reluctant to make any sort of judgment. At the moment , she could think of nothing to say.

"I went in search of those places where I thought I could enter the past once more," he said, "and finally release myself from it. And certain people I made a special effort to see for the same reason. Only I couldn't seem to get free of them. I wanted to clear my mind for other things. . . . Does that make any sense to you?"

"Yes," she said gently. "I understand that." Could she say she was any better off then he? It was a continual struggle to keep afloat, she acknowledged, and not to be invaded by the past.

He nodded. "I think there is something I have not yet experienced, but I know it exists."

She wanted badly to know what it was, but she knew better than to ask what it might be and that, even if he knew, he wouldn't tell her. Some things had to work below the surface. But she also knew that, for the moment at least, she couldn't leave.

"Maybe it has to come before I know what it is." Koenig said, and added in a low voice, "if it comes at all."

The conversation had evidently settled something between them, at least temporarily. Florrie now spent part of the morning walking a Great Pyrenees owned by an elegant Dutch woman away on a visit to her family in Amsterdam. And she was also becoming fond of the pair of Burmese cats whose owners had gone to the south of France. She was glad to be earning a little money and to have some sense of purpose that took her out of the apartment. She was continuing her journal.

Koenig was putting his mind to finishing an article about the efforts of certain writers he knew who were trying to reestablish themselves in the current scene. "They're having a hard time now figuring out what to write about," Koenig told her. "Before it was easy—they had a common enemy."

After their morning's work and mid-day meal, they returned to the pattern they'd first established—exploring various parts of the city or wandering along the river.

She was glad to see his renewed interest in his work.

Though she enjoyed these outings and their conversations about the book Koenig proposed to write about the transition from a dictatorship to an open society, she felt as if everything still hung in the balance. She was at loose ends, not knowing where she belonged or what approach to take. Waiting for something to happen seemed an empty gesture. At times she was restless and dispirited. She'd put aside any further attempt to inquire about the prisoner, though she'd put his notebook back on Koenig's desk. He had not mentioned it.

In spite of the moment of openness that had passed between them, Koenig never alluded further to what had happened to him in the street or how it might be connected to his previous life. She thought of the comments and accusations that had gone around when they'd been in the factory.

By now she knew she would never get a clear picture of him, only occasional hints and guesses when almost in spite of himself some piece of his inner world escaped him.

In spite of that, he was, as he had always been in an important way there for her, ready to take her in, available whatever her situation, generous in what he offered her. She had demanded a great deal of him, both materially and psychologically. And she knew that on some level, they both were afraid to give themselves to each other.

He would always be in some sense a very private, deeply inward person. She knew he had suffered greatly, been betrayed and caught, no doubt, in the diabolical machinery of betraying others.

Any portrait of him she would have to create herself in careful degrees from what he revealed and the rest from what she could imagine—without asking what he might finally mean to her. And the story she'd begun to invent she would simply let go off on its own. Maybe, for some obscure reason, that was what she needed to do, let something be revealed—so she could leave and begin to remake her life anew.

She took it up again and wrote:

> *While he was lying there, someone came along and kicked him in the head. Suddenly his sight was restored. But he couldn't make*

out a single object. His eyes were besieged by a jumble of colors, a
confusion of objects. When finally his eyes adjusted to them, they
were so dark and the landscape so disordered it was clear that
blindness would be a benediction.

A discovery of the most ordinary sort, it occurred to her. But you always had to be kicked in the head to make it. She continued to write:

He could see, but he could see only chaos and, deprived of the
familiar ways of taking in experience, he had no words for what
he encountered. The voice no longer spoke into his ear whispering
tempting promises. He stumbled along as before.

Gradually, his vision cleared: things took their shapes and the
edges no longer blurred. But he wondered that the world was
such a dark place; he had not expected it would be so dark.

Everyone praised the miraculous cure he had experienced from
being kicked in the head. And each year a public celebration was
held and he was made to go through the motions of his blindness
and the wonderful restoration. He became an important figure
in the public schools, explaining to the children the workings of
a just society. For his sponsors used him to prove that only here
could such a miracle occur. And though he questioned that what
had happened to him had any connection with the society he lived
in, he was somehow redeemed, and no longer an outcast.

But in a fit of jealousy over his astonishing success, a malcontent
from one of the schools pushed him down a set of cement steps.
When he recovered from the fall, one leg was shorter than the
other and so weak he could barely stand.

At this point, she felt she had reached an impasse. She didn't know what to do for her creation or how he might get on with his life, or, for that matter, how she should get on with her own. She'd certainly besieged him with difficulties enough to tie him in knots. Now she wanted simply to throw away the notebook and forget she'd ever gotten him into such a fix, but she couldn't abandon him. All this struck her as very stupid.

❖

One afternoon, after she and Koenig had crossed the bridge over the Vltava and were wandering the streets going toward the Castle, she said, "You told me you moved from the countryside to the city and grew up here. How old where you then?

"About six or seven." He looked at her as if she had caught him up short.

"I'd like to see it—where you were a child."

"It's a very long time since I've been there," he said. "It's hard to find a way back even when you think you know it. Like here in these streets—I was so sure I'd know the lane that led to my father's shop.

"Curious," he said, as they turned into a street where they hadn't been before. "It seems so close, as though I could reach out and touch it." They were standing alongside a stone wall that enclosed a garden. He leaned back against it, then ran his hand over the stones. "Maybe this is the wall," he said with real excitement. "I'd go out of my way to come up here. Certain things I had to do or dire things would happen. I had that game with myself. I'd lose my favorite toy; the dog would die. Only this wall would save the day. And for good measure, a certain carving just up the street—a Moravian lion. I had to touch its mane." They walked in that direction. "Now we turn off to the right."

They entered a long curving street, shops and apartment buildings intermingling. Once there, Florrie could see that he forgot her presence, as though he were back in that time again and was seeing the faces that belonged to it.

For a time she looked around at the houses, wondering which might have been his. Clearly he was looking for it. He kept pausing, studying the facades.

"Do you recognize anything?"

"I'm not sure. Everything has changed so much. It seems to me the German woman lived in this neighborhood."

"Who was she?"

"Oh, just a poor unhappy war-bride. She used to give me nut cake and sometimes a little money if I'd take notes to an officer at the barracks."

"Her husband?

"No, her lover. She'd married a Czech soldier who brought her back here. But he was killed early in the war, and she lost her home. I've no idea what happened to her. Strange I should think of her."

His manner had changed, as though all his senses were heightened, ready to seize on anything, like those of a cat on the hunt. Occasionally, he murmured something to himself she couldn't catch. She walked alongside in silence, not wanting to disturb him. She tried to imagine being a boy here. She watched him as he kept looking into the faces of passersby as though for clues as to whom he might have met once on the street.

A little explosive laugh caught him up. "My God," he said. "Madame Novak! That house—it's all divided into apartments now, but it used to have a garden and a couple of fruit trees. I used to steal apples and pears. She never caught me, but her husband almost did. He chased me and yelled at me. I was scared and never went back."

She looked at him caught up in his amusement. And watched it fade.

He paused again. "My best friend lived there on that corner, though the facade has changed. I'm sure that's the place. We used to get into such arguments when we were both at university. A group of us used to get together and discuss politics and philosophy—you know how that is. He was such an ardent Communist he couldn't tolerate any criticism of his beliefs. I once asked him if he thought that killing off your opposition was justified. And he said, 'Yes, if it's a threat to the new order you were trying to create.' He was big on the New Order. And you know what happened?—he was denounced

243

at some point over an internal disagreement within the Party and had to flee for his life. He always wanted to be a doctor," Koenig added ruefully. "Never got to use his talents."

As they rounded a curve of the street, Koenig came to a halt. She saw a look of dismay, as though he expected something to be there. "That's strange," he said. "It was here—right here. I know it was."

The street ended with a building that housed certain offices, nondescript, of recent history, that took up the whole block. A small park created a space between it and the house on the other side. The park itself was rather neglected, with some few struggling trees and shabby wooden benches set around. Several elderly pensioners occupied them now. Koenig walked on a little farther, turned back, looked around again, to gain a perspective of the street.

"It was a seventeenth-century house, but it's gone. They probably let it fall apart here in this little back street. And when it became a hole they put this monstrosity in its place."

For Koenig the house had left a hole in the present, but it was nonetheless inescapably real. No doubt there was a lot more evoked by this house, this street that she could only imagine. "So much for his family home," he said. "It was a fine old house.

"We do it all the time where I come from," Florrie said. "And seldom give it a thought—until it's too late."

They left quickly and turned back down the street.

"It had two floors and an attic," he said. "I was always begging to go up to the attic so I could look down at the street."

"And did you?"

"Every once in a while. But it was a very dusty place."

He made some comment about the way his mother always kept the window boxes full of flowers. "She had a great love of color and especially like geraniums and petunias." Then he was finished. His expression returned to an impassiveness she had come to recognize, and she didn't know where the experience, this touch of the past, left him, though he still seemed caught up in it.

They went to sit by the river until the sun set and the clouds began to darken. When they returned home, they had a quick supper of bread and cheese, and Koenig went to his desk to do a little work on his book before bedtime.

Florrie sat in silence for a time and tried to revisit the day and what it revealed about Koenig. It left him with a certain satisfaction, she felt, to find a few links to his past. Beyond that, she couldn't say. Finally, she took out her notebook. She had to do something to get her man out of the predicament she'd left him in. She plunged in.

Walking, or rather lurching forward with downward thrusts of his hip made him a spectacle for the townsfolk, especially the children. He hated their jeers and laughter, their efforts to imitate him and even to go him one better. These ingenious twists and turns made them double over in paroxysms of laughter. Alone, he wept.

Of course, she thought, and then wrote:

He might have endured if only they cared for him, but, except for a few who looked at him with pity, for the most part, he was only an object of ridicule.

The one real exception was an old woman who often cooked supper for him and gave him one of the hounds she kept to be his companion and protect him. She encouraged him to continue his search.

But were people the same everywhere? he wondered. Well, he would have to be cannier now, look around with a careful eye. But perhaps he had to approach things differently as well. Suppose, he thought, those he encountered could become part of the joke while he would be there to create the setting for laughter. He came up with a scheme.

He found his way to a poor village where most of the children had holes in the soles of their shoes. Though they regarded him questioningly when he entered their midst, they did not laugh at him but instead petted his dog. Their parents willingly gave him shelter and a little food.

He told them he was a Party Master and that he would set up various games for birthday parties and other celebrations in exchange for a place to sleep and two meals a day. Meanwhile he taught the dog, Kingpin, a few tricks to amuse the kids.

For the first party, for a boy named Ned, he made a sign: Be prepared for the Kick-Butt Alternative Walking Competition and put the sign up on the door of the school house where the party was to take place. For the party he demonstrated a few curls of his longer leg around the shorter, a couple hops in that position, and then turned the kids loose for their own inventions. A girl named Sheila, a slender blonde girl of eight, who bent herself into the most disjointed set of knots and twists imaginable and taking only one step forward to qualify them as a walk, won the prize, a papier mache monkey mask. A few years later, after she won stardom as a contortionist, she always spoke highly of the Party Master as the inspiration for her career.

His success inspired his creator, and now Florrie went on with a flood of ideas.

After that, no party was arranged without him, and the children themselves came up with hi-jinx for him to try. The parties had all sorts of new competitions and prizes. The mothers held a contest for the best prize that could be knitted or crocheted, and the fathers had a contest for the best one that could be made out of beer can tags. Soon the adults had him arrange their parties as well. His reputation spread to many parts of the country, and the kind of freedom he engendered became a powerful influence—so that he was followed by spies, and the rumor went abroad that he might be apprehended for dangerously undermining the social fabric and the order of things. When it appeared the Party Master was in danger, his friends began hiding him, moving him from one place to another. The parties took place in secret, but with diminished freedom and pleasure. Occasionally, the authorities got wind of some event about to take place, and several were arrested before the group could disperse. A reward was posted for information about the Party Master's whereabouts, an invitation to betrayal.

It was time to act, his supporters decided, for everyone, both children and adults to fight for all the Party Master stood for—the freedom to be. All their numbers would march in protest, hold a great rally, take over official buildings and flood the city with posters giving their declaration.

The Party Master was behind their efforts, but he was uncertain of the outcome, even though they were within their rights. He didn't want his friends getting arrested or even killed on his account or what they now stood for. He had the sense they no longer needed him and that he might even be a liability.

Florrie came to a pause. No doubt her man longed for escape from the hidden life he had to live, always under threat, dependent on others. Would he try for it, difficult though it would be with such an uncertain outcome? Or would the longing for some other chance for life make him take the risk? Would he make it beyond despair or death at the mercy of the great forces he faced? At the moment she had no answer. She put her notebook aside and got ready to go to feed the two dogs in her charge and take them for a walk.

Koenig was occupied with his own affairs. When she asked him if he was making progress with his book, he made a grunt that was neither here nor there. She saw that he was holding a train schedule, but he didn't elaborate.

Koenig wouldn't say where they were going, although he insisted now that he'd told her about it long before and this was the place. There had been a subtle shift in his mood since their visit to his old neighborhood. Sometimes she caught him in the same state of abstraction she had come to recognize, and didn't try to pull him out of it. Now there came a certain excitement: he wanted to show her something. She had no idea what to expect—she decided not to expect anything. The time was growing short, she kept thinking. Something was about to be finished. She sniffed the air for change, for some sign, and she hoped she'd be ready for it. She couldn't borrow the excitement that was in the streets, not in any permanent way. She wanted something of her own.

They were to take a little excursion, that's all she knew. She hadn't even accompanied Koenig to the shops and didn't know what was inside the backpack he carried with them—their lunch. One more time he was intent on giving her something to eat. She reminded him of that, and he agreed that this seemed to be his purpose in life. A certain irony came with his levity.

They took the train from Prague, watched the environs of the city disappear and then were in the country. Several stops later, they descended at Karlstejn and left most of their fellow passengers to cross the bridge and make their way up to the castle, where its extensive rooms had housed the great patron of the capital, King Charles, who'd founded the university and cultivated learning and the arts. Fought his wars and captured territory. And prayed, Koenig told her, in a chapel decorated all in gold, studded with amethysts and carnelians and rubies and diamonds, as though he were trying to create the inside of heaven.

"Maybe that's the only way to get there," Florrie commented, "if you have enough loot."

"He did have a certain advantage."

They were going to walk towards the next village, along the road, the river not far below them. For it was the river they'd come to see as well as the village. The Berounka. And she remembered now—a long time ago, it seemed, when he and the Czech poet in Copenhagen were reminiscing about this part of the country. Now

Koenig was coming back there. She tried to read his expression, but he didn't give her any help. This was the place he wanted her to see—before she left.

It felt good to be in the country. Meadows and fields of young corn stretched down to the banks lined with plane trees and willows. Their great trunks towered up along the river, and their leaves formed a scrim of green and golden light as the sun played with them, bringing up the yellows, shifting over onto the greens, dazzling. It left a brilliance on the open fields, kept the only shade beneath the circling foliage of the trees. Fields led down to the river, and beyond the fields on the other side, the bluffs rose in solid shapes. Between them, the river was a silver ribbon.

They continued along the road, losing the river behind the trees.

"We need to get down closer," Koenig said. "There should be paths we can take along the river."

"Yes," she agreed. She would like that.

It would be quite a walk. The open air had awakened her hunger and she had thirteen kilometers to Beroun to stave it off.

Above the road, on their right hand, were cottages, most of them with gardens. The irises were blooming in great variety and profusion, and they stopped to admire the colors: pale blue and lavender, yellow and bronze. They found tulips on tall stalks, and daffodils. She bent over to catch their scent. All these blooms kept company with the newly sprouting corn in the fields. She had never been in a place where they all came together. The light was soft, expectant.

"There should be a path that will take us down along the river. It has been so long ago—my God, how many years! But perhaps I can remember."

For some reason, he kept looking off to the right as they walked, pausing here and there. Then he said, "It's here, I think, that we turn off."

They took a path that led them up into a thicker growth of trees as they headed away from the road. The path divided into a number of narrow offshoots after they followed it briefly, and

Koenig was faced with a series of decisions about where to turn. But they plunged onward, climbing higher. In some places the path disappeared entirely. They paused to inspect a small cave where a spring had made the ground squishy. It was dark there, and cool, the ground matted with leaves.

"I remember this," Koenig said. "There are many caves in this region. It can't be far now."

She had worn sandals, not at all suitable for climbing, but she managed to keep up with him. They climbed the side of a hill and found themselves at the edge of a large circularly plowed field. The corn plants were only a few inches high.

Koenig paused and surveyed the area in some perplexity. "My God, how stupid of me," he said suddenly. "This isn't the way at all. You've have to be coming from the opposite direction to want to turn to the right. What a dumb thing to do! I don't know my left hand from my right."

She laughed. "We'll get a workout anyway," she offered.

"The main thing is how to get down from here," he said. "It looks to me like we've got to the top of the bluff on this side of the river."

"We could go back," she suggested, though she didn't much want to retrace their steps—it seemed a great waste. She sat down at the edge of the field while Koenig walked on ahead to see if he could get his bearings. He stood looking down at her when he came back. "I have no idea where we are," he admitted. "Perhaps if we go back to the other side of the field, we can see where to go next."

She was glad they did not have reverse their steps. They moved across the field, stepping over the young plants. Once they were on the other side and had found their way through the surrounding trees, they saw they were high above the road. The wall of rock was too sheer to allow them a way down.

"Damn!" Koenig said. "What a mess I've got us into."

Except that she wished she'd worn more sensible shoes instead of sandals, she wasn't at all unhappy. Being out in the air enjoying the landscape made her feel buoyant. She'd forgotten her hunger. "Don't apologize," she said. "It's quite—"

"But you must be starved," Koenig protested. " Considering that my purpose is to see that you're fed, I'm doing a poor job of it. And we're still a long way from where we're going . Do you want to stop and eat?"

"No," she said. " No, not yet. Let's find our way out first."

They continued on, though the walking wasn't easy. There were low bushes and brambles to work through, and they had to pause now and again to detach a bit of cloth from the thorns. After the bushes, they worked their way through a copse and then could see a stretch of land ahead of them rising and falling with the hills. They were still well above the road and could look out over the roofs of the houses on the other side of the river.

"It looks like we're coming to the edge of the village," Koenig said. "And just ahead I think I see another road."

She couldn't make it out at first. Several sheds that looked to be constructed of corrugated metal sheets, all quite rusted, lay below them. Some chalky piles that proved to be a fall of rocks lay in their path; they had to get around those.

Koenig tried to find the edge of the pile. "We can climb down here," Koenig said. "See, there's the road." He looked greatly relieved.

He went ahead and helped her down from among the rocks. It was steep in places even with the bare ground, and she hoped the leather soles of her sandals wouldn't cause her to slide. The rocks were big, and sometimes she knelt and slowly felt her way down. When they reached the bottom, they saw the road not far below them. They were almost at the level of the rusted corrugated sheds they had seen. Now they noticed great blocks stacked on one another, slabs lying haphazardly, some broken. "It's a quarry," Koenig said, "only it looks abandoned."

"Yes," she agreed. "But look," she said, surprised, "They've got all sorts of colors scattered over them. "

They hurried over to examine the slabs more closely and saw that the surfaces were encrusted with gemlike crystalline stones: some dark, a greenish-black; others amber, pale blue, green, lavender and clear. A few looked like pale pink confections, crystallized sugar

"They're beautiful!" Florrie exclaimed. Her eye had caught something on the ground and she bent down. "They're scattered here," she said, excitedly, then stood up to hold her treasures up to the light,

Koenig yielded to the same impulse, and in another moment both of them were wandering among the piles of slabs looking for the brilliant fragments, pausing to show them to each other. "Look at this blue one—look at the way the light comes through it."

"Wait a minute—look at this." Collecting them, stopping to admire each new addition, they set them into little piles on a flat smooth space on one of the rocks. They forgot their hunger, forgot they still had to find their way to the road, forgot everything. They were like children in their search for treasure, eagerly looking for more.

"And this one," Koenig said. "It's just a thin blue vein in white stone embedded on this rock, but what an exquisite blue! I wish I had a hammer—I can't get it loose."

"Here's a piece of it," Florrie said, picking up a fragment from the ground.

"No, keep it. That's one you must have. Absolutely."

"I can always find another. That one's yours."

They began laughing at themselves, at what they were doing. Then buoyed up by laughter itself, it was as though they couldn't stop. When she looked into his face, she saw that his cheeks were flushed and his eyes shone brilliant blue. Their expression made anything she might say evaporate. They threw their arms around one another and held each other as if they would never let go.

When they stood apart smiling at one another, she said, "I'm so happy you lost the way. Otherwise, we'd never have found this place."

"Yes," he agreed. "How lucky we are. Only now I'm starved."

"And so am I."

How extraordinary these abandoned slabs, the testimony to some failed purpose, should have been there with such jewels to catch the light and bring them to an opening in the day and something beyond.

She looked back once more as if to memorize the scene, to make sure she'd carry away the image of the gems glimmering there, all abandoned. Her pockets were heavy with the stones she'd gathered, and she had taken off her hat to carry a few that didn't fit.

"What will we do with them?" she wanted to know. They were caught up in another burst of laughter. What were they doing after all?

Now they came to the dirt road that would take them back to the paved road into the village. Once they were on it, they discovered a path that led them easily down along the river. They were at the outskirts of the village. Among the cottages along the road, chestnut trees rose above them, covered with white candles. other trees she didn't recognize were full of red blooms.

It was getting warmer, the sun full on them now, and they were not alone in having been lured to the river. Several youths were climbing the bluffs or sitting on the banks talking and smoking. Families had come for bathing and some of the children were splashing their feet in the water, though it was too cold yet for swimming.

She and Koenig reached a grassy knoll between the trees, set down their things and unpacked their lunch. Koenig gave her a cloth in which two wine glasses were wrapped, and she spread out the cloth after handing him the glasses. He also took out from his backpack bread and ham, sausages and cheese and a bottle of red wine.

"I hate plastic cups," he said, as he opened the bottle. "The wine will taste much better in these glasses."

They sliced the cheese, unwrapped the ham sausages and bread and made their sandwiches. Florrie leaned her back against a tree, a large willow, and began to eat. Though she was hungry, she ate slowly. A sparrow landed close by looking for crumbs, and she pulled off a bit of bread to throw in its direction. She watched the river flowing past, slowly, lazily, with little eddies. She didn't have to move, just sit there. Just below her, a fisherman stood in hip boots, his line in the water, not far from the bank. No hurry for him or the fish. No hurry for any of them. They could pause for a moment with the light on the water, just watching it flowing past.

"This is where I used to come with my grandfather or my parents," Koenig said. "After we moved, we'd come back for visits. I loved it here. I'd wander through these fields and down along the river."

So now he'd come back, after all that had flowed between. He wouldn't speak of that now. He was sitting with his hands clasped loosely around his knees, legs slightly apart. The blue shirt he was wearing sharpened the blue of his eyes. The boy had come to this river, grown into the young man. She could see him, something pure and determined in his expression, all caught up in the excitement of ideas, ready to transform society into the perfection of the idea. Heady stuff. And then trying to convince those who shared his beliefs to create the reality—the greater good. She could imagine him torn apart by mistakes and failures, the bitterness of betrayal. She wondered if now that he'd handled the various pieces of his life, they'd come together in some kind of unity and he'd been reconciled to himself and what had happened.

She gathered all the stones together in one sparkling heap and took them out one by one to examine them again, her treasure. Pieces of glass. Fragments of color, these stones. From a quota of building blocks perhaps. No doubt intended for something. All the specifications given. Taken from the depths of the earth and brought to the surface. To be found worthless. Thrown down in dismay. Of no use at all. To wait there for them

She could imagine him with his great faith in technology: A means to progress and the perfection of humanity. Trying to engineer everything, impatient with a father who wanted only a bit of something of his own, a little shop full of wiring and electrical parts.

She began playing with the pieces of glass, putting some of them into a circle, arranging them into various patterns. "I'm fascinated with the clear ones and the greenish black ones," she said, as Koenig was stretched out on the grass, idly watching her.

"They're like ice, and the others sit like little towers. There's something mysterious about them."

She could imagine him—betrayer and betrayed. She moved the stones around until she found a pattern that she liked. When she moved them all together, the various fragments, something flowed between them. Down below, they had been formed in a great heat, molten matter. In Bulgaria they took the prisoners to the quarries and shot them and threw their bodies in—for some reason She remembered that.

Far below the surface of the earth, things melted together and solidified and made these stones, little pieces of leftover creation. And all the things down there rose again, old urges and instincts

It was no doubt impossible to find a single square of ground that didn't bear some taint. Yet the light of early afternoon glowed in everything. She'd have been content to stay there until darkness fell and the stars came out. Brilliant stones: Orion's belt, Venus and the moon. All the fascinations a Kepler could contemplate: stars and snowflakes, which would never give up all their secrets. Sheer power that kept it all together, continuing on.

It was after dark when they arrived back in the city, leaning together sleepily on the train. They stopped for a bite to eat and sat with a glass of wine, rejoicing over the day . They were tired when they went to bed, but still lay talking to one another. "I meant to tell you—I forgot—I finally had a letter from my friend in Basel. He's planning a book of writings from various people after things went bad here. He's very much interested in seeing Bauer's notebook. I'll send it on to him."

""I'm very glad, " Florrie said, "And tomorrow, I'll read you the story I've written. I'm not sure about the ending, though."

"Is it a love story" Koenig wanted to know.

"I'm not sure you can call it that."

"Then I'll tell you a story," he said. "It's a very old story and it doesn't need words."

"Sometimes the old stories are the best," she said and moved closer.

In her efforts to explore what the imagination can offer as a way of knowing, Gladys Swan has published *The Carnival Quintet*, a trilogy of novels set in New Mexico, and eight collections of short fiction., including *The Tiger's Eye—New & Selected Stories*, and *Jungle*, ten stories from the *Sewanee Review*. Her fiction, poetry, and essays have been published in various literary publications here and in Europe, such as the *Kenyon Review, Sewanee Review, Virginia Quarterly Review, Shenandoah, Manoa, Ohio Review*, and *Prairie Schooner*, where she was awarded the Lawrence Foundation Prize for Fiction. In 2001, she received the Tate Prize for Poetry from the *Sewanee Review*. Her artistic efforts extend to creating the cover paintings for a number of her books, as well as exhibiting her art work. She was awarded one of the first Open Fellowships from the Lilly Endowment for a study of Inuit art and mythology and has held residencies at Yaddo, the Fundacion Valparaíso in Spain, the Chateau de Lavigny in Switzerland, and the Martha's Vineyard Writers' Residency. She has received various fellowships for residencies in painting at the Vermont Studio Center, where she has also been a Guest Writer.